GETTING TO MR. RIGHT

This is a work of fiction. Names. Characters, places and incidents are either a product of the author's imagination or are used fictitiously, and any resemblance to actual persons living or dead, business establishments, events, or locales, is purely accidental.

Copyright ©2014 by Carol Balawyder.
ISBN number: 9780993934612

Also by Carol Balawyder

Missi's Dating Adventures
Café Paradise
Not by Design
The Longest Night Months
Mourning Has Broken
Warning Signs

Just Before Sunrise

Chapter 1

Missi Morgan hoped this weekend would bring the magic back into her marriage with Max. She pictured the resort where they were going with its indoor pool, sauna and Jacuzzi and imagined how relaxed they would both feel, their daily preoccupations forgotten as they focused on the pleasure of being together. She couldn't even remember their last romantic getaway.

As she selected a pink, lacy bra from a drawer in their walk-in closet, she felt a pang of regret. In the early years of her marriage, the closet had been her office when she still had dreams of becoming a published novelist. The years wore on and after a baby and piles of rejections arrived, it had made more sense to transform the space into something useful.

Her cell phone rang, interrupting her thoughts. The caller ID showed "Skipper Jacobson." The name was familiar to her but she couldn't place it.

"My name's Skip. I'm Sheri's husband," a male voice jumped right in after her tentative hello.

"Sheri?"

"Yeah. Sheri Jacobson."

Of course - the waitress who worked at Max's bar. Missi felt her stomach tighten. Had something horrible happened at the bar? Was Max alright?

"What is this about?" she asked, her heart racing.

"Your husband and my wife are having an affair."

For a brief moment her mind went blank. Then she made Skip repeat what he had said.

"Max and Sheri are sleeping together," he said, punctuating each word with an expulsion of breath.

Maybe Sheri was having an affair but it surely couldn't be with Max. She relaxed now, picked a turtleneck off her bed and placed it in the suitcase on top of a bathing suit. "I'm sorry," she said softly. "I think you have the wrong number."

"You're married to Max Morgan, the guy who owns the Jazz Bar?" he asked her. His harsh tone made her feel like she was being interrogated, as if being Max's wife were a crime.

She twisted the pearl dangling on a pendant in the hollow of her throat. Then, "Um...Yes."

"I thought you should know that your husband and my wife are getting it on."

Getting it on. Such an offensive term. She imagined the caller as a pitiful man who had nothing better to do than to cause trouble, and she immediately distrusted him the way she distrusted drunken people or people on drugs. She gazed out her bedroom window. The large glass panel ran floor to ceiling and offered an unobstructed view of the harbor. The windows were one of the features that had attracted them to the condo. That, and its walking distance to Max's bar.

It had begun to snow. Only small flakes, nothing that would prevent her and Max from leaving before the Friday afternoon traffic.

"What makes you think they're getting it on?" she asked, shaking out a peach-colored cardigan that had fallen on the floor with more force than necessary.

"He came to the funeral."

She vaguely recalled Max telling her that he'd needed to work later hours because he was short of staff. Sheri's mother had died. She didn't recall any mention of his attending the funeral, though.

When she didn't answer, Skip kept talking. "He had no right being there." His voice rose and had a scathing tone.

Missi felt a need to defend her husband. "Max is her boss. It's only normal that he attended the funeral," she said, her lips pressing tightly together.

"It's the way he was with my wife. Comforting her."

"Comforting her?"

"You should have seen them. I felt so humiliated. There they were in the corner, whispering to each other as if I wasn't even there. She should have come to me."

Missi thought she might have heard a whimper in his voice and felt a little pity. "People in grief can behave strangely. I'm sure it's a misunderstanding," she said. But as she said those words, another thought superimposed itself on the first, racing through her mind: she herself had met Max while waitressing at his jazz bar.

She forced herself to remain calm. "Is this what your wife told you? That she's having an affair with my husband?" She sat on the bed, her hand fidgeting with the zipper of the suitcase.

"She doesn't have to tell me. All the signs are there."

"The signs?"

"They've been calling each other. I checked her cell phone. I called that number. There's no misunderstanding. And she's been coming home later and later."

Missi sucked in a lungful of air. If the phone calls were real, Skip had to be wrong about the cause. There had to be a logical explanation.

Why should she believe this stranger over her husband? In the eighteen years they'd been together, they had built a foundation of trust.

Max loved her. He would never betray her. Max having an affair? The whole thing was absurd.

There was a pause. A pause that was meant for her to say something. But what was there to say? Then he said roughly, "Just tell your husband to lay off my wife." He hung up and she held the phone next to her ear for a good while, listening to the silence.

As they approached the Vermont border, Missi felt her body clench. What if Skip was right? Did she really want to know? Yet to hide from the truth was cowardly. But what was there to hide from? Max would never do this to her. They were best friends. She had helped him build up his jazz-bar business. Had encouraged him in his music, although that had not turned out so well. The bar and restaurant took up so much of his time that he was forced to set aside his music aspirations. She wondered if he blamed her for not having fulfilled his dream of being a musician. Had she pushed him too far, into the arms of a woman who empathized with him, who believed his dream was still possible?

If the affair was real then they would go through this together. They wouldn't be the first couple to have this happen to them; obstacles like this could strengthen a marriage. Taking a long deep breath, she clutched the edges of her car seat. "I got a call from Sheri's husband this morning," she said.

Max turned to look at her. She tried to evaluate whether it was fear or surprise she saw in his eyes but couldn't tell. The sun was beginning to go down and cast a pale-yellow sheen on the snow banks along the highway and inside the car, across his face.

"Skip?" he said, tucking in his upper lip.

"He told me that you and Sheri are having an affair." She released her grip on the seat and rubbed her hands along the outsides of her thighs, as if trying to ward off the chill that swept through her.

Max reached for the hand closest to his and said, "Sheri's been telling me about Skip. How he's been acting weird lately. Overly protective of her; obsessively jealous. I think he's mentally unbalanced. Might have something to do with a drinking problem. It's not the first time he's done this to her."

"Skip said you went to Sheri's mother's funeral."

"Everyone working at the bar went. I wanted to pay my respects. Nothing wrong with that."

"But you didn't tell me."

By now, the sun had already sunk behind a mountain and that ash tone that came just before darkness shadowed his face. "Didn't I? I thought I did," he said. "I'm sorry, honey. I know I've been working a lot of hours. This weekend together is going to do us a lot of good."

"Skip also told me to tell you to lay off Sheri."

"Christ, he's a madman."

She thought about what Sheri's husband had told her, hesitating before she spoke. "Skip told me that you've been calling Sheri."

He blinked his headlights at the car in front of him. "These Sunday drivers. Don't they know to stay in the slow lane?" The car moved to the right lane and Max accelerated. "I call all my staff," he said. "Sometimes I have to change shifts around or have someone come in earlier. You know that."

Missi had been twenty-three when she married Max ten years her senior. She looked at him. At fifty-one, with his longish grey hair and deep dark eyes he was the kind of man that got more handsome with age. Missi had never loved him more than she did now.

"It's not true?"

Squeezing her hand, he said into the windshield, "Of course it isn't."

She leaned her head on his shoulder and said something that sounded like a line in one of the stories she used to write for Real Romance Magazine. "Oh, Max, I love you so much."

It was to save her marriage that she'd stopped writing. At first, she had believed Max was jealous of the virile, sexy men that she made up in her romance stories. He accused her of being dissatisfied with their sex life. Then, as years went by, sexless weeks turned into sexless months. Then, Missi blamed her low libido on the baby. It was well known that a having baby could be a strain on a relationship. But as baby Randy became a little boy, then a teenager, sex with Max did not much improve. Of course, there was wild lovemaking on those drunken nights, with slightly tamer sessions on birthdays and Christmas Eve. But generally, physical intimacy with Max had left her dissatisfied. At times, she had secretly turned back to her romance writing, hoping to ignite the sensual feelings of the early years of their relationship.

She gazed out of the window into the night winter landscape and thought that maybe she could write a story about this misunderstanding. Now that Randy was at college, she had more time on her hands. For the remainder of the ride, she thought of how she'd given up not only the short stories but her dream of writing novels. This phone call from Skip had curiously ignited her desire once more. Perhaps it was meant to shake her up this way.

It was almost eight by the time they reached the resort. They unpacked their bags and went into the dining room for a meal where they both drank too much: two martinis each and a bottle of wine, followed by a scotch for Max. They stumbled back to their room and fell into bed as well as into each other's arms.

On Saturday morning, her head pounded as she made her way into the washroom, where she splashed cold water on her face. She vaguely remembered having sex with Max last night. Picking up her toothbrush, she spread a half inch of toothpaste on its bristles. As she slid the brush along her teeth, she wished she hadn't drunk so much last night. That kind of sex never made her feel special. Was this the problem between her and Max? She'd stopped feeling special to him.

It turned out to be a glorious day, exceptionally warm for February. The bright sunshine on the snow blinded them. They cross-country skied on the trails behind the resort; it was so warm they skied without gloves. They went for high tea at the Trapp Family Lodge, where they sat outside and admired the view of the mountains in the distance. They made love in the late afternoon before going for dinner, this time without being intoxicated. At night before they drifted to sleep, Max gently touched her face and stroked her neck and shoulders. His tenderness felt like a long embrace, which reassured her and made her feel desired once more. A man having an affair wouldn't show such tenderness for his wife, she thought as she lay next to him. She cast aside her misgivings about the conversation with Skip. He was a madman; she wasn't going to let him ruin her holiday, and especially not her marriage. She snuggled up next to Max's warm body and heard him softly snore.

The next morning, she and Max went for a swim. Later, in the hot tub, their feet touched like teenagers. I am one of the lucky ones, she thought. There were yearly trips to Indonesia with their son, Randy. Seasonal shopping sprees in Milan and Paris. Dining in the best restaurants in Montreal. Flying to New York for a weekend of Broadway shows. Scuba diving on the island of Bonaire in the Caribbean, where they rented a condo.

"Do you still love me, Max?" she asked, her foot floating up his calf. What she really wanted to ask was if he was still in love with her, but she couldn't get those words out. What if he said he wasn't? Besides, the giddy magic that happened when you first met someone, that feeling of falling in love, transformed into love itself. In the end, she told herself, it was love and not falling in love that mattered.

He leaned over, slid his wet arm around her shoulder and kissed her firmly. "Are you still thinking of Sheri's crazy husband? You shouldn't let him bother you."

She was aware that he hadn't answered her question but didn't dare ask it again.

On the way home, they stopped in Burlington, a college town, where they walked around the pedestrian main street. They held hands, something they hadn't done in a long time. Years even. They went into the mall where they passed by Victoria's Secret.

"Let's go in. I want to buy you something sexy," he said.

She was surprised but pleased. He had never bought her lingerie before, although she had often written about male characters buying sexy lingerie for their wives or girlfriends.

Checking out the bras and matching panties displayed like candy, while Max stood next to her, was sexually stimulating. They roamed around the store, his arm around her shoulder, picking out racy underwear. She felt shy about wearing such underwear. It seemed a bit too young for her. But she wanted to please Max, so she finally settled on a violet outfit. The salesgirl pointed out that the bra and panties came with a cover-up and Max said, "Wrap that up as well."

He kissed her as they left the store, she carrying the pink striped bag - a symbol, she thought, of their marriage.

Once they were home a few hours later, she started unpacking their luggage while Max put their skis and boots away. Tucked into a corner at the bottom of Max's suitcase, she found a small package wrapped in silver paper with a blue bow around it.

"What's this?" she called out.

There was a moment of silence before Max said, "You weren't supposed to find it," he said. "It's a Valentine's present."

Valentine's Day was a week away. It had been years since Max had bought her something besides a last-minute bouquet of flowers for the occasion. "Oh," she said, noticing disappointment in his face. "I've ruined the surprise, haven't I? I'll wait then."

"No, open it now, over drinks," he said. "I'm going to make myself a scotch. White wine for you?"

"That would be nice," she said. She followed Max into their living room, where he took a good bottle that came from his wine cellar. He uncorked it, poured her a glass and then made himself a scotch.

She opened the package carefully, not wanting to tear any of the wrapping paper as if that would symbolize the tearing apart of her marriage. Inside was a bottle of Chanel's Chance. Not cologne. Not eau de toilet. But perfume. Missi removed the cellophane wrapped tight around the box, opened it and took the cap off the pretty bottle. She dabbed a few drops on her wrist and sniffed the fragrance as if it were filled with Max's love for her.

"You must have bought this while I was trying on the lingerie," she said. No, he couldn't have – Victoria's Secret didn't sell Chanel products. She smiled as she remembered that the boutique at the resort sold them. Max must have gone there while she showered.

"Do you like it?" he asked. "I know it's not your usual perfume, but I thought you might like a change."

"I love it," she said. Maybe this gift was a good omen. As they sipped their drinks, she thawed out a package of smoked salmon and bagels. Later, she showered and sprayed her body with the new scent before snuggling naked next to Max. He was fast asleep.

The following Monday Missi received another call from Skip. "So, did you tell your husband to lay off my wife?" he asked her.

"He's not having an affair with her," she said.

"That what he told you?"

The weekend had left her in such good spirits that she hated Skip spoiling it for her. Her instinct was to hang up on him but then he said, "Can you meet me for coffee?"

She hesitated. What harm would it do? She would tell him about her weekend with Max and reassure him that he and Sheri were not having an affair. Maybe he was like her cousin, who suffered from a mental illness. Missi had always shown compassion towards the mentally ill; every year she wrote out a check to the Mental Health Association. It was wiser to listen to him. There was no telling where his illusions might lead. She didn't want to be indirectly responsible for any violent act.

"I can see you this afternoon," she said. "Where do you want to meet?"

"There's a Café on the corner of Laurier and Park Avenue," he said. "I'll be there at two."

After taking special care with her make-up, she put on a woolen sweater with a girly frill. She even wore the lingerie Max had bought her. Why did she go to such pains? She realized that she needed to feel beautiful. Certainly, she wanted to convince Skip that Max would never leave a woman like her, but part of her wondered if she were also convincing herself.

Skip was a big man, over six feet tall with a hefty frame. He wore a ski jacket and a pair of army green pants tucked into a pair of heavy black rubber boots. He took off his jacket, revealing a plaid flannel shirt. His hair was blond, thinning and long. This was not the kind of man that women noticed.

Missi placed her fur hat, a hat that used to belong to her mother, on the table for the reassurance that came with familiarity. Soon she sat facing Skip, with mugs of steaming coffee between them.

"Why can't you believe me," he said, anger sharpening his voice. "We've got to stop them."

Missi thought of her cousin. She knew that it was useless to argue with someone who was delusional. He imagined that Max and Sheri were having an affair and she doubted if she could say anything would make him change his mind.

"I'll speak to Max again," she said gently.

"But you told me he denied having an affair. Why would he admit it now?"

She didn't know how to respond.

"Maybe you don't care about this thing ruining your family, but it's ruining mine. Sheri is all I've got. If he takes her away from me, I've got nothing."

"I do care about my family and I love my husband. Nothing is going to happen."

"Something's already happening," he said. "You just don't want to believe it."

It felt as if she were betraying Max sitting here with Sheri's husband. As if she were plotting something against him.

She studied him, trying to determine if he shared any traits with her cousin. Two similarities occurred to her - his eyes bulged and it was impossible to reason with him.

"I'll talk to Max again. Make sure he stays away from Sheri," she said. "Your wife needs you to be strong for her; she just lost her mother. This is no time for you to be falling apart."

When their coffees were almost finished, Skip looked at his watch and said, "I've got to get back to work or they'll wonder where I went," he said. "I have to find another way to deal with this. I'll figure something out."

"Listen, Skip. There's nothing to figure out. Sheri just needed someone to talk to because of her grief. It was normal for Max to show up at the funeral. He's her boss."

"Why couldn't she talk to me?"

"Sometimes it's easier talking to a stranger than to someone you're close to."

"But all those phone calls?"

"Did you ever think they could be about you? That Sheri might be worried about you?" she pointed out.

"Why should she worry about me?" His eyes narrowed at her in suspicion and disbelief.

"Maybe something about your work. Or about your feelings for her. Couples go through different stages. Maybe she talks to Max about saving your marriage. What if you're misinterpreting everything?"

"I'm not getting anything wrong," he said. He took one last sip of coffee, shoved his cup across the table, and turned to leave.

Randy was still at school when she reached home. She had planned on spending her afternoon writing, but her meeting with Skip had depleted her energy. At four o'clock, he called again as she was slicing vegetables on the cutting board in her kitchen. "Have you spoken to Max?" he asked.

She felt a headache begin at the side of her head and put down the knife to massage her temples. "Not yet," she said, trying to keep her voice even. "He doesn't come home this early."

"Sheri called. Said she wouldn't be home until late," he said. "She usually comes home for supper."

She let out an exasperated breath. "Well, it is Valentine's week. That's one of their busiest times at the bar."

"Maybe they're celebrating together," he said.

Missi regretted her words. Now Skip had something else to worry about. As she balanced the phone against her ear, she became aware of the heaviness in her limbs in spite of her diet. Extra pounds were difficult to get rid of, just like Skip's arguments.

In the background, Beethoven's *Silence* played, her attempt at finding solace as she worked. She had always loved silence and felt that if others couldn't understand her need for it, then they couldn't understand her, either.

"You've got to stop imagining there's something between my husband and your wife."

"You think I'm making it up, don't you? Well, you'll see who's right."

He hung up on her, but ten minutes later he rang her again.

"Now what?" she said.

"I just called Sheri. She's not at the bar. Call your husband and see if he's there. Maybe they're shacked up in some motel."

She wasn't about to call Max. She didn't want to choose sides or decide who was telling the truth. Sometimes it was better to leave well enough alone. If Max told her that there was nothing between him and Sheri, then why should she try to disprove him?

"Don't call me anymore," she told Skip. "I don't want you bothering me with your fantasies. If you don't stop harassing me, I'm going to make a complaint to the police."

Missi didn't tell Max about her meeting with Skip or about the phone calls. Her husband had worked overtime all week and she had hardly seen him.

Then, on Thursday, as she and Max sat in the living room having drinks and looking out over the Saint Lawrence Seaway, Max said, "I need to get away."

A surge of happiness coursed through her. She'd love to get away from this cold weather. "Why don't we go to Bonaire?" she said. "Snorkeling always helps you unwind."

He shifted before looking straight at her. "I mean alone," he said. "There's a lot going on at work and I need to figure things out on my own."

Alone? They'd never gone on separate holidays. She thought of her conversations with Skip and their meeting. She had to trust Max. Then she thought of their weekend in Stowe and their lovemaking.

"When?" she asked.

"This weekend."

"But it's Valentine's," she said. "Your busiest time at the bar."

He frowned. "Christ. Valentine. The bar is going to be crazy. But if I don't go away, I'm the one who's going to go nuts. I'll make it up to you, I promise."

"Where are you planning on going?" she asked, attempting to keep her voice light.

"I'm not sure," he said. "Just take the car and drive."

She felt a knot in her belly when he kissed her goodbye the following morning. Until then, she had hoped that he would change his mind and ask her to come along. But after he was gone, she thought of what Skip had told her. For the first time, she pictured Max in bed with Sheri. The image wouldn't leave her.

She needed to speak to someone about this. It wasn't as if she had a number of friends she could call. The women in her yoga class were only acquaintances; she didn't even know their names. Long ago, she'd also met women in a writing class but had never become friends with any of them. It struck her that she'd really dedicated her life to being Max's wife and Randy's mother.

The only person she could think of calling was Campbell Jones. It had been months since she'd spoken to her. Campbell had been so busy with her research on some Prince Charming myth that she had no time to socialize. Missi punched in her number.

"I think Max is having an affair," she told Campbell.

"Oh, no," said Campbell. "What makes you think that?"

"Max went away alone for the weekend. It's not like him to leave the bar on one of the busiest weekends."

She told Campbell about the phone call she'd received, their weekend in Stowe, the lingerie he'd bought her and the bottle of perfume. "All the signs point to him <u>not</u> having an affair," Missi said, "but something feels very wrong."

"Do you think he might have gone away with someone else?" asked Campbell.

"I don't know," said Missi, "but there's one way to find out. Meet me at Max's bar."

Chapter 2

Campbell was the first to arrive at the bar in Old Montreal. She ordered a glass of Chardonnay and glanced around the room. When she had last come here, it had been for cocktails during the week, when the place was filled with out-of-town clients and regulars from the near-by courthouse – defense lawyers, judges and their staff. The latter had likely returned to their suburban homes for the weekend. The bar was now packed with a younger Friday evening crowd, the place buzzing with lively conversation and the clinging of glasses. A number of young women mingled in the bar, probably hoping to meet their Price Charming.

She thought about her research and the last five years debunking the Prince Charming myth. Taking a sip of her wine, she smiled to herself. In less than three months, she would receive an award – not to mention long-awaited professional recognition – at the annual Women's Studies Convention held in New York City.

"I hope you haven't been waiting long," Missi said, squeezing into a chair at Campbell's table as a jazz duo tuned up their instruments.

Their friendship had started at university, where Missi had taken Campbell's psychology tutorial as an elective. After-class discussions developed into meeting for coffee and when the session was over, they continued seeing each other.

"Is that Sheri?" asked Campbell, regarding the young barmaid opening a bottle of wine for a couple seated across from them.

Missi shook her head. "I've never seen her before."

"What can I get you to drink?" The barmaid smiled at Missi.

"Where's Sheri?" asked Missi. After the other woman told her that Sheri was off for the weekend, there was a stiff moment of silence.

"I'll have another glass of Chardonnay, please," Campbell said. She turned to Missi. "Okay with you?"

Missi nodded. As soon as the barmaid turned away, she said, "I think I'm going to be sick."

"Oh, honey." Campbell took her friend's hand.

"I feel like such a fool," said Missi.

Campbell drew a tissue out of her handbag and handed it to her. She waited while Missi dabbed at the tears at the corner of her eyes.

In the years Missi and Max had been married, she had seen Max only a few times. It had always been in the company of other people: a birthday celebration or barbecue. She had never had a real conversation with him. It wouldn't surprise her if he were having an affair. She had witnessed the way he flirted with other women and how he enjoyed their attention. Of course, she wasn't about to tell Missi that. The man she'd believed in all this time was not who she thought he was. With time, she'd find the strength to accept the truth.

"Max has been coming home later than usual. But he always has good excuses. I never doubted him."

Campbell took a sip of her wine. Although she felt sorry for Missi, she also felt a sense of satisfaction. Here was further proof that she was better off living alone. Somewhere inside, she was glad that this was happening. Not because Missi was miserable, but because this could be a wake-up call, the one they all got sooner or later. Maybe now she could focus on her writing dreams and stop placing Max on such a pedestal.

"Come to my group," Campbell said. "I'm starting a new one on Tuesday evening."

"What group?"

"For my research on the Prince Charming myth. This will be my last group before I go to New York for my award."

"Isn't it unethical to treat a friend?' Missi put down the tissue.

"It's not therapy. It's just a group for my research study. It's no different than if you were in one of my classes."

"Max is my Prince Charming," she said.

Campbell leaned over and whispered, "I know," thinking that, in her eyes, he certainly wasn't Prince Charming material.

"Seven o'clock. I'll e-mail you the address. It'll do you good to get out of the house. Also, you'll be helping me out. I haven't had much response so far and I need a certain number of people in the group. "

"Maybe I'm wrong. If Max said nothing's going on, then I ought to believe him. What's marriage without trust?"

Campbell patted Missi's arm with her free hand. "Everything is going to be alright," she said, although she knew from experience that problems didn't fix themselves like that. Especially for someone like Missi, who attached so much importance to being Max's wife. She would have to wean off him like one weaned off a cocaine habit. The psychological craving would linger long after the physical one faded away. This could take months or even years in Missi's case.

By the time they left the bar, the blizzard that had been forecast was so heavy that they could hardly see two feet in front of them.

"You're welcome to stay over at my place," Missi said.

Their talk had exhausted Campbell and she didn't want to wake up in the morning only to listen to Missi's troubles all over again.

"Thanks, but I'll hail a cab," Campbell said. Around the corner there was a taxi stand and she reached the one cab waiting there at the same time as someone else.

"Where are you heading?" asked the man.

"North," she said.

"You mind if we share? It's on my way. I live in the McGill ghetto." He had a pleasing face, with dark, thoughtful eyes. Snowflakes sprinkled on his black hair and long eyelashes. She wondered if the stubble on his chin was intentional or simply a way-past-five-o'clock shadow. Whatever the reason, she found it sexy.

She hesitated. Something about him persuaded her to accept his offer. Maybe it was his accent; she felt it her civic duty to be kind to tourists. In any case, there was no harm in sharing a ride.

He looked too old to be a student. Perhaps he was a professor. Inside the cab, he started to ask her questions. First, how her evening had gone.

His straightforwardness put her on guard. She never discussed her personal life with strangers.

"Fine," she said. "I met a friend."

"A boyfriend?" he asked. "I would imagine a woman as beautiful as you would have plenty of suitors." He smiled at her, displaying straight white teeth.

Who said "suitors" these days? Yet she found the word endearing. "A girlfriend," she said.

He nodded, then asked if she were married.

She laughed. "No, are you?" she asked.

"I'm still searching for the right person. The older I get, the pickier I tend to be."

She was surprised at his openness. Most men she met bragged about how many women they could get.

"You sound like you're already an old man."

"I'll be forty next month," he told her. That was two years older than her.

His name was Chandrashekar. "But everyone calls me Chand."

"Thank God," she said. "Your name must be hard to remember."

When she offered her own first name, he laughed and said it sounded strange.

"It's Scottish," she said, annoyed. "Named after my maternal grandfather."

When the taxi driver pulled up in front of his apartment building, Chand dug into his wallet and handed Campbell a twenty-dollar bill. She looked at the meter. It was just over eight dollars. She was about to reach into her handbag for change when he touched her hand.

"Don't worry about the change," he said. "If it's okay, I'd like to see you again." He handed her a business card. "Call me if you feel like it."

As the taxi drew away, she felt the soft imprint of his fingers on her hand.

His business card said *Chandrashekar Rajumar*. He was manager of a downtown hotel. She called him the next afternoon to thank him for the fare. "I owe you four dollars," she said. "Even with the tip it didn't come to twenty dollars."

"You can buy me a coffee the next time we see each other," he said. "I know this cafe where they make the best espresso."

She had planned on spending her Saturday afternoon working on her acceptance speech, but that could wait. She had to eat anyway. She told him she'd meet him in forty minutes, feeling a warm tingling inside. It had been a long time since she'd felt this kind of attraction for a man. Her neck felt a little tense and as she rubbed it, she began to find fault with Chand. Finding fault with the men she dated was a long-standing habit.

For one thing, he was Indian. Not that she had anything against dating men from other cultures. She'd dated Egyptians, African Americans, Persians and even a man who had turned out to be a transsexual. But never had she dated a man from India, and his culture, although interesting from a touristy perspective (she'd always wanted to go to India) was much too risky for her. Hadn't she read on the internet stories of how Indian men married white girls for money or visas? Not that she had any money. But Chand didn't know that. As for a visa, he had told her that he'd been living in Canada for the last ten years, but anyone could say anything.

Then there was the matter of his job. Coming from India, she'd expected him to work in IT or engineering or physics. Wasn't that what Hindus were good at? She then hated herself for her prejudiced thinking. Besides, it didn't matter to her what he did. It wasn't as if she were going to begin a relationship with him.

As she waited for Chand in front of the cafe, she spotted her father jogging towards her with two other men. She started to turn away but it was too late. He had seen her and called out to her. To make matters worse, she saw Chand crossing the street to meet her.

Now what was she supposed to do? Of all things, she didn't wish to explain how she felt about her father. If only she could hide, but her father was already jogging on the spot before her.

"What are you doing here?" Her question came out too harshly, as if he had no right to be on the street, especially on the same street as her, especially when she was meeting a man.

"This is our jogging route," he said, catching his breath. He was wearing a fashionable winter jogging suit which Campbell thought was too young on him, and when he smiled at her she wondered if he'd had his teeth capped. It had been more than six months since she'd last seen him.

"Hey, guys, meet my daughter, Cambie," he told the men who were also spot jogging next to him, both breathing heavily.

Cambie? She felt something twist in her chest. The name brought up memories of when she was a little girl and he was still living at home. Happy times which had been suddenly shattered by his leaving them to live with another woman – someone he had got pregnant. She had always felt jealous of baby Abigail, even now that Abigail was an adult. Why did he have to call her Cambie? Was it just a pretentious show of affection to impress his buddies?

"My name is Campbell," she informed the men.

"If you've got a problem, you can go to her. She's a therapist."

"Counselor," corrected Campbell.

"And a damn good one at that," her father said.

What did he know whether she was good or not? His phoniness irked her. Oh, how supportive and encouraging he pretended to be! Making himself look like the ideal father to his friends.

All the same, she politely shook hands with her father's friends as Chand came up to her. Introductions were made and Chand in his overly well-mannered Hindu style said, "So very pleased to meet you, sir."

Sir? Her father didn't deserve such respect. Her father's buddies started asking her questions about her job, which she answered with one ear tuned into Chand's conversation with her father.

It annoyed her how Chand played into her father's hand, making animated gestures as he spoke.

"I've always wanted to go to India myself," she heard her father say.

Just like him to exaggerate his interest in Chand's work and India. Why couldn't he be as interested in her? He rarely called her and when he did, all he talked about was his work as a judge. She couldn't bear his hypocrisy another minute.

"We better get going," she said, pulling on Chand's arm.

"I hope to see you again soon, son," said her father as he placed both of his hands on Chand's shoulders.

Son? Oh, my God how could he even say such a thing? Worse, he then turned to her and whispered in her ear, "Nice gentleman."

As he jogged away, she felt an ache in her heart. In spite of her frustrations with him, she hoped he would turn around and wave to her. He didn't.

How many times had she stood by the window, way past the time he had agreed to pick her up? Waited there until her mother wrapped an arm around her cold shoulders and tried to lead her away? Instead, Campbell stomped into her room, refusing to let her mother witness her anger. Sure, he had called all those times and promised to be there for her the next time. But when the next time came, he was never there. Eventually, she stopped hoping for things to change; it was just too painful. It was easier to put distance between them and get him out of her mind.

Her reaction to him now, years later, surprised her – how she still longed for a sign of his affection or to hear him say he was sorry.

"Nice man, your dad," Chand said as they made their way towards the café.

She didn't want to hear how great a man her father was and especially didn't want Chand referring to him as "dad."

"He left my mom and me to live with a woman he got pregnant," she said.

"I thought I sensed some tension between you and him. Well, to be honest, mostly from you."

"I still haven't forgiven him for ruining my childhood. I don't think I ever will."

She looked wearily at Chand. Should she tell him what she'd learned about how a father's abandonment affected a daughter's subsequent relationships with men? No. He would only ask questions about her own life and she didn't know him well enough to trust him with her feelings.

Chand held open the door of the café for her. They chose a quiet table by a window. He helped Campbell remove her coat and placed it on the back of her chair. Then he unzipped his leather jacket, leaving it on as he sat next to her. For a moment, they both gazed outside, where a soft snow had begun to fall. He reached for her hand

and held it tenderly in his. "Promise me one thing," he said.

"What?"

"That you won't confuse me with your father."

Chapter 3

Suzy Paradise was up early. She dressed, brushed her teeth and looked outside at the bright sunshine. It was the kind of winter morning she adored. She went into her kitchen, walked over to her fridge and took out a large box. As she opened the box, she admired the dozens of pastries as if they were precious jewels. For Suzy, the pastries might as well have been rubies, emeralds and sapphires.

Each Saturday, the box was filled with a different assortment of her gems: mocha meringues, chocolate truffle shells, banana croustillant or luscious lemon tarts. One thing was certain. The box always contained her famous coconut cupcakes: fluffy white cake with a topping of buttery vanilla bean icing, laced with fresh flakes of slightly roasted coconut on top.

Suzy slipped on her coat and boots. Careful not to disturb her masterpieces, she carried the box to her car and placed it on the passenger seat. The cold, crisp air exhilarated her. She drew in a large lungful and smelled its freshness. At seven o'clock, the easy drive across the mountain to Victoria Avenue allowed her to take in the snow-covered branches on the evergreens and the thick ice dripping on the huge boulders lining the road.

She parked in front of La Patisserie Lyse – a warm, friendly shop with gleaming windows showcasing the day's fresh pastries.

Lyse opened the door for her. Except for her widow's peak, her dark hair was set in place by a net and even at this early hour, drops of sweat beaded her forehead. Small laughter lines as well as tiny ones over her upper lip betrayed her advanced age.

When Suzy handed her the box of pastries, Lyse placed it on a table behind a counter. She looked inside the box and let out a joyful cry. "Ah, you made chocolate macaroons, this time," she said sliding her hands along a crisp apron. "I know what everyone says about your coconut cupcakes but these are my favorite."

Suzy grinned. "I made them especially for you."

She had met Lyse last fall at a charity bazaar benefit at the high school where Suzy substitute taught. Lyse, whose daughter was a senior at the school, came up to Suzy's stand and tasted one of her chocolate macaroons. Right on the spot, she'd said, "You have to bake for my shop."

Flattered by the invitation, Suzy had laughed. La Patisserie Lyse was one of the city's most famous pastry shops. "I already have a full-time job substitute teaching," she told her.

"Well, how about if you simply brought in some pastries on Saturdays?" Lyse then asked.

Suzy had always dreamt of becoming a pastry chef. But things got complicated. First, her parents had disapproved. Both being academics, they wanted her to follow in their footsteps. Then, Kevin came along and for years she'd put aside her dream of becoming a patisseriere until Lyse had serendipitously appeared.

Lyse took two chocolate macaroons and hid them behind a coffee machine so that they wouldn't get sold. "Oh, these hearts are adorable." She placed them on a white porcelain plate next to the cash, probably as a reminder to her clients of Valentine's Day. Then she poured Suzy a cup of moccachino coffee.

Suzy took the mug and sat at one of the tables lined against a wainscoted wall. At least once, she'd have to come in the evening to see the shop lit with its the turquoise lamp shade sconces.

She enjoyed these Saturday mornings with Lyse. Although they had started with a business relationship, they had become fast friends.

"How's the man hunting going?" asked Lyse.

Suzy shrugged and took a sip of coffee. "You know. Same old."

"You still on the dating sites?"

"Ugh...Afraid so."

Lyse laughed. She was in her early sixties, with a solid marriage that Suzy admired and envied.

"Sometimes I think I'm not ready for a relationship. Or maybe I make myself believe that I need one," Suzy said. "I've tried almost every type of dating: a dating agency, going out to singles clubs (ugh), going to conferences on love and burning candles and incense at home. None of it has worked."

Lyse shook her head. "You're a beautiful woman. Why wouldn't any man want to be with you?"

Having men like her wasn't the problem. The problem was finding a man whom she liked. Men always disappointed her. How much effort she'd wasted trying to find a man who wasn't self-absorbed. She would never admit this to anyone, not even Lyse, but what she really hoped for was a man who would dote on her, who wasn't afraid to put a woman at the center of his life. The kind of man she had read about in the biographies of George Sand, Frida Kahlo, or Mary Wollstonecraft. These were women who made romantic love their highest aspiration. If only she could meet a man like Frieda's Diego.

"Maybe I'm just too old for this. The men my age are stoical, overweight, bitter, and boring.

Where are the great lovers? The men capable both of strength and tenderness? Men unafraid of passion, unafraid to allow their women to be the sun around which their universe revolves?" she asked. "I'll tell you where they are. They're looking for the fountain of youth in women twenty and thirty years younger than me."

"Nonsense," said Lyse. "Love knows no age."

Suzy shook her head. "A woman my age longing for romance is seen as pathetic. Soon I'll be fifty. It seems like I've been on these horrific dating sites forever."

"Queen of the dating sites, are you?"

"I certainly haven't had much luck in finding my king. The other day I met someone who talked for a whole hour about fishing. I got a full lesson in floating jogs, rubber tails, rods and reels and lines. The guy was absolutely crazy about fishing. That's all he talked about. Didn't ask me one question about myself. Know what he said when I finally said I had to go?"

"What?" Lyse asked, as she artfully arranged Suzy's pastries on long silver platters and placed them in the display shelf next to a basket of fresh croissants.

"Said I was a great conversationalist. Can you believe it? As far as I'm concerned, stimulating conversation certainly doesn't mean that I'm the one doing all the listening."

Lyse laughed. "Maybe good conversation isn't what you need a man for," she said, wiping her hands on her blue and white striped apron. "That's what girlfriends are for. Better in your profile that you replace interesting conversation with interesting in bed. Maybe you ought to date younger men."

"That's what I've been doing. But even that has been unsuccessful. Next to their strong bodies and good looks, I feel old and spent."

"What else did you put in your profile?" asked Lyse. She finally poured herself a cup of coffee and came to sit at Suzy's table.

Suzy thought of all the different profiles she'd composed about herself. "I said that I'm looking for a tender, loving relationship. With a kind man. Someone who inspires trust."

Lyse sighed. "You've got to be more specific. Hold on." She rose and made her way to a bulletin board at the entrance of her shop. After untacking a piece of paper, she brought it to Suzy. "This might interest you," she said. "A woman posted it the other day."

Suzy held the paper in her hands. Her eyes fell on the line: *Are you a woman searching for Prince Charming?*

She carefully studied the words before her:

Are you a woman searching for Prince Charming?

Can daughters of unavailable fathers find love?

If you would like to be part of this study, please call

Campbell Jones for more information.

"If I could find a charming man, that would be enough for me," Suzy said. "Never mind a prince."

Nevertheless, she tore off the phone number and stuffed it into her handbag. Maybe it was time to confront her relationship with her father.

Customers started to come in and soon the place was crowded. Suzy looked at her watch.

On her way home, the breathtaking vistas of the city helped clear her mind as she drove over the mountain. She thought about what Lyse had said. What kind of compatibility did she need with a man? Did it have to do with the sports they played? She wasn't much of an athlete, although she liked men who were. The kind of lifestyle she wanted to lead? Where she wanted to live? How she liked to travel? She realized that Lyse was right – she had not been specific enough in her profiles. No wonder she had drawn a series of Mr. Wrongs.

At home, she cleaned up the mess in her kitchen, putting away her pastry-making equipment, cleaning bowls, flexi pan forms, dough sheeters and decorating combs. Suzy loved the opportunity for creativity that pastry making provided. It was in the art of baking that she derived her greatest pleasure; she looked upon it as a celebration of life. With her fingers smothered in butter and her hands twisting dough, she completely lost herself and, in the process, came in touch with who she really was.

She stopped at the fridge to look at the vision board which she'd made last spring. As background, it had a photograph of sunshine coming through a bright, modern kitchen window, falling upon beautiful woodwork and state-of-the-art appliances. Images and words which symbolized her dreams and goals were superimposed on the collage: names of cities she wanted to visit. Bora Bora. Berlin. Casablanca. Except for a lay-over at the airport in Berlin, none of the wishes on her collage had materialized.

Suzy looked at the photo of her dream kitchen. She still made her pastries in a cramped kitchen. With a start, she realized that she'd neglected to include an image for her dream of opening her own pastry shop. Why hadn't she? Partly, she realized was because she didn't believe enough in her talent as a pastry chef and the other part was still hoping to meet a wonderful man – preferably one who either possessed his own to-die-for kitchen or was good in renovations. How much of her life had she put on hold waiting for Mr. Right to appear?

She made herself a cup of coffee and carried it with one of her heart-shaped sables into her living room. Balancing the cup and saucer, she sank into her white leathered sofa. What exactly, she wondered, did she need a man for that she couldn't provide for herself? Was it the romance? The feeling of being in love? Sure, she wanted to be desired but it had been so long since she had felt desire for someone. Years really. Could she still hope for romance and passion at her age? In less than four months, she would cross the half century mark. What it came down to was that she wanted a man for resurrecting sex. But she wasn't about to put that in her profile. She remembered the phone number she'd stuffed into her purse at Lyse's. She took it out and pressed the numbers on her phone. A woman answered.

"I'm calling about the ad you placed for participants in your study," Suzy said.

"I'm doing research on the Prince Charming myth. I'm focusing on how a daughter's relationship with her father affects her relationships with men. A new session begins this Tuesday evening."

That could be interesting, thought Suzy. She still harbored anger towards her father for rejecting her son, Kevin. Perhaps in this group, she would also find help in dealing with the hole her son's death had left in her heart and finally find closure. In a few months, it would be Kevin's tenth death anniversary

Chapter 4

Felicity Starr awoke in a state of panic. She hated Saturdays. Especially Valentine weekend Saturdays. How had she reached thirty-two alone? There had been a time when she'd looked forward to Saturday afternoons, roaming around the department stores and boutiques with her girlfriends to try on the latest fashions; browsing in art galleries and going to afternoon plays, then grabbing a bite to eat afterwards. Now, all her girlfriends were busy with either boyfriends or husbands. Some of them already had small children. The few single ones were often off travelling for their careers. And for some reason, she had not been able to connect with women at work or in the business program.

It was not only that she had no one to share these activities with, but her interest in them had vanished.

She could no longer melt away her loneliness with a new pair of shoes, a Hermes scarf or a Chanel lipstick, or by checking out the art galleries on Sherbrooke Street. The department stores bored her; fashion and make-up had become irrelevant. Going to art galleries and looking at what other people had achieved left her feeling empty.

Wearing a pair of boxer shorts and an oversized t-shirt, Felicity made her way to the kitchen. She reached for the bottle of Clonazepam on the counter and took out a pill, popped it into her mouth and swallowed it with a glass of juice. She repeated the procedure with a second pill. Lately, she'd noticed that the medication had less effect on her and she found herself exceeding the dosage in her prescription.

She rested her forehead against her kitchen window as she waited for the pills to work their magic. The coldness of the glass against her skin was oddly comforting. Outside, the bike path connecting Nun's Island to Notre Dame Island was covered with snow and from her fourteenth-floor apartment, she made out people – like tiny bugs – skiing on the path. An edginess fluttered in her stomach. She turned away from the window and the skiers below. Why couldn't she relax and enjoy the day as it unraveled before her? It seemed that every Saturday morning was the same: always in a rush for the day to be over.

Felicity's apartment was rented by her father, supposedly for out-of-town clients, and claimed as a company tax deduction. In the six years that Felicity had worked at her father's company, there had not been a single out-of-town client and she knew there never would be.

Her father owned Starr Movers International. Felicity had never planned to work at the company. Her dream had been to study at the School of Design and Fashion in Milan, but her father had convinced her that business was a wiser choice.

"Just think of it, Princess, in business you'll study marketing. You'll then have the know-how to sell your sketches."

Amazingly, she did exceptionally well in business school. Although she found the subjects useful, if not particularly interesting, her heart was not in it.

Upon graduation, her father had offered her a position in his company. "One day," he told her, "All of this is going to be yours."

What was there to complain about? She travelled to Europe, Asia and South America. Her father provided her a handsome salary, a very generous expense account, a sports car, and shares in the company. What thirty-one-year-old had all that? Yet, deep down, she resented that she had traded her father's dream for her own.

She plucked a grapefruit from a bowl on the counter and cut it into bite-sized pieces. Sucking on one of them, she paced around her apartment, scowling at what she saw. She might as well be living in a hotel, she thought. Nothing here reflected who she was. The furniture and wall hangings – although of good quality – had been selected by a designer hired by her father. Her own paintings and sketches of futuristic outerwear were carefully bubble wrapped and tucked away under her bed and at the back of her closets.

Picking up her smart phone, Felicity punched in the weather forecast app. Sunshine and below freezing temperatures. More of the same, she thought glumly. Still, she needed to get out. An idea popped into her mind. She would go skating at Beaver Lake.

The pair of ski pants she slipped on seemed looser than they were the last time she'd worn them, only a few weeks ago. She pulled on a thick sweater, her white parka and a matching white tuque and mittens -- a gift which her mother had given her for Christmas. How in the world had her mother found woolen hats, scarves and mittens in Mexico City? Probably on one of those online shopping programs that appeared at one or two in the morning.

She had hardly seen her mother since she'd left to live with a man fifteen years her junior. Even when her mother was still married to her father, Felicity didn't see much of her. Her mother, a real estate agent, was always racing out on weekends and evenings to show homes.

"I wasn't meant to have children," she had told Felicity, as if that could console her, when explaining her decision to move to Mexico.

Felicity had been fourteen then and pity for her father had led her to accept a role that she realized later was unsuitable for a daughter. After witnessing his fury over his wife's infidelity and then his sadness, Felicity silently vowed to never disappoint him.

It was a fifteen-minute drive to Beaver Lake. Felicity wore a pair of sunglasses to shield herself from the glare coming through her windshield. Once she got to the rink, her desire to skate disappeared. It all seemed too much of an effort, so she sat on one of the benches along the rink and watched the skaters go by. Teenage lovers holding hands. Mothers training children to skate. Young boys filled with hopes of becoming hockey stars. She viewed them all with a feeling of anguish.

A woman wearing a smart three-quarter-length coat came to sit beside her. Wisps of grey hair fluttered below her purple woolen hat.

"Wonderful day, isn't it?" said the woman, whom Felicity judged to be in her seventies.

Felicity smiled at her. She was happy to have someone to talk to. Being an only child had always made her feel lonely, but these days her loneliness seemed to have deepened.

"Look at all those skaters. When I was young, I had dreams of becoming a figure skater. Dorothy Hamill and Peggy Fleming were my idols. An older cousin of mine handed me down a pair of skates. They were a bit too large for me, but I stuffed them with tissue."

Felicity surreptitiously tucked her ice skates, with their sleek design, under the bench.

"Of course," the woman continued, "my parents were too poor to give me skating lessons, but we had this rink on the lake where we lived and I taught myself to skate. I would watch the skaters on TV and then imitate their spins and jumps. I managed pretty well too on my own."

The woman wore a happy expression, showing a joie de vivre which Felicity assumed came from a stable life filled with love.

"You don't skate anymore?" Felicity asked.

"Oh, no. I broke my hip a long time ago and had a hip replacement. When you get to my age, dear, you start taking care of your bones."

A dashing older man wearing a bright red Anorak approached them. "Here comes my honey," the woman said. "He brings me here every Saturday because he knows how much I love to watch the young one's skate. They bring back memories, they do."

She held out her hand to her companion and the way he reached for it reminded Felicity of days when men asked women for the pleasure of a dance. The elderly woman rose from her seat. "We're going to head downtown and have lunch at the Ritz," she told Felicity. "I struck gold when I met this man."

Felicity watched them walk towards the parking lot, holding hands like teenagers. Why couldn't she meet someone she could be in love with forever? Why couldn't she, too, strike gold?

The mittens her mother had sent her were angora, hardly thick enough to keep out the cold. She went into the chalet and ordered a hot chocolate just so she'd have something warm to wrap her hands around. When the cup got cold, she dumped it, still full, in the trash can.

The conversation with the woman, although a stranger, had made her feel connected, but now she was alone again. Her shoulders grew heavy as she made her way to her car. Knowing that she still had half a day with nothing to do filled her with dismay.

As she drove home, Felicity passed by Le Sports Club. It was a club which her father had urged her to join; she had resisted because she knew that he'd been more interested in the tax deduction for his company than for her well-being. But now she wondered if she might meet an interesting man there. Maybe she would strike gold.

The heat inside the sports center contrasted sharply with the bitter cold outside. She yanked off her tuque and mittens and took a moment to glance around the reception area. A huge crystal chandelier overhead cast a yellow glow on a dark varnished desk, behind which stood a middle-aged woman in a lime green jogging suit.

"May I help you?" she asked.

When Felicity inquired about a membership, the woman eyed her from head to toe and said, "This IS a private club."

Felicity never bragged about her income or status as future president of Starr Transport but couldn't stand the woman's haughty manner. Clearly, she had no idea who she was dealing with.

"I know," she said. "My father told me about this club; he sends his out-of-town clients here."

The woman gave her a frozen smile. "And which company is he with?"

"You probably haven't heard of it," Felicity said. Of course, almost everyone knew of her father's company. Its transport trucks were all over the city, its name on billboards. "Starr Transport." As the woman's eyes widened, Felicity continued, "He owns the company and I work there, too. Here," she said, handing the woman her business card after pulling it out from the wallet tucked into an inside pocket of her ski jacket.

"Hold on a sec," the woman said, her manner suddenly alert and business-like, "and I'll page one of the trainers to show you around."

In no time at all, a short, muscular woman appeared and indicated that Felicity should follow her. The hallways were filled with people in shorts and t-shirts, leotards and colorful spandex tops. They passed by a lounge that included an aquarium with exotic fish and a counter where one could buy fruit juices, smoothies and healthy snacks. A few men in their forties chatted on one of the leather couches, their foreheads beaded in sweat, towels draped around their necks. One of them gave her a cursory glance before turning back to his friends. In that moment, Felicity felt judged, found lacking and dismissed. How rude, she thought.

The trainer led her past the tennis courts and along the enclosures of the squash courts. The sound of the squash ball hitting the wall reverberated in Felicity's head, causing it to ache. She glanced at herself in the glass window. No wonder the receptionist was skeptical. With her ripped jacket, her too-large ski pants and mussed up hair with its purple streak, she looked unkempt.

They came to a room at the far end of a hallway. The door was closed, but they watched women jumping up and down through the glassed panel. Just watching them exhausted Felicity. Up a flight of stairs and they arrived at a room the size of a basketball court.

"It's all state-of-the-art equipment," said the trainer, pointing out stationary bicycles, leg presses and outer and inner thigh machines, and upper and lower arm curls that looked like they came from another orbit. Felicity's focus, though, was not on the equipment but on the men using it. As she and the trainer passed several of them, she caught snatches of their conversations on bonds and securities, while the screens on their machines showed graphs of their workouts. The room felt confining and the air stuffy. She found herself walking a little faster. Not only did this not seem like fun, but did she really want to meet another businessman?

"Let me show you the ladies' locker room," said the trainer. They passed shelves stacked with fluffy white towels, a sauna, a whirlpool and a steam room before coming to a door. Behind it was an Olympic-sized swimming pool surrounded by lounge chairs and tropical plants. Felicity noticed a few well-groomed women stretched out on chairs next to their boyfriends or husbands, the Saturday paper folded to the sports page. At the far end of the pool, an elderly man held out a towel for a woman half his age, embracing her as she came out of the pool.

"What do you think?" asked the trainer as they made their way back to the reception area.

Felicity thought of the fluffy towels perfectly stacked and the men in the gym talking about their investments. It was all so orderly and had a sterile, homogenous feel to it. She had not seen one client of color and it reminded her of her job with its rules and ways of functioning that she had to obey. How could she come here in her off-time? It would only be a continuation of the business world that she had come to hate.

"It's certainly luxurious," said Felicity, "but I don't think it's for me." Maybe her life was lonely but at least it was hers to spend how she chose.

On her way out of the sports center, her eyes caught an ad on the bulletin board.

Are you a woman searching for Prince Charming?

Can daughters of unavailable fathers find love?

If you would like to be part of this study, please call

Campbell Jones for more information.

Yes, she was searching for Prince Charming. She thought about how none of the men she'd dated had won her father's approval. He had been so quick to point out their flaws that she inevitably lost interest in them.

She ignored the part of the ad about unavailable fathers. If anything, her father was too available. Below the text were little tags with a phone number to tear off. None of them had yet been taken. Felicity guessed that the women who came here already had their Prince Charming. She tore off one of the numbers and crammed it into the pocket of her parka.

When she got home, she called the number but only got voicemail. She left a message.

Felicity was in the shower when Campbell called back, telling her about the first session on Tuesday evening. She jotted down the particulars.

Finally, six o'clock arrived. Things didn't bother her after six. As a teenager, when her parents went out to concerts or to see friends, she loved having the house to herself. Playing her music as loud as she wanted to. Practicing dance steps. Drawing. The memory of this time of freedom had stuck with her; she'd always enjoyed staying home alone on Saturday evenings.

She inserted her iPod into her docking station and turned it on to shuffle. A few songs came on as she chewed on a protein bar. Ringo Starr's *It Don't Come Easy* filled her apartment. For a long time, she'd been unable to listen to any of The Beatles' songs. Flopping onto the couch, her naked feet up on the coffee table, Felicity allowed herself to return to the past when she was a chubby ten-year-old.

Her father had told her that she was related to Ringo Starr, The Beatles' drummer. When she bragged about that at school, Patti Lambert – the most popular girl in the class – had said, "You're nothing but a fat liar. You can't be related to Ringo Starr. His real name is Richard Starkey." After all these years, Patti's dreadful words still stung.

When she had come home and told her father about this, he'd said that he only wanted the best for her.

How could the best for her be based on a lie, Felicity wondered as the lyrics *I don't ask for much, I only want trust* floated around her.

Chapter 5

Campbell gazed out the window of the National Library in the Latin Quarter. She had come here to work on the speech she was to deliver in New York at the end of May. It was such a big moment for her, such a coup to be invited. She was determined to give an amazing talk. More than that, she was getting an award.

She loved working in this library, loved its energy, its potted palms, the displays of new acquisitions, and the comings and goings of people. They reminded her of travelers in a train station, en route to destinations in the imaginations of writers and great thinkers. As usual, she chose a working area by the window on the third floor and settled her legs under a varnished desk. Like all the others in the row, it had its own emerald green lamp.

It always dismayed her how many women still believed in Prince Charming, how so many of her clients had come to her wanting to find a man who would sweep them off their feet and solve all their problems - emotional, financial and even psychological. Campbell rarely found a woman who was determined to be her own hero. In her five years of researching the Prince Charming myth, she had come across hundreds of women who still hoped for a knight in shining armor to appear and rescue them.

Rescue them from what? From a past filled with pain, humiliation, abandonment and emptiness? From a future of fear, solitude, dying alone and the realization that, after all, there was no one to love them? Or were they simply hoping for that one last chance at rapture?

She could understand the motivations of the girls she had counseled at the center for troubled youth. For the promise of a better life, they willingly engaged in promiscuous behavior or risked addiction and depression. She could see why they would trust in pimps who promised them luxury and security and made them feel special, at least in the beginning.

Her work had never been easy with these girls. Dignity, self fulfillment and integrity couldn't compete with their needs to feel secure and taken care of. Campbell had succeeded in persuading some of them to pay attention to a higher level of need. With others — those she had at times run into as young adults hustling their bodies along the strip joints – she saw despair and hopelessness etched in their faces. There was no need to tell these women that Prince Charming wasn't coming. They had long ago given up on that myth and on the prospect of any sort of rescue.

It was her clients, both in her private practice as well as her research study, who were the most difficult for Campbell to comprehend. These were women in their thirties, forties and fifties who had careers and were financially independent. They had the ability to take care of themselves, to do whatever rescuing had to be done. Yet they were still waiting for the beast to turn back into a prince so that they could continue their happy-ever-after lives, or for the prince to show up and somehow make it all effortless. Why couldn't they trust their own abilities? Or rely on themselves?

Sitting at the desk with her back to the window, she opened her lap-top. As she waited for it to boot, she received a text message on her cell. It was from Chand. She felt her mouth stretch into a spontaneous smile.

Chand: What's up?

Campbell: Working at the library.

Chand: Have 2 tickets to the premiere of The Wolverine. Want to join me?

Campbell: When?

Chand: Today. 7 o'clock. I get off work at 6:30. We'll meet in front of Forum at 6:50.

Campbell: Sounds like fun.

Chand: ☺

She turned off her phone and clicked on her Prince Charming file. Inside were hundreds of pages of notes, interviews and research. She began to comb through the text, highlighting passages to use in her speech:

Women often see men as their rescuers, their source of happiness.

Women need to remain true to themselves and not give up their value in order to please a man.

With the absence of a male figure in her childhood, a woman will create a fantasy about what a relationship should look like – secure and ever present. No real-world relationship will match her fantasy. As a result, the woman will always be waiting for a man who never arrives.

A slight quiver started in her stomach, moving upwards into her chest and constricting the muscles of her throat. Campbell stopped reading. Why had she said "yes" to Chand when she knew she needed to work tonight? She shifted in her chair, leaned away from her laptop, then stood and faced the window. She glanced at the Comfort Inn across the street and watched the traffic slowed down by the snow. A woman, or was it a man — she couldn't tell from this distance — was tossing snowballs for a dog to fetch in the park down the street. Along the west side of the park, the homeless lined up, waiting for the food bank van to arrive. From her working experience, she knew that most of them, primarily the men, had been let out too early from mental institutions. It always amazed her that while they might rage and vent the rest of the day and night, in their wait for their daily meal, they formed a peaceful and respectful line. Grateful to be fed.

These men would never be anybody's Prince Charming. She wondered if, as young boys, they'd ever had such dreams. Surely some of them must have. And now look where they had landed. She too had had such dreams. The white picket fence, the three children (two girls and one boy), perhaps a golden retriever named Sunny. And of course, the man, the husband, the ever-loving father whom you could always count on. Life hadn't been as harsh for her as it had been for some of the homeless in that bread line. But it had squeezed out of her any desire to be rescued. It had proven to her that she could only count on herself.

There had been two men in her life who could have filled the Prince Charming mold. There was Josh, whom she dated in her last two years of high school. It occurred to her that somewhere in her house, though she couldn't remember where, was a long list of criteria for the man she sought. Being good at math had been one of the items.

Although the list had not yet been compiled while she was with Josh, she was disappointed with him. Though good-looking, generous and in love with her, he had trouble understanding physics and that had prevented her from loving him.

The second man she had met at university. He was what they called "madly in love" with her. Apart from being smart, funny and athletic, he treated her kindly. She rejected him as well. This time, though, it was because he wasn't tall enough. She had simply been unable to get over the fact that she could never wear high heels when they went out.

Campbell gave into her curiosity and Googled Josh. His name came up on several sites. A wave of regret washed over her as she read that he was the director of the entrepreneur business department at Ryerson University. He had been a very successful businessman, starting his own sports apparel company, and was now on the board of directors of several businesses and charities. She then Googled the boyfriend she'd had at university and read that he was one of the top lawyers in New England, defending victims of medical malpractice suits.

It was a sobering discovery – two accomplished, high-profile men who had loved her and whom she'd rejected for stupid reasons.

The clock on the wall said five-forty. She calculated that it would take her no more than twenty minutes to reach the Forum by subway and meet Chand. That left her almost an hour to work. She went back to her Prince Charming file but found herself unable to concentrate.

Wasn't saying "yes" to Chand exactly what she counseled women not to do? She had planned on spending the evening working on her research project. Instead, she'd placed Chand's wishes before her own. She didn't even like adventure movies. And she hardly knew him. They'd been on only one date.

Why hadn't she told him that she was busy and that she didn't care that much for those kinds of films? Her heart began to race. She had said yes to please him. His needs had become more important than hers – after just one date. Campbell pulled in a deep breath. She could always text Chand back and tell him that she couldn't make it. After picking up her phone, she set it down again.

She returned to her file on father/daughter relationships. Based on years of research, she had concluded that girls who were fatherless – whether physically or emotionally — developed a fear of commitment as a defense mechanism. To place themselves in the vulnerable position of being rejected again was too risky, too painful.

Was this what she had been doing with the men who'd come into her life? Those brief affairs that sooner or later led to her finding fault? He was too old. Too young. Too dull. Too conservative. Not conservative enough.

The men she couldn't count on formed the majority of her failed relationships. She was especially tired of those who told her they'd call and never did, leaving her feeling rejected and disappointed. Men who called at the last minute to cancel a date with no consideration of the many hours she'd spent getting ready, not to mention the money she'd put into a new outfit. She was disgusted with men who told her that they wanted a long-term relationship and when the subject of commitment arose, flew like a rooster lit with a firecracker. Didn't they know that long term implied commitment? That without commitment there was no relationship? Ignoring that was the most glaring fault of all.

At times, she had felt like Goldilocks looking for the man who was just right. He, of course, had never materialized. Instead, she had given up and plunged into her research with the aplomb of a woman wildly in love. In love with her career.

Campbell turned off her laptop. She wished she'd worn something more elegant than the ratty old sweater that practically reached the knees of her woolen leggings. And her hair. She looked at its shadow in the window. My God, she thought, had she ever had a good hair day in her life? It was flat from having worn her winter tuque and, although it was impossible to tell its color from the shadow, she knew that the claret red needed a fresh washing.

The subway station was beneath the library and although she had no need to put on her coat, she did so to disguise her carelessness in dress, and then walked down the stairs to the crowded platform.

As she rode the subway car, the problems created by a father's absence preoccupied her. Repeatedly, she'd seen its crippling effects not only in her clients but in her own life. Although she had come to terms with her solitary state, she had used her experiences to help other women navigate this murky reality of the non-existent Prince Charming. At least some good had come out of her own situation. She was at the peak of her career and an expert in her field. She could almost hear the applause from an enthusiastic audience in New York.

Chand already waited for her when she reached the cinema. Her breathing accelerated as he held out his arms to her. Of their own volition, her arms wrapped themselves around his slim waist, accepting his embrace. He was about the same height as her, she realized, maybe even a bit shorter had she worn her sexy boots with their two-inch heels. She recalled the other short men she had rejected and just as quickly dismissed the thought. Campbell felt comfortable in his arms, like one piece of a puzzle fitting perfectly into another. She had never felt anything like this before.

He drew back and handed her a book. "I got this for you."

She studied the cover. It was a novel by Anita Desai. Campbell was not much of a reader of fiction. Her personal library was made up of mostly psychology and social science books and her living room table was piled with magazines such as Behavior and Relationships, Psychology Today, Scientific American. When she read the odd novel, it was usually a mystery that she could escape into for a few hours. She derived tremendous satisfaction at guessing who the murderer was. And almost always did.

"Thank you," she said, touched that he had thought of her. She turned to read the back cover. "Anita Desai's sensitively portrays the inner feelings of female characters."

"You've read this book?" she asked, surprised that a man would be interested in such a subject. Most men she knew had little concern for feelings, whether those of a woman or their own.

"No. No," Chand said, as if embarrassed. "I e-mailed my sister and asked her to recommend a book written by an Indian writer that women might like. I picked it up at the book store on my lunch hour."

Campbell pressed a hand to her heart. "Thank you," she said again. "I'll let you know what I think about it."

She placed it into her handbag as carefully as if it were a delicate flower that she didn't want crushed.

Chand rested his hand lightly on her elbow as he led her inside the cinema. "Have you ever been to India?" he asked.

"No, but it's one of the countries I've always wanted to visit," she said.

Her interest in India stemmed not from a curiosity about its culture but because Carl Jung had spent time there. But she had never travelled there, or overseas for that matter, for she was terrified of flying. Her anxiety had always been a source of embarrassment and had caused her to miss two important conferences on father/daughter relationships: one in Scotland, the other in Brazil.

"Well, then you can come with me, if you wish. I am going back home in mid April."

"India?" she said, stunned at his request. "For how long?"

"Three weeks."

She had exactly a three-week gap between her last research group and the conference. But why was she even considering it? Besides her flying terror, hadn't the literature on her research clearly demonstrated that people who were in love risked everything for their partners? She couldn't allow that to happen to her. And why in the world was she thinking that she might be in love with Chand? She barely knew him. Had met him only three days ago. She was not a believer of love at first sight. People who fell head over heels upon meeting someone for the first time were merely encountering their demons. It took time to know a person.

"I don't know you well enough for that," she said.

"It will be a wonderful way for us to get to know each other," he said, as he gave the tickets to the usher at the entrance. "You can meet my family and I will show you around my province. India is a large country. One needs a guide to really appreciate it."

It sounded wonderful, but she wouldn't let herself fall into that trap.

"Perhaps," she said, and stepped into the darkened theater.

Although Campbell couldn't concentrate on the movie, she enjoyed sitting next to Chand. She found herself leaning her head against his shoulder, inhaling his intoxicating scent of spices and soap. She braided her arm around his. She felt like she was sixteen again — or rather how she should have felt when she was sixteen but never did.

Her teenage years had been a horrible period for her. A period of anger mixed with fear. For six years she had watched her mother slowly die and when she finally passed on, Campbell was filled with relief, guilt and grief. And always anger. It was during the last years of her mother's illness that she had met Josh, and not long after her mother's death that Campbell left him. What need was there for an anchor when the ship had sunk?

"I feel too much grief to love you or anyone else," she had told Josh, offering an excuse for their break-up. His difficulty in physics had only come to her later, although it had been sitting in the back of her mind all along.

After the movie, Chand insisted on going with her the extra four stations to see her home. For most of the way, he talked about the movie and she listened with admiration to his analysis of the cinematography, the sound effects, the special effects, and the music. She wished she'd paid more attention during the movie, for Chand's enthusiasm made it seem like a remarkable film.

"The next stop is mine," she said, gathering her bag and buttoning up her coat.

He got off with her. She assumed he would just traverse the overpass to the tracks on the other side for his ride back home. Instead, he began to walk towards the escalators that led outside.

"You don't have to walk me home," she said.

"I know," he said. "But I want to." He placed an arm around her shoulders.

She loved this feeling of being protected and yet she feared being drawn into risky waters. If she let herself get swept away, all her research would look like a sham, like something she didn't really believe. She stopped suddenly. She was so close to the pinnacle of her career, to recognition, to the sense of belonging that would come from being in the inner circle of experts. She slipped away from Chand's side and continued to walk towards her home, careful not to touch him.

When they reached the front steps of her house, he said, "I better get going. It's late and I have to be at work early tomorrow."

She looked down. "Thank you for the movie, the book and for taking me home," she said, her voice tight with disappointment that he did not want to linger.

He reached for her then and held her in his arms. When he lifted her chin, she gazed straight into his eyes, seeing the undeniable warmth in their depths. This time he pressed his lips against hers. They were soft and gentle, pushing her research far away.

"Want to do something tomorrow evening?" he asked.

For a second, she thought of cancelling her research meeting, then came to her senses. "I can't," she said, grateful to have a legitimate excuse. "My research group starts tomorrow."

Campbell had avoided telling him about the Prince Charming myth. The last man she discussed her research with accused her of being a feminist bitch. It wasn't so much that she associated with being a feminist. She didn't like to box herself in. She was merely a woman who believed in equality for everyone.

Chand nodded, reminded her to think about the trip to India, and walked away.

Under the warm blankets of her bed, her imagination drifted to images of Chand's strong hands on her breasts, making their way down her stomach and thighs. Thinking of him started an electric charge vibrating in her veins that triggered her entire blood system. *India, with a handsome Indian guide!* And then she shook her head. No. She wasn't going to let these sexual feelings ruin her career and what she had toiled over for so many years. Chand was sweet and sexy and she loved how he made her feel special, but he had walked into her life at the worst possible time.

She switched her focus to the women in her new group. She wondered what they would be like. Felicity on her voicemail had sounded as tremulous as a teenager, filled with anxiety. Then there was Suzy, whom she'd spoken to. Such a lovely voice, though Campbell had detected notes of sadness in it.

She took out the book that Chand had given her and began to read it, hoping to be lulled to sleep. But it was about India, which only made her think about his offer to travel with him. She realized that she already missed him. After closing the book and the light, she lay on her bed and stared at her ceiling in the dark. It was silly of her to think that there was anything between her and Chand. Things had never worked out with men, so why believe they would this time? How could they? The absence of her father's love had left a trail of mistrust. That was what her research was all about. She was proving it with empirical evidence and she was proving it in her own life.

This brought to mind an autobiographical article she'd written for the Journal of Social Science. It related how she'd always rejected the men she dated. She had linked this to her fear of reopening the early wound of being abandoned by her father. Then she had explained how a father's absence instilled the feeling of never belonging. Because of the lack of a positive father figure, a woman didn't see herself sailing off into the sunset with her dream man. The irony was that, consciously or unconsciously, she constantly sought this.

Chapter 6

Campbell dreamt she was seated in the back seat of a car. It seemed to be her car, although she'd never owned a car in her entire life. In front, her mother was reading Joyce Carol Oates' Blonde – the inner life of Marilyn Monroe.

A phone shrilled. By the time Campbell realized it was in real life and got up to answer it, the dream was firmly planted in her memory. A dead mother reading about the life of a tormented woman.

Campbell picked up the phone.

"I hope I didn't wake you," said Tina, her father's latest girlfriend. She had always liked Tina. In fact, had she not been living with her father, she was the kind of woman Campbell would have enjoyed having as a girlfriend. She was smart, fun to be with and only a few months younger than her own thirty-eight. What in the world she was doing with her father puzzled Campbell. She wondered how long her father's roaming eyes would begin to wander once more.

Campbell glanced at the clock on her night table. It was past noon.

"Listen," Tina said, "I'm planning on having the family over to celebrate your father's birthday."

"How old's he going to be?" Campbell asked, as she made her way into the kitchen.

"Sixty."

"Is this a surprise party?"

"No," Tina said. "Just a family get together."

Campbell felt her stomach harden. Why hadn't her father mentioned the party last Saturday when she ran into him?

"Couldn't he call me himself?" she asked, although she had no desire to talk to her father and endure his fake interest in her. Why give him the satisfaction of knowing anything about her life? Having abandoned her years ago, he'd forfeited that right. That he hadn't called himself was further proof that he was unworthy of her attention.

"You know how busy he is," said Tina.

"I met him the other day. He could have mentioned the party," Campbell insisted. She turned on the tap in the kitchen sink, her bare feet chilled by the coolness of the faded green linoleum, and filled a kettle with fresh water.

"He told me that he ran into you. Said you were with a very nice gentleman. Why don't you bring him along?"

"No," she said too quickly. "I mean we're not that close."

After her phone call with Tina, she took her cup of tea into her living room, where she stretched out on her couch next to the front window. With the cup of tea in one hand and Anita Desai's novel in her other, she began to read. The sensitive, elegant writing soothed Campbell until she read this passage: *All of us, every one of us, has had a moment when a window opened, when we caught a glimpse of the open, sunlit world beyond, but all of us on this bus have had that window close and remain closed.*

She put the book face down on her lap to glance around the living room – the same room where she had spent hours with her mother during the last months of her illness. Since her mother's death over twenty years ago, Campbell had slowly made changes to the house. It was a good, solid duplex and because of its location near the Jean Talon Market and the subway station, she had never had any trouble renting the upper part. She'd used the little money she inherited when her mother died to renovate the upper duplex so that it would bring in more rent. Her intention had been to update her own kitchen and enlarge the tiny bathroom but somehow, as the years went by, she'd never had enough money or the energy to do so.

Practical. That ought to be my middle name, she thought.

Campbell stared out the bay window of her living room. Small snowflakes, the size of faraway stars, were floating down from the sky. She thought about Anita Desai's words. Was she, with Chand, closing the window that had unexpectedly opened in her life?

Chand was different from the other men she'd dated. She felt his genuine interest in getting to know her. Other men never bothered asking questions about her life, but Chand did. It felt as if he wanted to see into her soul.

The moment she formed this thought, her stomach tightened; she realized that she liked him more than she wanted to, more than she should. Yet she had gotten along fine until he came along. Maybe her life had been a struggle at times, having to take care of the maintenance of her house on her own. A man, of course, could make her life easier, but at what cost? A good relationship took time and she barely found the time for her clients and her research. Besides, she could just hear the women from her research groups asking, wondering if Campbell walked the walk or only talked the talk.

She placed her book aside and went into her bathroom to shower before putting on a print-flowered blouse and her favorite brown skirt. She wore a wide head band to hide her silver roots, and with extra care, applied a thin line of brown eyeliner along her upper eyelids. Her eyes, brown with glimmers of yellow, were her best feature. She picked up her handbag and headed for the door. Focusing on her dream of exposing the Prince Charming myth and helping women to lead fulfilling lives on their own, she made her way north, closing the short distance between her and the Women's Center.

Chapter 7

The first woman to arrive stood by the doorway as she peered cautiously into the room. She wore a tailored navy cloth coat and leather boots. "I'm here for the Prince Charming study," she announced.

"You came to the right place," said Campbell, walking towards her. "I'm Campbell Jones. And you are?" She extended a hand to her, but the other woman ignored it, panned the room and said, "Felicity Starr."

They stood in a large, rectangular room in a building that used to be a clothing factory. Eight folding chairs were evenly spaced around a card table. Campbell had placed a box of tissues and a white scentless candle on the table as well as African violets on the windowsill, hoping to offset the bleakness of the room.

She told Felicity to take a seat, reassuring her that the others would arrive shortly, and pointed to a series of hooks along the wall where she could hang her coat.

Felicity stared at the rusty hooks. "That's alright," she said. "I'll leave it on for now." She chose a seat at the table opposite the place where

Campbell had left her notes and slid the box of tissues away from her.

"Where did you hear about my study?" Campbell asked.

"On a poster at a gym. So, is this something like AA?"

Campbell shook her head. "Not at all. I mean we don't have the Serenity Prayer or anything like that, but I do encourage women to become more resourceful and to share with each other. What made you decide to come?"

Felicity fiddled with the buttons on her coat. "I am so ready to find my Prince Charming."

"This isn't about finding your Prince Charming," Campbell said with a patient smile. "It's about giving up the myth. Giving up the desire of being rescued."

"Oh," said Felicity, disappointment on her face. "Why would anyone want to do that?"

Campbell knew it would take more than two minutes to defend her thesis. "Why don't you stay for this session and then you can decide whether this is the right place for you?"

"How long is this...um... going to last?"

"Twelve weeks."

"I mean tonight's class."

Her question reminded Campbell of those obnoxious students in the tutorial class she'd given years ago. They had to endure her if they wanted their credits, but Felicity didn't have to be here. She focused her attention on Felicity's Hermes watch. "We should be finished by nine."

Before things got more awkward, the second woman confidently strode in. She was tall, slender, had straight, platinum blonde hair to her shoulders and a very white smile that must have cost a fortune. "You must be Campbell," she said, extending her hand. Their warm handshake was of equal strength. "We spoke over the phone last Saturday. I'm Suzy Paradise."

"Yes, of course," said Campbell, surprised at her age. From her voice on the phone, she had pictured a woman in her late thirties, like herself. Not someone closer to fifty.

"Where can I hang my coat?" she asked. Her opened coat, elaborately fur-trimmed, revealed a short black leather skirt and a silk print scarf. Both the fur and the leather looked real. This, Campbell thought, was definitely not a woman concerned with animal rights.

"By the door," said Campbell.

After she hung her coat, Campbell introduced her to Felicity. The latter gave her a wave, brushing aside her handshake offer.

Suzy settled into a seat facing Felicity. "Aren't you going to take your coat off?" she asked, "It's so hot in here!"

"I'm cold," said Felicity and moved her chair slightly away.

Campbell smiled warmly at the women, hoping to dispel the tension. She then fixed her eyes on the newcomer and asked, "So, Suzy, what draws you here?"

Suzy loosened the knot of her scarf, allowing the silk to drape over her shoulders. The colors accentuated the violet of her eyes. "It may seem silly, but I'm attracted to men much younger than me. It's not that I have anything against a woman dating someone younger. I mean, men do it all the time, so why shouldn't we? It's the way they all leave me feeling empty."

Campbell had been right about the sadness she'd heard in Suzy's voice over the phone. It was like a scent that seeped out of her pores and lingered in the air around her. It was similar to the sadness she had sensed in hundreds of girls she'd counseled at the center for troubled youth.

"Why don't you try dating a man your own age," Felicity blurted.

Suzy gave her a tight-lipped smile. "Maybe it's because men my age are only interested in dating women your age."

Felicity groaned. "Just because older men are attracted to me doesn't make it easy. When I saw your ad about Prince Charming," she said, addressing herself to Campbell, "I said to myself, 'that woman is all wrong.' No offense. But if you met my daddy, you would know what I mean." She finally unbuttoned her navy coat, revealing a matching woolen dress with a pearl necklace. Then she removed her outer garment entirely and placed it on the back of her chair.

Her ultra conservative outfit puzzled Campbell. The purple streak in her hair clashed with what she was wearing, and to Campbell, signalled a streak of rebelliousness.

"What do you mean?" she asked Felicity.

"He is the genuine Prince Charming."

"Isn't that a bit incestuous?" asked Suzy.

Blonde bitch, Campbell categorized her in her mind. She knew the type well. She had been one herself in her undergraduate years. She felt smug at the prospect of how astonished her professors - those who'd pegged her as a dumb blonde - would be when they heard about her research. Of course, now her hair was no longer blonde. In a reactionary attempt to become *au naturel*, she'd let it grow out in its claret-hued shade, and no longer bothered taming the wild curls. The blonde hair had been an experiment of hers; she'd wanted to see whether blondes did, in fact, have more fun. Her sad conclusion was that, as a blonde, she'd dated more times in six months than in her entire life as a redhead, even after adding in the "bitch factor" for the sake of her research. Blonde bitch trumped graceful, understanding redhead every time.

Felicity gave Suzy a murderous glare. "Really?" she said. "That's all you can think of?"

Campbell saw Suzy's eyes narrow and her hands clench as she prepared to respond. These were the sort of remarks that led to conflict, or worse, violence.

"Let's not get into that right now," Campbell said, clutching her Styrofoam cup from coffee purchased on her way here. Doubts snaked into her mind, questioning her competence and ability to remain calm and professional, undermining her faith that she could control an unruly situation if need be.

Fortunately, Missi walked in at that moment. Strutted in was more like it, thought Campbell. The other women turned to stare. Missi, who had always taken care of herself, looked more strikingly beautiful than usual. Yet Campbell knew it was all for show; she was trying too hard.

After introductions were made, Missi asked Felicity, "Would you like me to hang your coat while I hang mine?"

Felicity shook her head quite forcefully and said no. There was a moment of silence before she added, "Thank you."

The dress Missi wore showed off her bust line; her legs were encased in a pair of stylish knee-high boots. In spite of the care she'd taken with her appearance, no amount of foundation could mask her swollen eyelids or the pinkness in the whites of her eyes. She's probably been crying since I spoke to her last night, thought Campbell.

Missi sat near Felicity, placing her oversized red patent leather tote bag on the chair between them.

When it became obvious that no other woman would show up, Campbell fought to hide her disappointment. Having a small group wouldn't be fair to these women. Ten women had assured her of their participation. Now, only three were here. If they weren't going to come, why did they say they would? She knew the answer to that: it was easier to lie than to let people down. Whatever happened to personal integrity?

Campbell took out a booklet of matches, struck one and lit the candle. She then looked at the notes before her, cleared her throat and began. "I'm sure this is going to be an enriching experience for all of us." She paused and gave them what she hoped was a confident and encouraging smile. "Thank you all for coming. I'm so happy that you're here. I'll begin by telling you a bit about myself and my research."

She told them that she'd been working at the Women's Center for years and that they were her sixth and last group. "I've counseled hundreds of women in the midst of what I call a 'man crisis.' Women who place all their hopes and dreams on a man rather than tap into their own strengths." She explained how women often sought the love of a man for their validation, and this wasn't only the uneducated or impoverished. These were also women who had good jobs. Lawyers. Advertising executives. Bankers. "I want to prove to you that we don't need a relationship with a man to feel whole about ourselves."

"Are you one of these man haters?" asked Felicity.

Campbell counted to three before she replied. "I don't hate men," she said. "And I still believe in love. That's not what my research is about. We've bought into this love-ever-after fairy tale. And believe that this kind of love will conquer all, solve all our problems. There are many of us out there who are perfectly happy without being in a relationship."

A series of thoughts raced through her mind. Had she attached herself to this Prince Charming myth only to justify her lack of a man in her life? Clinging to theories having to do with being strong and doing it all on her own? Worse, was she sabotaging her relationship with Chand to prove herself right? Her heart pounded. It both shocked and frightened her to realize how quickly her values and beliefs could vanish with the prospect of a Prince Charming.

"Is this one of those feminist approaches?" Felicity persisted.

Campbell ran her hand through the unruly curls in her hair and felt the beginning of a headache. "Basically," she said, forcing herself to speak slowly, "I'm interested in the relationship between a father's abandonment and a woman's adult relationships with men. I am working on a theory that..."

Felicity sat up straighter and broke in, "My father didn't abandon me."

"Not all abandonment needs to be physical," Campbell explained. "There's also emotional neglect and psychological abandonment. Just because the father is physically present, doesn't mean that he hasn't abandoned his daughter on another level."

Now Felicity studied her nails, as if she didn't care what else Campbell might say. Campbell adjusted her chair before leaning forward. "Most of the research I've looked at points to a correlation between a father's abandonment and a daughter's inability to find her 'Prince Charming.'" She decided not to mention that her own experience with her father had led to the same conclusions.

At the mention of Prince Charming, Missi let out a whimper. Her eyes filled with tears. "I'm so sorry," she said. "It's just that I believed I would always be with Max. He was my Prince Charming. He's gone now and I just ... I don't know ... I feel like a failure as a woman."

"Gone?" asked Campbell.

Missi went on to explain Max's affair to the other women. "When he came back from his weekend, he admitted that he'd gone away with Sheri and now he's taken an apartment. He needs space, he told me."

Felicity reached out to stroke Missi's arm, as if she were stroking the back of a cat, and Missi erupted into sobs. Everyone sat silently watching. When she finally stopped, it was Felicity, not Campbell, who spoke first.

"One day you'll be grateful he left," she said. "You'll find a better man who'll sweep you off your feet."

"Being swept off your feet ...," Campbell began, but Missi looked up at Felicity through teary eyes. "I don't want another man," she said softly.

Barely fifteen minutes had passed and already Campbell felt mentally exhausted. Spreading her hands over the table without touching it, she tried again. "Being swept off your feet only leads to falling on your back," she said.

"You can't be fulfilled when your happiness is tied to being loved by a man."

She thought of Chand and how she felt with him. The idea of a relationship frightened her. All her relationships with men had left her disappointed or heartbroken. No, it was better to stick to her usual arguments; no sense rocking the boat. "Until you can count on your own self-fulfillment, you'll always be hoping for that illusive fairy tale. The research is very clear on this. My colleague, Doctor...."

"What's wrong with wanting a fairy tale?" Missi blurted, as she took out a mirror and a cleansing pad from her tote bag and wiped the mascara that had smeared below her eyes and down her cheeks.

"It's a fairy tale — not real life," Campbell said. "That's what's wrong."

Felicity rolled her eyes to the ceiling and Campbell pretended not to notice. What was happening to her? Why was she getting so riled? She took in long, steady breaths in order to calm down.

"There are so many women who want to be saved by a Prince Charming," she said. "The truth is that it's never going to happen. The more I tried to find out why this myth is so pervasive, the more clearly, I saw a pattern emerging. Most of these women had absent fathers. There's a very strong correlation between women who believe in the Prince Charming myth and father rejection."

"Not the case with me," said Felicity. "My father treats me like a princess. He's always buying me gifts."

"Of course," murmured Suzy.

Campbell's headache sharpened and she massaged her temples. "My goal here is to make you feel whole about yourselves. To see that your lives are worthwhile and rich without a man. Or gifts."

The women stared at her, disappointment on their faces. She was used to this. The women who came to her sessions were all seeking a man to save them. Campbell had made it her professional goal to help them realize that their strengths lay within themselves. It was what she was best at.

She knew there was always a price to pay for having a man take care of you. Hadn't Missi sacrificed a writing career for Max? And what was she left with? An empty house, a broken heart, and a once-sharp writing skill that had gone to seed. This was a story which Campbell had heard repeatedly over the years. Woman latches onto Prince Charming. Who, after a few decades of "bliss," frees himself from his aging wife. Wife is left clutching the hope that her Prince Charming will return. He never does. And then her sacrifices become glaringly obvious. And she has to start from scratch figuring out who she is, what she wants, and what she needs to do to get it. Far better to depend on yourself from the start.

"All right, let's get started. I want you to fill out this questionnaire on your relationship with your father. Just answer as honestly as you can," she said, handing them each a copy. She had found the questionnaire in Cosmo and although it wasn't a foolproof, scientific one – which study was, anyway – it was exactly what she needed. She retyped it and made a few changes to the wording, praying that none of the women had come across it in Cosmo.

As the women filled in the questionnaire, Campbell flipped through her notes. Her eyes fixed on lines she had highlighted: *women who had difficulty getting attention from their fathers will choose the same type of men for romantic partners.*

Chand's words – "Don't confuse me with your father" – jumped into her mind. Thankfully, he was nothing like her father.

Her mind shifted to the adjacent part of her research, the part she most cared about: did absent fathers make for absent romantic relationships later in life? She had plenty of anecdotes to support that theory. She'd read books on the subject, dissertations and blogs dedicated to the absent father. And hadn't her own unlucky record with men and her absent father supported the theory?

"I'm finished," said Felicity with a pleased expression. "The test proves how important Daddy is in my life. Says I see him as a protector. I've always felt protected by him."

Campbell thought of her evening with Chand. She had felt protected. She thought of his offer to take her to India. Going on her own or with an organized group were not options for her; she hated being pushed around like cattle. But with Chand next to her, she would have no worries. He would take her to see the Holy City of Rishikesh along the Ganges, where she could see with her own eyes why the river was considered divine.

Yet, wanting a man to protect her was exactly what she'd been working so hard to prevent. She prided herself on being an independent woman. She'd seen what dependency had done to her mother – left her a shell of a person at the end of her life, unable to find fulfillment in work or to meet people without downing her collection of anti-anxiety pills along with a stiff drink, unable to let go of her bitterness towards life and trapped in her loneliness - and had vowed never to be in that situation herself.

"You can't just commit to a man because you feel protected by him," she felt compelled to say.

She turned towards Suzy. "What did you learn from your questionnaire?"

Suzy's results were the complete opposite of Felicity's. "The test points out that I dislike my father. No ground-breaking news there." She crossed her arms and Campbell noticed her face flush. Was it anger? Disappointment? Contempt? Or all three?

Missi's results indicated that her father was someone she might not even recognize if she met him on the street. This had actually happened to her. She reached for the strap of her tote bag and began to wind it around her fingers as she explained.

"I was six or seven years old. My sister Emily and I were on our way to the movies when a strange man stopped us and began to talk to us. Turned out he was my father. Of course, I couldn't have known. I was only an infant when he deserted us."

"It's rough being disappointed by a man," Suzy said, "but more than rough when that man is your father."

"The research studies show that a father's rejection sets the stage for all the other men that follow," said Campbell.

"Could be rough the other way around, too," said Felicity. The other three women waited for her to continue. "Just because you have a father who adores you, is no guarantee that you'll meet a man who also adores you and treats you like a princess."

Chapter 8

Campbell felt herself bristle whenever the phone rang. That evening Chand called. And he called the next evening, too. She had to make a choice – either Chand or her research. His presence in her life was upsetting her findings. As much as she wanted to be with him, she knew that she couldn't have both. She was in control of her research whereas with Chand, who knew … it might only be a passing thing and she was not ready to give up something tangible for something that could be as fleeting as star dust. She needed to tell him that she couldn't keep seeing him.

"I hope you miss me half as much as I miss you," Chand said as soon as he heard her voice.

Her feet felt like they had floated two inches off the ground. Campbell bit her lip. Be strong. Be strong, she commanded herself. "Listen, Chand, there's something I need to tell you."

"Oh, no," he said. "Not the 'we need to talk' lecture."

She thought of the spineless guys who'd broken up with her over the phone and even through e-mail. Or even worse, those who'd given her the silent treatment. She had better manners than that. "No … nothing like that," she lied.

"For a moment I was afraid you would want to stop seeing me. As long as it's not that, I can take anything. I've gotten attached to you."

She rubbed the back of her neck with cold fingers. "How can that be? You hardly know me." But she already knew the answer, for she herself felt the same way.

"I know. Isn't it weird? I've never felt like this before. Well, there was this one girl, but that was a long time ago."

A pang of jealousy shot through her. "What happened? I mean between you and her?"

"She left me for some other guy. I thought I'd never get over that pain, never love again. Not that I didn't want to love again. I thought I'd never find someone else I could love as much as I loved her."

There was a long moment of silence. "Love is like that," Chand said. "You kind of graduate from one level to a higher one. Have you ever been in love?"

Campbell shut her eyes. Had she ever been in love? She didn't know how to answer. Yes. No. Maybe. I don't know. All of the above.

When she failed to answer, she heard him ask, "What is it that you want to tell me?"

"I'd rather tell you in person," she said, no longer certain of what she wanted to tell him or whether she should say anything at all. It flattered her that he found her appealing in a romantic sense.

"Not a problem. How about going out for a drink? I'll pick you up."

"Don't be silly, Chand," she said. "You don't have a car. Let's meet half way." How could he be her Prince Charming when he didn't own a car? Everyone knew that even though Prince Charming didn't come with a chariot, he came with a snazzy sports car. She didn't really believe this anymore, but it had been one of the criteria on her long list.

"I'm still a gentleman. I'm sure there are plenty of nice places around your home where we could go for a drink. I like discovering new places. Anyway, as long as I get to spend time with you, I don't mind the subway ride."

She wanted to believe him, but how many men had delivered similar lines to her only to desert her after she'd slept with them? If she was to protect her heart, she needed to be cautious.

Half an hour later, they sat in a back booth at the Irish Pub two blocks from Campbell's house. The pub was filled with late afternoon shoppers carrying bags from department stores; she noticed The Body Shop and Roots.

They ordered beers on tap. An amber one for her, a stout for him.

In the dim lighting, Chand's eyes gleamed. He looked incredibly hot in his crisp white t-shirt and jeans. Sitting next to her in their booth, he leaned closer, put an arm around her shoulders and pressed his lips against her forehead. She was aware of the strong muscles in his arm and acutely aware of his hip touching hers under the table. Waves of warmth suffused her. Did she really want to stop seeing him?

Maybe she could just keep him as an experiment in her study of the Prince Charming myth. Another proof that things would never work out. Why should he be any different from all the other men she'd dated? Wasn't she doomed from the start? Didn't all the studies on absent fathers show how nearly impossible it was for their daughters to find lasting love? Her failure with Chand would be another anecdote in her long list of anecdotes about men who had abandoned her. A feather in her cap, so to speak, though she didn't feel that triumphant about getting it.

"Are you going to tell me what you wanted to say or will you keep me in suspense?" he asked as he snuggled next to her.

"Let's keep the suspense for awhile," she said.

"No problem." He gazed at her. "Tell me about yourself."

"What do you want to know?"

"How long have your parents been divorced?" Chand asked.

"Since I was eleven. My mother's no longer alive."

"I'm sorry to hear."

"She got cancer right after my father left us." The facts sounded cold and dreary, even to her own ears.

When the beers came, he reached for her hand and drew it to his lips. He placed tiny kisses on each of her fingertips and gave her his irresistible smile, his white teeth perfectly contrasting against his chocolate-colored skin. "You think your father's leaving was the reason for her illness?"

Campbell took a sip of beer. "Haven't you heard of stress causing cancer?" she asked.

"The evidence is not clear. Apparently stress accelerates the cancer that's already there. When did your mother die?"

"Over twenty years ago."

"And you're still blaming your father for that?"

Sure, there had been a time, a long time, when she'd been angry with her father for having deserted them; a time when she'd truly believed it was his fault that her mother had taken sick. Wasn't that what her mother had said when she asked her why she was always so sad? *Your father broke my heart, sweetie. I don't think I can get over it.*

"My mother wasn't a strong person. She didn't want to live without him."

Chand reached for her hand. "I suppose you can go on resenting him. But that won't turn him into the father you wish you'd had."

"I no longer blame him for my mother's illness. I see it differently now."

What she really blamed her father for was her shitty love life. But she couldn't tell that to Chand. She didn't want him pitying her.

"But you still resent him."

She took another sip of beer. "Yes. For leaving me."

Were her bitterness and anger towards her father keeping her from forming a healthy relationship with a man? What if she discovered that her father's leaving had nothing to do with her lack of success in love? What would happen to her research? And what would it mean about the choices she'd made? It was all too confusing and she felt her head spin. "What about you? Are your parents still married to each other?'

"Yes," he said with a note of pride in his voice. "They'll be celebrating forty-five years together."

"I can't imagine being attached to someone for so long."

"I know. It's amazing."

"Do you see them often?" she asked Chand.

"I go to India about twice a year. I would go more often if it wasn't so far away." He paused. "Will you reconsider coming with me this time? I'd love to take you there. You'd see the real India, not the touristy one."

"I started reading the book you gave me. The author does a wonderful job describing India. I feel like I'm there. She writes about the sights, sounds and tastes, giving me a sensuous feel of the country."

He smiled. If only he weren't so damn sexy. "It's even more sensuous when you're actually there. Please say you'll come with me. My father is an engineer for Air India. I can get us tickets. It wouldn't cost you much. We could stay with my parents and India is really cheap."

When she didn't answer, he said, "What is it that you most want to see?" He finished his beer and signalled the waiter for two more.

There were so many things about India she wanted to see: the beaches in Goa, the brilliant-colored saris the woman wore in Rajasthan, the Himalayas. "The Ganges River," she said.

"That filthy water. I never could figure out the attraction of watching people brush their teeth and wash their hair in such polluted water. You know they burn dead bodies along the river and sometimes body parts don't get burned enough and end up in the river."

"It must be because of its healing properties," she said. "No other river in the world can claim that. I heard people have gone there with incurable diseases and leave cured."

"I promise I'll take you to see the Ganges, even though I have no interest in it myself. But I do have an interest in making you happy."

It was a tempting offer and she promised Chand that she would think about it. She had not travelled very much. There was, of course, her fear of flying but in spite of her independence, travelling alone was too much of a hassle. The arrival in a foreign city, the booking of hotels and the possibility of being mugged. Of all the countries in the world, India held the most appeal for her. She had contented herself by reading travel books on it, and yet the more she read, the more her desire to be there intensified. With Chand next to her, she'd have nothing to worry about.

"So...what is it that you need to tell me? That you are falling hopelessly in love with me? I hope so, because I'm really falling for you."

"Is that a cultural thing, for Indian men to be so direct about their emotions?"

He placed the softest of kisses on her lips. It felt delicious. "Only if they mean it," he said.

She drew her fingers through his thick, luscious dark hair.

"Hair like yours is really wasted on a man," she murmured.

"That's what you needed to tell me?"

Campbell shrugged. She couldn't bring herself to tell him that she didn't want to continue seeing him. "Uh..." She hesitated, and then said something that surprised even her: "I want to tell you that I need a commitment."

He looked at her with curiosity in his dark eyes. There was a long moment of silence and she wanted to take back her words, but then Chand let out a hearty laugh and squeezed her hand.

"What kind of commitment were you thinking of?" he asked.

She was speechless. She had no idea why she had said that. All she knew was that she'd felt compelled to say those words.

When she failed to answer, he said, "It's a bit too early for marriage but in my culture, men and women get married all the time without even seeing each other."

"Well, of course it's too early for marriage," she said. "I was thinking more about...well...you not having sex with anyone else."

Where had that come from? Did she even want to have sex with him? Of course, she did. How could she deny the dampness between her thighs when he'd kissed her? It had been years since a man made her feel sexually alive. The men she had dated, and there had been a good many, left her libido in a state of flat line. So much so that she once wondered if her body had shut down in that area. But then she remembered her father/daughter relationship theory and although it had not consoled her, she'd at least found an answer for her frigidity.

Chand nodded. Why did he have to be so damn handsome? She wondered what he looked like naked. What it would be like to lie next to him. Maybe she should suggest they go to her place and have sex right now. Get it over with. Get him out of her system, so that she could once again focus on her research of the Prince Charming myth.

"And when were you proposing that this commitment take into effect?" he asked.

Proposing? A marriage-related word. She shrugged her shoulders. Was she out of her mind? She had come here to break off with him and here she was, suggesting a commitment. A heaviness in her body planted her in her seat, unable to move. She needed to say something, but her mouth was clamped shut.

Chand leaned over and kissed her gently. Then he drew back and looked serious as he said, "You are an amazing woman, Campbell Jones. I like that you don't play these relationship hunting games, making the man chase you, pretending that you don't care. I appreciate your honesty and admire your going after what you want." He slid closer to her, his lips against her ear and whispered, "Your proposal is very tantalizing and sexy. Like you." A nibble on her ear lobe sent immediate sparks down her spine.

They finished their beers and walked along the side streets of her neighborhood near the Jean Talon market. In summer, the market was bursting with colorful fruits and flowers, but this was February. It felt like a ghost town. They talked and minutes turned into hours. Conversation flowed with him and he was also a great listener. They discussed Anita Desai's writing and other books; Chand was a history buff. She learned more about his life growing up in India and his early struggles in Canada. She asked him about his relationship with his past girlfriend.

"Everything felt perfect to me with her and when it was over, I figured that I had my chance. But now you come along." They were holding hands as they strolled along and he squeezed hers tighter. "I didn't realize how lonely I had become. But your coming into my life is like sunshine coming through the clouds. Oh, God, that sounds so cliché, but it's the way I feel. When you walked up to where I was waiting for a cab, I knew that you were the one for me."

"Now, that's a cliché," she said.

They came to an apartment building and Chand stopped walking. "This is where I live," he said. "You want to come inside?"

"I don't know." She was so afraid to get close to him. So afraid that the closer she got to him, the farther she'd get from her research.

"Come on," he said. "I promise nothing will happen."

"I've heard that one before," she said and laughed.

"It's a grave offense in India for someone to refuse to enter someone's home," he said.

"Now I know that you're joking." She trusted him. It was herself she didn't trust. Yet, what would it hurt to see how he lived?

His teasing put her at ease and she took his hand as he led her to the elevator. It was an old rickety elevator with accordion black metal grids, the type she'd seen in war movies. The elevator, barely big enough to hold two people, jerked and he held her close to him. She felt desire for him swell in her abdomen.

The hallway to his apartment smelled of curry and cumin. This kind of building was often populated by Indian and Pakistani immigrants, along with students.

"Welcome to my home," he said as he slid the door to his apartment open.

Chapter 9

"What are you doing with that?" Missi asked. She eyed Max's saxophone case in Randy's hand, noticing that he held his father's gym bag in his other hand. His fingers slid restlessly on the gym bag. Missi felt slightly nauseous as she saw her son's eyes shift away from her.

"I'm bringing these over to Dad's," he said.

When Max left, Missi had vowed that she wouldn't let her anger spill over onto her son. She didn't even want Randy to see her hurt, but it was hard not to get angry. Max hadn't touched his sax in years and the gym bag only meant one thing: Max was working out. How many times had she coaxed him into coming to the gym with her? How many times had she'd tried to get him to play his sax again? His answer had always been the same: "No time, Missi."

But now he had time, didn't he? Lots of time.

"You're going over to his place?" she asked. She immediately regretted her tone of voice. She might as well have said, *how could you betray me like this?*

She frowned and dug herself in even deeper. "Where is it?"

Randy mumbled the name of the apartment building. His face was drawn, showing his discomfort. She wanted to take him into her arms and hold him close, but doing so would only make things harder for him. As she felt tears well up in her eyes, she blinked them back.

"Don't you need to be at school?"

"I don't have a class until noon," he said.

She nodded. "How's school going?" she asked, trying to make up for putting him on the spot. He was really a sweet boy, always had been. Although he had Max's height, she'd always prided herself on his having her sensitivity.

"Cool," he said. "I think I'm cut out to be an architect."

"You'll make a great one." Ever since he was a little boy playing with his Lego set, he knew what he wanted to do. Some people just knew. It wasn't the case with her. Except for her writing, she had never thought of a career for herself. She was content to be a homemaker. Taking care of Max and Randy had filled her with joy.

"I really have to go, Mom."

"Okay," she said. She reached to touch his hair. Its curls still had a baby-fine silkiness to them. Her heart expanded with love for him. "Will you be back for lunch?"

"I'll need to come pick up my stuff. But I'm going to join my friends at the cafeteria."

As soon as he left, Missi went into Randy's room and sat on the edge of his bed. She wished she could go back in time when he was a little boy and they were a happy family. She heard the traffic below and went to the window. For a moment, she watched the tourists in caliches wrapped in thick woolen blankets and businessmen rushing to meetings, their heads bent against the harsh wind. Then she studied Randy's collection of miniature cars lined along the window sill. She picked up a yellow race car. One of these days, her son, too would be moving out; that would be worse than Max's leaving. Missi squeezed her eyes tight.

She went into the laundry room and took out a pile of Randy's polo shirts from the dryer. Of all the household tasks, ironing was her favorite. The back-and-forth motion of smoothing out wrinkles and the smell of fresh cotton always soothed her. As she passed the iron across the sleeves of Randy's shirt, her heart again filled with an intense love for him.

She was still ironing when Randy returned. "How did it go?" she asked. It was a stupid question and not what she really wanted to know. What she wondered was what Max's apartment was like: was it gloomy or filled with sunlight? And had Sheri been there?

"Okay," Randy said.

Where had all the years flown? Just yesterday, he'd been leaning his head on her lap as she caressed his hair. Now there was dark stubble on his chin. Her son was becoming a handsome man. She imagined that her own father might have looked like Randy when he was his age.

For years Missi had made allowances for her father, making up her own reasons for why he had left. The most believable to her young, vulnerable mind was what her mother had told her: he had moved to another country, while they had moved so many times. How could he possibly know how to find her? It was years later when her sister, Emily, told her that their father lived in the same city.

Missi was enraged. How could her mother have lied to her? Slowly, the knowledge that he'd known all along where she lived but made no effort to contact her began to sink in, bringing up surges of anger and resentment that were so strong, she pushed them away. Now, similar emotions arose in her concerning Max. Would he too one day forget her, as her father had?

Following her son into his bedroom, she watched him pick up his books and place them into a packsack. The drawings on his desk caught her attention. She picked up a sketch he'd drawn of a building. "This is good," she said.

He tossed a set of keys and a wallet on his desk and came up to her. "I know this is difficult for you," he said, "but I don't want you to worry about me. All my friends' parents are divorced so now I feel normal."

She faked a smile, knowing he was trying to cheer her up. When he folded her into his arms, she hugged him back. He was so caring. But it shouldn't be this way – the child comforting the parent. In spite of the sorrow that threatened to overwhelm her, she told him that she'd be okay.

He left soon after and that was when the anger hit. By noon, it had intensified too much to be ignored. The thought of calling Skip crossed her mind, but what would she say? That he was right and she'd been a fool not to believe him? Besides, he couldn't give her what she wanted: to bring Max back.

She brought the colorful pile of neatly folded polos into Randy's room and lay them on his bed. About to exit his room, she spotted the keys that Randy had left on his desk. Keys to Max's apartment.

An idea occurred to her: she could sneak into his apartment. At first, she told herself that she was being foolish. What would be the point? To make certain that Max was living comfortably? She had loved taking care of him, but that part of her life was over. Her anger turned to rage. She grabbed her phone, punched out the number at his Jazz Bar, and asked to speak to Max.

At his hello, she felt her heart break into a thousand pieces.

"Max, it's Missi," she said, her voice shaky. She didn't know what to say. The only reason she'd called was to find out whether he was still at work.

"Hi, Missi," he said. That he said her name so gently only made it worse.

She waited one beat, then two. "I miss you," she said. She hadn't intended to say that but the words had flown out of her mouth. Nor had she intended to cry. All the same, silent tears coursed down her cheeks. Missi swallowed hard. Max obviously didn't miss her; he had Sheri to comfort him.

"I'm unable to talk right now," he finally said. "It's really busy. Lunch time, you know."

"I understand," she said, the palm of her hand wiping the tears from her face. "Sorry I called."

She grabbed a bucket and some rags and then as she was about to leave, she spotted the bottle of Chance that Max had given her as a Valentine present. It dawned on her that the perfume hadn't been meant for her at all but as a Valentine's present for Sheri. Yet he had wanted her to find it. What a coward he was. She grabbed the bottle and threw it into the bucket along with the rags.

Dressed in a pair of old jeans and a sweater under an even older ski jacket, she wore no make-up. Her dark brown hair was pushed back in a tight pony tail. She walked along the rue de Commune, until she reached the apartment where Max lived. She didn't know the exact apartment number or what she was going to do there. All she knew was that something was pulling her forward, making it impossible to resist. She rang the janitor's bell.

"I'm here to clean Max Morgan's apartment," she said into the intercom. The janitor, a tired-looking, fiftyish woman, came and opened the door for her. Missi smiled at her as she entered the lobby. Dangling Max's keys, she said, "He just moved in and I'm his cleaning lady. Can you remind me of his apartment number? I forget what he told me." She was surprised at how calm she was, as if she'd done this sort of thing hundreds of times.

"It's thirty-six," the woman said, and began to gather the junk mail left on a shelf in the lobby. It stunned Missi how easily the woman gave out this information.

Once in the apartment, Missi felt her palms sweat. She took off her gloves and tossed them into the bucket that she left on the parquet floor of his entrance. She paced around the apartment, not certain what she was looking for. She had never done anything like this before and knew that if she got caught, she could be charged for breaking and entering. She tip-toed around the room even though she knew she was alone.

The table in the living room was covered with Jazz magazines and CDs. She picked up a few of them. There were names she didn't recognize: Tigran Hamasyan, Dhafer Youssef Quartet, Paolo Fresu. It saddened her that he already seemed like someone she didn't know. Then her eyes fell upon a series of unframed and loose photographs tossed onto a side table. They were of Sheri. Cute, perky Sheri. Missi felt her stomach clench. Sheri on skis with Max's arm around her. *When had Max taken up skiing again?* Sheri in a low-cut cocktail dress, slim and gorgeous. Sheri with a towel wrapped around her head and Max's bathrobe around her body. Missi took the one of Sheri holding a glass of wine, her upturned face smiling at the camera – smiling at Max – and stuffed it into the pocket of her ski jacket.

She went into the bedroom. The bed was perfectly made. In all the years she had been married to Max, she had always made their bed. She stood at the edge of the bed, pressing her fist to her mouth. As she bit down on her bottom lip, she felt her body crumple. Her legs went limp and she fell forward onto the bed. She passed out for only a second or two, but when she regained consciousness, she felt disoriented. When she realized where she was, anger surged through her once more.

Missi took the bottle of Sheri's Chance out of her bucket and began spraying the pillows and sheets, emptying a quarter of the bottle as if it were bug spray. There was nothing more for her to do here. It was best to leave before she did more damage. She picked up her bucket and rags, locked the door and stole out of the building.

Her own apartment felt empty. Empty of Randy. Empty of Max. Empty of life. She made a cup of tea and carried it into the living room, where she built a fire. She sat in front of the fireplace, clutching her tea cup with both hands as she stared at Sheri's photo on the coffee table. It lay between her and the flames. After setting her cup on the table, she picked up the photo. Her hand trembled and she could almost hear the thudding of her heart. Everything seemed in slow motion as she walked towards the fireplace and tossed Sheri's photo into it. She watched its edges curl in the flames, Sheri's face disintegrating into ash. Then she sat on the floor, lowered her head into her arms, and wept.

Chapter 10

"What's this?" she asked, letting her kitten heel shoes sink into the ribbed carpeting.

The offices of Starr Transport veered on luxurious, located on the seventh floor of a modern building in the north end. She had mixed feelings about being back at work – grateful for the sense of purpose it gave her, but resentful at having to be there.

"Theo's wife left him a few months ago," the receptionist said. "He's looking for a new girlfriend."

"Theo?" Felicity said.

"He's my cousin. I asked if I could give you his number, seeing as you're always complaining about how difficult it is to find someone. "

"I'm not desperate," Felicity said.

"Of course, you're not. It's just that a guy like Theo will get snatched up quickly. If I didn't think you might find him special, I wouldn't suggest him to you. Call him. What have you got to lose?"

"Alright. But don't blame me if it doesn't work out," Felicity said before heading for her office. She tried to remember the last time she had felt passion for a man, but drew a blank. Maybe with this Theo guy, she'd feel something. This time, though, she wouldn't mention him to her father. At least not until she was certain of her own feelings. Her father's criticism had a way of deflating any new romance before it got started and she wanted to give this a chance.

Still thinking of Theo, she phoned *Today's Trucking* to place an ad in their magazine. The idea of placing an ad seemed a waste of money. Starr Transport already had more customers than they could handle. It had gained a reputation as one of the best transport companies in the city, with unbeatable prices. Felicity often wondered how they pulled in so much profit, considering their overhead. She'd once brought that up at a board meeting but was told by her father, "Just good business sense."

She spent the rest of the day online, placing other ads and booking a booth at this year's trade show at The National Truck Show. Finally, she left the office the same way she'd come, in her business suit. In winter, she appreciated being able to drive from the company's heated garage to her own underground spot at home without the need for a coat.

On her drive home, she thought of the women in the group she had met on Tuesday. What was with Campbell? She seemed so uptight, trying to convince them how futile it was to chase after a Prince Charming. It was like an anti-dating club. Maybe Campbell hated men or she'd just had bad experiences with them. Well, that was understandable. It wasn't easy finding someone to connect with.

Then there was Missi. Her high-standing lifestyle reminded Felicity of her mother. But that was where the similarity ended. Missi seemed genuinely in love with her husband and terribly hurt. Felicity liked her and wondered if they could be friends. It would be pleasant to have a friend to do things with on weekends.

She braked sharply at a red light. While she waited for the light to change, her mind wandered to Suzy. She bugged the hell out of her. Just because Felicity was young, Suzy assumed it was easy for her to find a compatible man. It simply wasn't true. All the men she met bored her half to death.

The ones who interested her — the artists, the musicians — stayed away from her. Sure, she could talk about the latest music groups and ask them questions about their art: how was their band doing? where were they exhibiting? In addition to talking about up-and-coming painters, Felicity could afford to buy their art. She actually had a few originals from her early days. The problem was she had too much money. Men, she had concluded, hated being with women who made more than they did.

At times, Felicity had lied about her profession. Instead of saying that she had given up her dream to follow her father's dream to one day take over Starr Transport, she would say that she worked as a receptionist or a clerk selling cosmetics in a department store.

She wondered if Campbell or any of the other women in the group had perceived her loneliness. She was usually good at hiding it, but had she been successful this time?

As she continued to wait for the light, she told herself that she hadn't joined that group to relive her past. What she wanted, what she was hoping for, was for a new beginning. She closed her eyes for a moment: if only she had the courage to be her true self. But she still didn't know who that was.

When the light turned green, she pressed the gas pedal to the floor and headed home to Nun's Island. After parking underground, she rode the elevator to her apartment. She immediately got out of her tailored suit and put on a pair of worn jeans and an old sweat shirt. The jeans carried stains from the days when she used to paint.

She remembered how eager she'd been to start a new painting. How she thought for days about the subject and then painted for hours, absorbed by the light and colors, without noticing the time. Was that her bliss? No, it was more than that. It was the sense of getting in touch with who she was.

Her marketing job at the transport company drained all her energy. Weekday evenings were spent watching movies on Netflix and when the weekends rolled around, so did her familiar anxiety. An anxiety that lasted from Friday evening until late Sunday night.

She thought she ought to eat, even though she wasn't hungry. She took out a package of crackers, some cheese and an apple. Although the cheese was of good quality and the apple had tartness to it, she didn't enjoy them. Food, for her, was merely nourishment. She swept the crumbs and tossed them into the garbage bin before settling on the couch to watch *When Harry Met Sally*.

In the middle of the movie, she thought of the phone number crumpled in her jacket pocket. It really went against one of her rules (where did she get that rule anyway?) which was to never call a guy up on a Friday night. This would give him the impression that she didn't have anything better to do. But if he were also home, then they'd be even, wouldn't they?

A deep, sexy voice answered the phone and told her she was speaking to Theo.

"I'm Felicity," she said. "Your cousin gave me your number."

There was silence on the line and she wondered how many other women his cousin had given his number to.

"Get out of here! I wasn't expecting you to call so soon."

Maybe this was a mistake. He was probably already thinking of her as some desperado.

All the same, the conversation began to flow. They spoke about the usual things that two strangers talked about. He taught ancient history at university. No, she didn't have any siblings. His two sisters lived in Toronto. She'd never been married. He liked to read political memoirs. She loved watching old movies. Romantic comedies, mostly. He played the cello. She used to dabble in art.

His energy and enthusiasm lifted her spirits. As she listened to him, she made her way to the fridge. She took out a yogurt drink, checked the label, unscrewed its lid and began to sip it.

"Tell me, what are you are looking for?"

She was taken aback by his forthright question. She thought of her support group and surprised herself by saying, "I'm looking for my Prince Charming."

"Hey, we're both looking for the same thing "I'm looking to be someone's Prince Charming."

After more chit-chat and laughter, she told him about her interest in art and he said, "Come with me tomorrow to the opening of my friend's art exhibit."

She asked what his friend's name was. She had never heard of him. "What does he paint?" she asked.

"Abstract art. But he's also into photography and this exhibit is on his photographs of tattoos. It'll be fun," Theo said.

They made arrangements to meet in front of the gallery at five o'clock the next day

Chapter 11

Campbell's cell phone rang. It was Missi.

"What's wrong? Why are you crying?" She stepped away from Chand to take the call.

"I burned Sheri's picture," Missi sobbed.

"What do you mean you burned her picture?"

Missi explained how she'd pretended to be the cleaning lady and had sprayed Max's bed with Chance – Sheri's Chance she pointed out – before building a fire at her apartment and watching Sheri's photo curl into ashes. "I feel horrible," she said. "I never thought I could be so mean."

"It's only a photo," said Campbell. "Don't make a big deal out of it."

"But it is a big deal. It's as if I wanted something terrible to happen to Sheri. I've never thought of myself as a vengeful person."

"You're not," Campbell reassured her. "You're kind and gentle and generous."

"If only I could believe that myself. I think I'm losing control," she whispered. "All I think about is Max. I can't get him out of my mind."

"I'm sorry you're going through this, but it's normal. Right now, you're hurting badly."

"I don't want to be normal," Missi said. "All I want is Max back."

"I know. You must feel awful right now," Campbell said.

"I don't know if I'm angry or sad. Maybe I should just have an affair myself."

"What's important right now, Missi, is that you take care of yourself. Eat properly and remember that what you're feeling now is not how you're going to feel in a few weeks. And remember, I'm here for you."

"Thank you," Missi barely got the words out. "I keep thinking of all the good times I had with Max. Just today I was looking at our wedding album. He was so handsome. There was this one photo of both of us in the garden and he was holding my hand. And then another photo where…"

"Missi, I'm not alone right now. I'll call you later on, okay?" Campbell wanted to avoid her play-by-play description of their wedding and honeymoon. She shut her cell phone and turned to Chand. "That was Missi. Her husband just left her."

Chand took Campbell's coat and hung it in the entrance closet. "It must be difficult having people count on you for solutions to their problems," he said.

"I don't always have solutions," she said. "Anyway, the whole point is to let the client talk and with a few questions here and there, they're usually able to find their own solutions. Missi and I have also been friends for years and she needs my support now. I'll call her later to see how she's doing."

She focused more fully on Chand and felt her excitement at seeing his home, a modest but impeccable apartment. "Are you going to show me around?"

"Of course. This is the main area." He pointed to the room before them.

His kitchen/living room was airy, with no table in the kitchen and a counter separating the two areas. There were two cushy arm chairs in the living room facing a flat screen TV and a state- of-the-art iPod sound system.

"Pretty unembellished," he said, "but I like it this way. It's easier to keep tidy. I don't like to accumulate a lot of stuff."

For the past few years, she had been unsuccessfully aiming at a clutter-free lifestyle. She'd turned down a few potential men because of all the junk in their homes.

The room smelled of incense and traces of lavender. She noticed a huge bouquet of lilies against his window sill. She leaned down to smell them. "These are lovely," she said sticking her nose into the flowers.

He laughed, then flicked some pollen off the tip of her nose.

"My father used to bring my mother fresh flowers every week. The house was always filled with them," he said. "I guess I've kept up the tradition."

"That's not the only Indian tradition you've kept up," Campbell said, reaching for a beautiful purple cushion covered with spangling paillettes, on one of the cushy arm chairs.

"Not too masculine, is it?" said Chand.

"Who cares? It's pretty."

"These cushions are all over our home in India. My mother brought them over for me when she came to visit last year. She thought it would keep me from being homesick." He wore a pensive expression.

"And does it? Relieve your homesickness?"

"I've been here long enough to get over it. What I don't get over is the loneliness I sometimes feel."

It was refreshing to hear a man admit his loneliness. "I know what you mean," she said.

He came closer and cupped her face in his hands before kissing her on the mouth. It was a gentle kiss. "Is this alright?" he wanted to know.

She drew away from him then. Was she sabotaging herself by believing that she felt something special for him? Was she fixated on him because she doubted that she was worthy of being honored for her work? A case of acute anxiety disguised as affection.

For a distraction, she gazed around his living room. Except for a few prints of the Taj Mahal and the Himalayas, the walls were empty. "What part of India are you from?" she asked.

"Pune."

"Is it close to the Ganges?"

"Not at all. But if you come, I'll take you there. Have you given more thought to coming with me to India?"

"There's so much work I have to do. I have to get ready for a conference."

"What conference is that?"

"A Women's Studies conference," she said. She told him that it would take place at the end of May.

"You'll be back in plenty of time for that," he said with a smile.

Things were going extremely fast for her. She could hardly breathe. Glancing around the room, she tried to think of something to say. Of course, going to India was tempting but how could she afford to take time off? Campbell noticed a fancy racing bike against his hallway wall. "Bike much?" she said.

"I do the Tour de l'Ile every spring," he said. "And as soon as the snow melts, that's my means of transportation." In spite of the fact that he didn't have a car (once a minus sign on her Prince Charming chart), she found herself attributing points to him for doing the Tour de l'Ile and being energy conscious. How ridiculous. Why was she even counting points with him?

His bedroom was off the living room. Campbell looked at his contemporary double-sized bed with its simple black headboard, the kind she had seen at IKEA. She imagined lying naked under the crisp navy sheets with Chand next to her, envisioned his mouth on hers, his hands stroking her skin. His body on top of hers, his sex swollen with desire for her. Trying to steer her mind onto a safer subject, she said, "Are your closets as organized as the rest of your apartment or did you shove everything inside?"

He opened the tiny closet. His jeans were painstakingly folded; his dressier pants hung tidily in a row while his shoes were smartly lined up, ready to slip into. Everything was so efficient that it made her own closet seem like it ought to be declared a disaster zone.

Chand wrapped his arms around her waist and whispered into her ear, "This proposal of yours. I presume it works both ways."

She had completely forgotten about her proposal that they not have sex unless he committed to her. Now she couldn't back out of it. "Yes. Of course," she said, and then to emphasize her sincerity, she added, "It's only fair."

Again, she thought of having sex with him. Then she remembered the underwear she had on. It was far from her best. As she drew away from Chand, she knocked over a golf bag. He caught her before she fell over. His skin smelled faintly of sweet butter and his arms around her made her feel safe.

"You golf?" she asked, straightening her body.

"Yes, do you?"

She nodded and smiled.

"My sister went to school with Smriti Mehra," he said, "Sometimes when I'm home and she's not on tour, I play a game with her. If you come to India with me and she's around, we can play together."

Smriti Mehra was one of India's most eminent female golfers. To play with her would be beyond Campbell's wildest dreams. "That offer may be too good to refuse," she said.

"Exactly my intention," he said as he pulled her towards him and began to place soft butterfly kisses on her neck.

In that moment, she imagined flying off to India with him and playing a game of golf with one of the world's top golfers.

No. No. No. She needed to focus. Focus on the women in her group. How could she face these women when she'd been preaching to them not to depend on a man for their happiness? She pulled away from Chand's embrace and began to walk out of his bedroom.

"Wait," he said, reaching for her arm. "Where are you going?"

She didn't dare turn to look at him. Caught by the hypnotic gaze of his dreamy dark eyes, she knew she would weaken. "I don't want to rush things," she said. "And I have some work to do. In fact, I should be going."

He stepped in front of her, forcing her to look at him. In his eyes, she saw desire mixed with disappointment. She resisted the urge to wrap her arms around him.

"What's going on, Campbell?" he asked in a hurt voice. "Why are you giving me these mixed signals? One minute you're in my arms, letting me embrace you and the next you're running away."

How could she tell him that she was afraid to love him? Hadn't she always believed in honesty, especially in a relationship? But what was the truth? That her career was more important than love? Yes. Yes, it was. At least no one but herself could disappoint her in her career. But with love, the one thing she could count on was that she would end up being hurt.

"Tell me, Campbell," Chand insisted. "Something's troubling you and I'd like to know what it is. Maybe I can help."

How could he help when he was the cause of her problem? He put his hands on her shoulders. "Your muscles are so tight," he said as he began to massage them. It felt good. "Relax and let it out. You'll feel better."

Campbell sighed. "Promise you won't call me a feminist bitch if I tell you," she said.

"I'd never call you that," Chand said. "I'm an honorary feminist myself, in case you haven't noticed."

She laughed softly. "It's about my research," she finally said. "My entire research is based on the Prince Charming myth and now you come along with a low handicap. You make me feel like I haven't felt in a long time ... and ... and it's screwing everything up."

"Your Prince Charming myth?' he asked her. He had stopped massaging her shoulders.

"Yes. I'm going to be getting an award for my writings on it at the conference I told you about."

He nodded. "That's terrific," he said.

She sat down on the edge of the bed, which was covered by a white fluffy duvet. He came and sat next to her, putting an arm around her shoulders.

"Now tell me. How am I screwing things up?" he asked.

"Because of you, my Prince Charming myth is turning out to be very different from what I imagined."

"And what exactly did you imagine?'

"That there is no Prince Charming," she said. "At least not for women like me."

"Women like you? What do you mean? You're one of the most attractive women I've ever met."

"Thank you, but it has nothing to do with that. I feel torn between you and my career."

"How so?"

She stared at the floor, feeling foolish. "What I feel for you is so real. It makes me think that maybe Prince Charming does exist after all."

He kissed her on her forehead. "And you see a problem with that?"

"Of course, there's a problem. A huge problem. I feel like a fake. All these papers I've written on the Prince Charming myth — maybe they were nothing more than my own unconscious wish for a Prince Charming. And now, what am I supposed to tell the women in my group? Or at that conference? How can I even face them?"

He took her hand and entwined his fingers into hers. "This award means a lot to you, doesn't it?"

She turned to him and said, "It's my dream. I've been working towards it for the last five years." She looked into his eyes. "I don't think I can keep seeing you, Chand. You're too much of a threat to my research."

"A threat?" She could tell by his tone of voice that he wasn't taking her seriously.

"Yes. I can't risk falling in love with you only to find out that I was wrong all along. I'm very familiar with this pattern of mine."

He took her hand and held it between both of his. "Maybe your research isn't about the Prince Charming myth."

Hadn't he been listening to her? "It's entirely about that," she said.

"What I mean is that maybe it's about how you're afraid to let a man get close to you and you use the Prince Charming myth as a shield."

Could he be right? That her fears were controlling her life? His words remained with her until he brought her home that evening.

A letter in her mail box informed her that her upstairs tenants were moving. Now, with everything else happening in her life, she had to find new tenants. Well, she would think of it later. Needing to relax, she filled her tub with hot water and poured some bubble bath in it. She slid into the bathtub with the latest version of her acceptance speech, which she re-read for the hundredth time. A surge of adjectives, metaphors and humor to insert into her speech spilled into her mind, no doubt flowing from her conversation with Chand.

How ironic that Chand, if he was indeed her Prince Charming, had inspired her to add sparkle to a speech that stated he didn't exist.

Chapter 12

It was after nine when Missi heard a knock at her door. She was already in her comfortable, old flannel pajamas and had taken off her make-up. Campbell, she thought. Good old Campbell coming over to comfort her. She thought of the bottle of Fuisse she kept in the fridge for moments like these.

But it wasn't Campbell – it was Max. Her heart pounded. He must have found out that she'd broken into his place; there was no denying the stench of perfume in his bedroom. Oddly, he seemed relaxed and she detected no anger in his expression or body language. "Are you just coming back from the bar?" she asked.

"Yes, I'm beat. It was extra busy tonight. I locked myself out of my apartment. Is Randy here?"

"He's got basketball practice," she said, letting out a deep breath. "He won't be home till late."

"He has a set of my keys. Do you mind checking if they're around?"

Grateful that she wouldn't need to defend her behavior that afternoon, she went to their son's room. There, she found the keys exactly where she had left them.

As she turned to leave Randy's room, she found Max standing in the doorframe. "I found them," she said, handing them to him. He looked confident and sexy in spite of his fatigue.

When he took the set of keys from her, his fingers touched hers and she felt her pulse race. "About what you told me earlier," he said. "I miss you too."

Her heart leaped. "I'm so lonely, Max. I miss us being a family."

He took her arm and drew her to him. She sniffed his aftershave; an unfamiliar scent. The thought that Sheri might have bought him the aftershave disturbed her. But as Max began to stroke her hair, she pushed the thought aside and enjoyed his attention. His hands slid to her neck. She loved the way he massaged it, making the tenseness of her day disappear. It was like the early days of their lovemaking.

Missi wrapped her arms around his waist and lay her head on his chest. She again felt safe and warm in the arms of the man she loved. Then he slid his hand under her flannel top and cupped her naked breast. It felt incredible to be touched.

As he pressed against her, she felt his arousal with a feeling of triumph. Right now, Max wanted her, and her sadness evaporated with that knowledge. After holding her face in his hands, he kissed her deeply, sliding his tongue along her teeth. She responded freely. His hands and fingers began to explore her, gliding along the sides of her body until he reached inside the bottoms of her pajamas. Missi gasped at the sensations he evoked. How she'd missed him. And how she'd missed this passion in their relationship.

She knew that she should have resisted him. But it gave her a perverse sense of satisfaction to realize that in having sex with her, he was now cheating on the woman he'd left her for. It didn't make it even-steven but somehow seemed to help, as if she were getting back at Sheri for wrecking her marriage. Of course, the woman had no clue about what was happening between Max and her.

"Make love to me," she murmured.

He led her to what used to be their bedroom but was now only hers. He laid her on the bed, peeled off his clothes and then pulled her pajamas off. Her hands continued to caress whatever part of his body she could reach. She knew that clinging to him fed his ego, making him feel powerful somehow.

Their lovemaking was more exciting and erotic than it had ever been when they'd been together. He came quickly, then slept for a short time.

She lay awake, thinking about how many times, in the midst of sex with him, she'd fantasized about the male characters in the romance stories. "Do you still love me, Max?" she asked when he finally awoke.

He circled her stomach with an index finger. "I'll never stop loving you, Missi."

"So why did you leave me?"

"I guess our marriage got too routine," he said. "The thing with Sheri just happened."

"Things don't just happen. People make them happen. Are you in love with her?"

He didn't speak for a long time. "I don't know," he finally said.

Missi felt a sharp pain in her gut. Max having sex with Sheri was bad enough, but being in love with her was far worse. She sat up quickly, her body trembling. Had he come here to seduce her, to try to manipulate her into a triangle? There was no room in her marriage for a mistress.

"It's either me or her," she snapped, hoping that he'd finished with his affair and would choose her. "You have to choose. You're either totally mine or not here at all."

He glanced at his watch. "I better get going. It's getting late." He got up and pulled on his work pants before shrugging into his crinkled shirt.

She looked at him sadly. Part of her wanted to yell at him to keep away from her, but a bigger part of her wanted him to stay.

Chapter 13

Suzy Paradise felt herself tense as she walked towards the Pizzatoria Restaurant a few blocks from her condo. After five years on what she called "infernal dating sites," meeting someone for the first time still unnerved her. She rarely met a man she wanted a second date with, let alone a relationship.

In her experience, older men were boring and stuffy. Give him a chance, she told herself. *Wayne is only two years older and his profile sounds intriguing.* Someone closer to her own age was more likely to be compatible. And that was what she wanted now, not just a roll under the sheets.

Taking a deep breath, she passed a strip of outdoor cafés and terraces on Bernard Street, places frequented by well-known artists and actors. Finally standing in front of the restaurant, she saw Wayne through the window.

He wore a pair of reading glasses and leaned over a book. So far so good, she thought. It was difficult to find a man who read beyond his golf scores or book reviews which he believed gave him sufficient expertise to discuss a book at length. Suzy waited for a confirmation. After a few moments, Wayne looked up, saw her and waved.

Before meeting, they had followed the usual protocol for online dating: e-mailing each other and talking over the phone; checking out each other's photo. She'd found his picture attractive and enjoyed the soft timbre of his voice.

Wayne got to his feet as she reached the table. Suzy's heart sank. His features looked much older than the image in his photo. She told herself not to be so judgmental. Yet she now noticed the horrible pair of pants he was wearing. They hung on him like an old pair of work pants from a time when he held more girth. According to his profile, he was born in Milan, the runway capital of the world. Suzy had expected to see him in a pair of slim, dark trousers tucked into black, soft leather boots – a mature version of the bad boy whom she'd always been attracted to. How difficult was it to put on a neat pair of trousers with a well ironed shirt?

She had gone on first dates with men who showed up with bellies squished under tight t-shirts with stains on them, wearing jeans that looked like they hadn't been washed in years. Still, she focused on the purple t-shirt under Wayne's creased shirt. Purple was her favorite color.

He told her he'd come in from St. Sauveur, a town about an hour's drive away. She already knew that he had worked as a creative director for an advertising agency and now lived in the country as an artist, painting nude women on bicycles. He had sent her a link to his web page and she'd been astounded at the beauty of his work.

"I have to admit that I lied to you about my age," Wayne immediately said. "That photo I posted is ten years old."

"How old are you?"

"I don't want to be boxed in. People have all kinds of preconceptions about age." He gestured for her to join him at the table as he sat back down.

Why couldn't he tell her the truth? She'd given her real age on her profile. More or less. Well, certainly not exaggerated by a decade as he had done. As she slipped into the seat across from him, she felt her jaw clench. This was why she didn't date older men. They were too insecure.

"I hate this blind dating charade," he said. "The site asks us to put in information that creates unrealistic expectations."

"What are your expectations of me?" she asked.

"I'm a free thinker and I'm looking for one as well."

The idea of multiple sexual encounters, mistresses and orgies coagulated in Suzy's mind. Not that she was a prude. While in Paris, her best friend, Fleur, had educated her on the art and pleasure of free sex. For the two years she had lived there, she had indulged in sex without guilt or attachment. When she returned to Seattle with the same sexual abandon she'd experienced in Europe, she quickly learned that sexual freedom was perceived differently in America. "What's the link between women and bicycles?" Suzy veered the conversation to his art.

He straightened in his chair. "Nothing has contributed more to the emancipation of women than the bicycle," Wayne said. "That's from Susan Anthony. 1896. The bicycle was a cheap means for women to get around. They were no longer bound to the home."

As she was about to ask why the women in the paintings had to be nude, he said, "I painted them nude to illustrate women's freedom from religious doctrines and their subservient role. I'm a feminist."

Suzy smiled. "A lot of men are more feminist than some women." She thought of Kevin, who used to say that he was more feminist than she was.

He told her how one gallery refused to show his collection because one of the paintings was of a woman holding her bicycle with one hand. In the background was the Taj Mahal Next to her feet, a canister of oil.

"The gallery was afraid of being blown up by a group of Pakistanis or Indians who didn't like being confronted with their practice of burning the wife after her dowry or her beauty vanishes. In this painting, I gave her control of the gas and matches."

"Are you suggesting that the woman set fire to herself?"

"Of course not. The gas and matches symbolize the power that she reclaimed from men."

He was so different from the men Suzy had dated. Although the younger men had flattered her ego, they were most concerned with their overflowing testosterone. Conversations with them lacked depth and there had been no opportunities to go to movies together, share meals in restaurants or enjoy weekend getaways. None of her sexually charged encounters with these men had developed into a relationship. This had suited her for a time, but now that she was approaching fifty, she wanted to find a life partner to grow old with.

Wayne could hold an intelligent conversation and she enjoyed the stimulation of exchanging ideas. As the evening progressed and they finished their food, she invited him over to her place for tea.

She made mint tea and lit candles in a pair of Tiffany silver candle holders. The room smelled of jasmine from the fresh bouquet that sat by the window sill. A large modern painting by Louise Carrier Nichols from her Australian series hung on the wall, overlooking a glass table holding the book *Louis Vuitton: Art, Fashion, and Architecture* and a tattered copy of Marguerite Duras' *The Lover*, along with the latest issues of Paris Match and French Vogue. Suzy set the tea next to her assortment of French pastries which had not turned out perfectly and therefore had been excluded from her Saturday delivery to La Patisserie Lyse.

She then settled next to Wayne on her couch to watch the news.

"We're like an old couple," Wayne said as he dug into his third pastry, not seeming to notice that the mille-feuille was disproportionate.

"We may not be a couple but we are old," Suzy sighed. The excitement she normally felt with younger men was absent with Wayne. As she looked at him, she couldn't imagine placing her mouth on his, let alone lie naked next to him.

He told her that he needed to be in Montreal the next day for business purposes. "I could stay at my daughter's place, but it's late and she has a young boy. I don't like bothering her."

Had he said this because he wanted to have sex with her, or did he just not want to drive back home? "You could stay here, if you want." The invitation flew out of her mouth before she realized what she had said.

Was inviting Wayne to stay overnight an act of rebellion on her part? And if so, who was she rebelling against? Or was she still trying to prove to herself that she was loveable, generous person? At the time, she was reading Piero Ferrucci's book on the power of kindness and was practicing being kind. Whatever her subconscious reason, it was mixed with feeling sorry for Wayne, knowing he'd have to drive to St. Sauveur and back into the city the next morning. If the roles were reversed, she would have appreciated such an offer.

As the minutes passed, she began to regret asking him to stay over, but she didn't know how to get out of it. Once they were in her home, their conversation dwindled and she no longer felt attracted to him. Mental attraction alone was not enough; she needed a physical attraction as well.

Looking at her well-manicured nails and letting out a wide yawn, she said, "I guess I better make your bed on the couch."

"Don't go through that trouble," he said. "I'll sleep in your bed."

Why did it seem like a reasonable proposition? She got into bed dressed in a t-shirt and a pair of jogging pants while he lay in his underwear.

"Don't you think we ought to kiss each other goodnight?" he said.

She turned and they gave each other a peck on the mouth and that was that. Before they fell asleep, he told her a story about when he was eight. An old woman on the street, a stranger, had asked him if he would mail a letter for her, for it was too difficult for her to walk to the post office to buy a stamp.

"I could have kept the money and bought candy instead," he said, "but she trusted me. Your hospitality reminds me of when I was eight."

That, Suzy thought, was probably what they were. Two eight-year-olds awkwardly sharing a bed.

The next morning, she made them bowls of oatmeal with blueberries, served fresh grapefruit with tangerine slices and cups of green tea. As she sat facing Wayne in her kitchen, the truth could not be denied. Her attempt at dating an older man had failed and all she wanted now was to be left alone.

"I have to leave early," she told him. "Parking on Sunday is free downtown until noon and I have some errands to do."

"Sure. Sure. I understand," he said.

Outside, next to his car, she said, "Keep in touch."

"You want me to keep in touch?" He wore a look of defeat.

"Yes," she said and sort of meant it.

After she returned to her apartment, she began to pull the sheets off the bed in order to wash them. She didn't want to be reminded of his smell. Although nothing sexual had happened between them, she felt the disappointment which she always felt after meeting a man who just wouldn't do. Wayne hadn't made her feel better and she hadn't wanted to hear about his past or what his bucket list consisted of. Was she becoming cold? Is this what disappointing dating did to a woman?

Did failing to connect with Wayne, someone who was more compatible in terms of interests, mean there was no hope of ever finding someone to share her life with? Perhaps Campbell was right in saying that it was unwise to count on a man for her happiness. But if happiness came from within, how would she ever find it?

Chapter 14

Felicity parked her sports car across the street from the art gallery. During the summer months, she loved this area – the Atwater Market overflowing with flowers, the antique shops on Notre Dame and the bike path leading to Old Montreal. But now, at five o'clock on a late February afternoon, darkness had already settled in. She could barely make out the silhouette of a man leaning against a red brick building off the Lachine Canal.

As she approached Theo, she liked what she saw. He wore a dark grey coat with a white, silk scarf loosely tied around his neck and blue velvet pants. He could have been a rock star in the same category as Rufus Wainwright, though only half as good looking. Certainly, though, as gay. She mulled over the possibilities – gay, bisexual or metrosexual – then decided that she wasn't going to let any expectations ruin her evening.

After she introduced herself, she said, "Your cousin didn't tell me you were so tall." "Six foot-two," he told her proudly, as if it were a personal achievement.

He motioned for her to take his arm, so she linked into his as they entered the building. The art gallery sat on the second floor above a jewelry store. They climbed a dim stairway and then passed through a hallway covered with graffiti of rainbows and butterflies. Inside, the gallery bustled with women in glittery dresses and men wearing dark suits. Felicity felt charged with electricity as she soaked up the once-familiar atmosphere of the art world.

Taking her hand, Theo guided her through the crowd. A waiter balancing a tray of champagne approached them and they each took a glass.

"You know, you and I are going to end up falling in love, don't you?" Theo whispered in her ear.

Felicity stiffened. To fall in love implied that she had no say in the matter. To fall in love was unreliable, for one could just as easily fall out of love. Felicity wanted her feelings for Theo, or any man for that matter, to be a conscious choice rather than succumbing to a half-dreamy state that she would awaken from after a few dates. Also, she instinctively knew that he was not the type of man whom her father would approve of.

The thought startled her. As she breathed in the ambience of the room, a wave of resentment rolled through her. Bad enough that her father had chosen her career for her; she would no longer let him control her love life. From now on, she would pick out the man she wanted to be with, whether Theo or someone else.

"I'm really not the woman for you," she said, taking a sip from her flute of champagne.

"With all due respect," Theo said, "I think I'm in a better position to know whether you are the woman for me or not."

She laughed, delighted at his comeback, but still far from sold. "You've got a point, but let's give it some time, okay?"

Strategically placed on the walls, hung photographs of different body parts covered with tattoos. When Felicity saw a section of artwork depicting kids doing hip-hop break dancing, she led Theo towards a painting of a young girl wearing a baggy pair of pants and a tuque. She leaned back on her hands, with one leg in the air. Felicity felt the momentum of her dance step.

"Do you like this painting?"

She turned to face a very large man, with a round face and a full, bushy beard.

"Eduardo," Theo said. Felicity watched as the two men embraced. The contrast between Theo's metrosexuality and Eduardo's extreme masculinity amused her. She realized that she liked Theo's energy. His presence calmed her in ways that her anti-anxiety pills could not.

"This is my friend, Eduardo," Theo said. "He owns the gallery."

The man's grey eyes sparkled at her. She held out her hand but he came closer, gently placed his hands on her shoulders and kissed her lightly on both cheeks, French style. The soft bristles of his beard tickled her cheeks.

"I love this painting," she told him. "You can feel the girl's focus as well as the movement."

"The artist is actually a young man. Enormous talent. Do you paint?"

She hesitated. "I used to. Nothing like this, though. I did ink sketches and watercolors of fashion design. Futuristic outerwear." Her next words made her wince. "I haven't held a paint brush in years."

"Futuristic outerwear, how fascinating," Eduardo said. "But tell me, why did you stop?"

"You haven't seen my work," she laughed.

"A woman with a beautiful smile like yours must have a beautiful soul. I sense an artist's sensitivity."

She recalled when a teacher in one of her art classes had told her that she had the sensitivity of a true artist. It felt good hearing it again.

"What made you turn your back on your art?" Eduardo persisted.

Felicity recognized his sincerity and desire to know more. Taking a deep breath, she said, "I got caught up in my father's business."

"Ah, the starving artist versus the successful business woman. Hard to make the choice." A photographer came up to Eduardo and asked if he could take a few photos. Before excusing himself, he turned to Felicity. "If you ever decide to continue with your fashion design, give me a call. I'd love to see your work. I'm always looking for fresh talent." He said goodbye to Theo before following the photographer to another part of the gallery.

Theo smiled at her and squeezed her hand. "You see," he said, "I knew he'd like you."

Felicity felt a surge of happiness. She loved the entire scene. Theo. Large Eduardo. The crowd and the paintings and photographs on the wall. They all uplifted her.

After they made the rounds, having each consumed two glasses of champagne, Theo said, "A French restaurant just opened around the corner. I've been dying to try it. You up to it?"

"I'm starving," she said, surprising herself.

The maître d' placed them at a cozy table at the far end of the restaurant, where paintings for sale hung on the wall. Candles danced their shadows on crisp white table cloths, their light glinting off the silverware. What Eduardo had said about her talent had encouraged her. Felicity wondered if the artists who produced the artwork along the wall were young, or old, new at their art, or seasoned. But more importantly she imagined her own sketches and paintings lining these walls.

When the waiter appeared, Theo turned to Felicity and said, "We'll be having white wine. Is that alright?" Then he added, "I thought I'd order seafood. You don't mind if I order for both of us, do you?"

"That's fine. I like seafood," she said. But it didn't feel fine. It bothered her that she allowed a man whom she'd just met to be making decisions for her. "Actually," she said, "what kind of seafood were you thinking of ordering?"

"The shrimp," he said.

She picked up the menu from the table and examined it. "I'd prefer the scallops, but a glass of chardonnay would be great." It was a small request, but she felt a sense of victory at specifying what she truly wanted.

When the wine arrived, Theo lifted his glass to hers. "I'm so glad you called me," he said. "After Valerie left I was devastated. I thought my life was over. Well, at least my romantic life."

"How long were you two together?"

"Twelve years."

"When did she leave?" Felicity took a sip of her wine. The rich, deep yellow liquid had a buttery taste she liked.

"Three months ago."

"And you haven't dated anyone since?"

"You're the first one," he said, as if she should be flattered. But she wasn't. She deserved better than to be a man's rebound chick. She knew she would dismiss Theo as soon as the meal was over. The meal, though, was divine. She had never dined on scallops that melted in her mouth like these did. Nor imagined that Brussels sprout could be so delicious. It had been a long time since she'd consumed a full meal. To add to her pleasure, Theo was charming and fun to be with. His remarks made her laugh and she found his knowledge about history admirable. It was a long time since she'd been so entertained by a man. A statement Campbell had made occurred to her: it wasn't a man's duty to entertain her. Still, she appreciated Theo's enthusiasm and liveliness and how comfortable she felt with him.

"Do you eat out a lot?" she asked.

"Every day," he said. "I can't cook to save my wife...oops, slip of the tongue. Let's forget about Valerie, shall we?" He lifted his glass to hers and said, "To our new love affair."

"You wish," she said and laughed.
Afterwards, he invited her to his condo. "It'll give you a good idea of my lifestyle and who I am."

Curious to find out more about him, she agreed. He paid the bill and, since he had taken a taxi to the gallery, they rode together in her car.

She wondered if he was luring her to his apartment for sex and felt flattered more than alarmed.

In his building, they took the elevator to the sixth floor before stepping into Theo's apartment. Felicity let out a very audible, "Oh my God! It's so spacious!" She removed her boots and placed them on a mat under a black lacquered bench. When she walked into his living room, she immediately recognized a Philippe Starck mirror by its sleek lines and silver frame.

Theo showed her a fabulous kitchen that featured two large sinks, cabinetry in blonde colored wood and a fridge camouflaged in caramel-colored wood.

"Valerie did all the renovations," he said. "You should have seen the place when we moved in."

Oh yes, Valerie, thought Felicity.

Past the living room came a bathroom. Felicity made a mental note regarding the makeup counter with the professional three-way mirrors and soft lighting that camouflaged your flaws. "How luxurious."

"You like it? I wasn't sure about the deep red ceramic. But it's Valerie's choice and her bathroom. Help yourself to the cosmetics."

Felicity started at the strange offer. She glanced at the shelves stacked with Dior, Armani,

Bobbi Brown, and Chanel. As if she wanted any of Valerie's makeup when she could easily afford her own.

"What if Valerie wants to come back?" she asked. "You shouldn't give away her makeup."

"It's over between us. I have to move on and you're helping me do that. Anyway, she took her best makeup with her."

"You're offering me her left-overs. All the crap," she said and laughed.

Leaving the red-tiled bathroom, she came face to face with a sketching on the wall. The artist's style looked familiar. She stepped closer to it. "You have a Renoir?"

"That belongs to Valerie, like all the paintings on the wall," he said. "I wish she'd come and get them. They only remind me of her and take up so much space." She felt his breath on her neck as he gazed with her at the Renoir.

Felicity ignored the small voice telling her that until Valerie moved out completely, Theo wouldn't be able to put the past behind him. But then, that wasn't her problem.

She followed Theo into his bedroom. Painted a soothing blue, it had wall-to-wall closets and built in cabinetry. A king-sized bed dominated the room, its only piece of furniture. Felicity glanced at the thick quilted down cover – probably Valerie's choice. Theo drew her to him and hugged her tightly. The contact felt good but ended much too soon.

She turned her face up to him but he was already turning away. "Let me show you the master bathroom," he said.

Disappointment dogged her steps as she followed him. Maybe she shouldn't have asked him to give it time. But what about his telling her that they were going to fall in love? Had he said that just because he was lonely? Because he missed Valerie?

This bathroom featured modern, state-of-the-art fixtures. It had blue counters and ceramic and beige tiles that perfectly matched the thick blue drapes in the bedroom. She realized that Theo's blue velvet trousers were made of the same material as the bedroom drapes. Could they have been fashioned from left over material? Apart from this oddity and the fact that Valerie had chosen the décor, Felicity loved every inch of his apartment.

"I better get going," she said.

Although she spoke firmly, she felt let down when he didn't try to coax her into staying. She didn't want to sleep with him, but she also didn't want to be so easily discarded. As she second guessed her decision, Theo walked her downstairs and said, "You're a very special woman."

On her drive home, Felicity felt her head swirl, whether it was from the wine or the prospect of a new romance. Theo had been so kind. So gentlemanly. So much fun. She felt her shoulders tighten. Of course, it would be foolish to get involved with him. He obviously was not over Valerie and she had not completely moved out. She thought about his brief hug and how it had communicated his loneliness. He hadn't even tried to kiss her.

As she unlocked the door to her apartment, her thoughts returned to the art gallery, Eduardo and his invitation to show him her art. Regret washed over her. What would her art have looked like now, had she not dropped out of fashion design?

She contemplated all the years spent in business school and working at her father's company when she could have been improving her craft.

Chapter 15

Suzy suggested naming Campbell's research group, "The Dating Club."

"More like The Anti-Dating Club," Felicity said.

Campbell stood by the window sill, her back to the other women as she tugged at some dried leaves of an African violet. The old radiator beneath the window made a gurgling sound, echoing her displeasure. She hated the idea of naming her research group The Dating Club or even The Anti-Dating Club. It was neither, but it was better to choose her battles.

"I brought us all a treat," Suzy said. She placed a pretty pink metal box on the center of the table. Then she carefully flipped the lid, revealing her signature fluffy butter icing on an assortment of cupcakes. Oohs and ahhs were emitted by the rest of the group.

"These are gorgeous," said Felicity. "So artistic. You must have a steady hand."

Suzy smiled. "All I can say is that I never drink coffee before getting started."

"But you can have some tea while eating them," said Campbell, turning to face the women. "I'll boil some water."

She made her way to the sink at the back of the room, where she filled a kettle with fresh water. While waiting for it to boil, she brought four cups to the table, along with a box of teas and a small flowered bowl to place the used tea bags in.

"Look at the intricacy of the frosting. It's too beautiful to eat," said Felicity.

"These are amazing," said Missi, selecting a cupcake with bright pink frosting. "You should sell them."

"I do," Suzy said. "To Patisserie Lyse. I bring over a batch every Saturday."

"Oh, I've been to Lyse's. That's a high-end tea shop," said Campbell.

"Haven't you ever thought of having your own shop?" asked Felicity.

"Lots of times," said Suzy. "I guess I just don't have the... I don't know what...the confidence. The belief."

"Belief in what?" asked Campbell, reaching for a cupcake with cream cheese frosting.

"That I can make it," said Suzy. "I mean, baking is a hobby for me. To think I could make a living from it is unrealistic."

"Maybe not," said Missi, her lips covered with pink frosting.

"Oh, this cupcake is even tastier than it looks," said Campbell, licking icing off her finger. "Change is always scary."

"If I were still in my twenties, it would be easier," Suzy said.

"But you're not that old," said Missi.

"I'll be fifty next May." Suzy fluffed her long, platinum blonde hair. "I feel like I've wasted half my life."

"Many women change careers during the second half of their lives." As the kettle whistle blew, Campbell rose and walked towards the back of the room.

After filling the tea cups with the hot water, she dunked a mint tea bag into her own cup. She glanced through her notes on careers and self-fulfillment as an antidote to yearning for Prince Charming. "Listen to this," she said as she read from her notes. "Women are obsessed with having a man in their life. They don't feel fully alive without one."

"I always feel more alive when I'm in love," Suzy agreed. With manicured fingers, she lifted the tea bag by its string and delicately placed into the tiny bowl. "Once you get a taste of it, you keep hoping it will happen again. It's like a drug."

"It's not that easy to find someone who will make us happy for the rest of our lives," said

Felicity. "Though I did meet a really nice man last weekend."

"Oh, what's he like?" asked Missi.

Felicity straightened in her chair. She had tied her hair back with a glittering clip and her single purple streak fell along her cheek bone. "A lot of fun," she said. "He took me to a gallery opening last Saturday. I haven't felt so alive in ages, though I see us more as friends. His wife left him just a few months ago and I don't think he's over her.

"Men can't seem to stay alone. As soon as they're over one relationship, they're already embarking on another one," Suzy said.

"Or they make sure they already have a new one before they leave," said Missi.

Campbell sighed. Things were not going the way she had planned. "I thought we could focus on your career accomplishments this evening," she said as she reached for a second cupcake, this one with blueberries sprinkled on top.

"What career?" said Missi. "I've been a wife and mother for the last eighteen years. Now I'm forced to go out into the marketplace. Who will want to hire me?"

For so many other women in her groups, going back to work and becoming self-sufficient was the silver lining in their divorces. But it was too early for Missi to see that now; she was still feeling raw.

"I'm very successful," said Felicity, "but it doesn't make me happy. Sure, Daddy pays me a good salary that comes with all kinds of perks. His company has been around for four generations and he expects me to carry it into a fifth. That's what he's been training me for during the last six years. Working in different departments so that I get to know the company inside out. He even sent me on management courses. Boring. I know you all think that I have it easy. But the truth is that I hate my job." Suzy rolled her eyes at her but Felicity ignored her. "Some days I don't even have the energy to get out of bed. I feel like something inside of me is dying."

"So why don't you quit," said Suzy in a flat voice.

"It's complicated."

Suzy let out an exasperated sigh. "What? Daddy will stop providing and you'll have to pay for the gas in your sports car?"

"What stops me is knowing that I'd really upset my father," Felicity said. "He's counting on me."

Missi blew into her tea cup. "Why can't we have both?" she asked. "A career and a man to love us?"

"I'll tell you why," said Suzy. "Men aren't attracted to smart women. We're a threat to them. They don't want a woman who's going to let her career come first."

"She's right," said Felicity. "How many times have I lied to men about my job simply because if I told the truth, they would no longer be interested in me?"

"And how has that worked out for you?" asked Campbell as she sipped her tea.

"I end up being bored with them. These men expect women to give up their lives to take care of them."

"What's wrong with that?" asked Missi. "I mean if that's what the woman wants."

"Well, look at what happened to you," said Suzy.

"Let's not judge Missi," Campbell jumped in. "Suzy and Felicity have a point. Having a career and a relationship is like having your cake and eating it too." She leaned back in her chair. These were the exact words her mother had often used with her. There was always a choice to be made. Chocolate ice cream or vanilla. Watch a television program or read a book. And now, career or man.

"Love is so fragile," she continued. "You can't count on it. Self-achievement is much more trustworthy as a source of satisfaction than any relationship with a man."

Missi reached for another cupcake and licked the icing. "I have a confession to make," she said. "Max came over the other night. I had sex with him. Ever since that evening, all I think about is having sex with him."

"It's always like that. As soon as a woman fears that she's losing her man, she starts feeling passion for him," said Suzy.

"What about Sheri?" asked Campbell.

"He's still with her," she said in a quiet voice.

"Aren't you setting yourself up to be hurt more than you already are?" asked Campbell.

Missi shrugged her shoulders. "Having sex with Max gave me some weird kind of satisfaction."

"It's like you're getting back at Sheri," said Campbell.

"I suppose," Missi said.

"I'm sure Sheri isn't aware of what's going on," said Suzy.

"You do realize you're feeding his ego?"

Missi nodded. "Maybe. But sex with Max was the most exciting and erotic that it's ever been."

"So, you're thinking of luring him back with sex?" said Felicity, nibbling at her cupcake.

"Maybe he'll change his mind," said Missi.

"What if he doesn't leave Sheri? How will you feel?" asked Campbell.

"French men have mistresses but stick with their wives. Maybe I just need to be more open."

"Think how it will make you feel, knowing that Max is with another woman after he makes love to you," Campbell pointed out.

"He already is," said Missi. "So, what have I got to lose?"

"You need to get your mind off Max. Okay, ladies let's all brainstorm for Missi. What are some job possibilities for her?"

Campbell went to the flip chart against the wall. With a green marker, she jotted down suggestions as the other women called them out: sell jewelry online, work as a receptionist, sell cosmetics at the Chanel counter (this got oohs from everyone), work in a home for the elderly, for the homeless, dog walker, house sitter.

"There's my writing," Missi said. "I sometimes wrote for Real Romance Magazine. Nobody knows about it, because they don't give you a by-line."

"So why did you stop?" asked Suzy.

"Max didn't like me writing for those kinds of magazines. He said that it made him look like an inadequate lover if his wife needed silly stories to fulfill her fantasies."

"Was he?" asked Suzy. "An inadequate lover?"

"Sex with Max often felt like my wifely duty. The passion was only there at the beginning. Then, whenever I had sex, I had to think of scenes for my romance stories to get aroused."

The women laughed.

"Stories Max didn't want you writing," Campbell said.

Suzy thumped her fist on the table. "As soon as a man feels that he's conquered you, all he cares about is himself. He wants you to satisfy him. To take care of him. I did it with my first husband and I promised myself I would never do it again."

"What happened?" asked Missi.

"We were young, of course, and I had my first teaching job. Sam was still at university finishing off a graduate degree in philosophy. He could have taken a part-time job to help pay the rent, but there was never anything good enough for him. It took me awhile to figure out that Sam's most important attribute was that he was unlike my father," Suzy said. "I never really loved him. I supported him longer than I should have, but only because I didn't want to give my father the satisfaction of knowing that he was right."

"But you'd like a man to take care of you?" asked Campbell.

Both Missi and Suzy nodded in agreement

"Are you going to eat that cupcake?" Campbell asked Felicity. When the other woman slid the cupcake across the table, Campbell reached for it. "These are sinfully delicious."

"Thank you." Suzy closed the lid on the empty box. "I'm of that generation that expects to be taken care of by a man, but I know it doesn't work that way anymore."

"What about your second marriage?" asked Missi.

Suzy told her that she'd married Alex because of a strong physical connection that convinced her she was in love, a *coup de foudre*.

"It's oxytocin," Campbell said. "That's the hormone released during sex. Because of its euphoric power, it can make you believe that you're in love."

"Oh, that's so depressing," said Missi. "We can't even trust our own feelings."

"Well, I shouldn't have trusted my feelings the other night," said Suzy. "I finally dated an older man."

"Did you sleep with him?" Felicity wanted to know.

"Yes, but we didn't have sex," she said.

"Like smoking but not inhaling," said Felicity.

"Something like that," said Suzy.

"You let a stranger sleep with you?" asked Missi.

"He lived up north and it was late. It didn't make sense for him to drive home, especially since he had to come back into the city in less than six hours."

When Felicity asked if she was going to see him again, Suzy said no.

"Because he's too old?" asked Campbell.

"It has nothing to do with age. Although he's a lot older than he said in his profile, I just didn't feel anything," Suzy said. "Well, that's not entirely true. When I first met him, I found him interesting. But then back at my apartment, it seemed we had nothing more to say to each other. By then, I'd already offered him to stay over. The whole encounter had ended in disappointment."

"We're always hoping to find The One," Campbell said as she refilled their cups with hot water. "That's why we're so enthusiastic when we meet a man for the first time. Only it doesn't usually last."

"Well, I can certainly vouch for that," said Suzy.

"So why do you keep going on those dating sites?" asked Felicity.

Something about her has changed, thought Campbell. She remembered how uptight Felicity had been at their first meeting. When she'd finally removed her coat, her matching woolen dress and pearl necklace had somehow felt inappropriate. Tonight, she wore jeans and a t-shirt under a hooded sweater, which suited her much better.

Suzy sighed. "I keep hoping, I guess." Ignoring Campbell's raised eyebrows, she said, "I hate to disagree with you and your research, but I'm still waiting for my Prince Charming."

"And then what?" Campbell asked as she dipped a fresh tea bag into her cup.

"And then she can be happy," said Missi. "Isn't that why we all want a Prince Charming?"

"But that hasn't happened, has it?" said Campbell.

"It's just so hard to make a good connection," said Felicity as she twisted her strand of purple dyed hair.

"Let's analyze this," said Campbell "Missi says that Suzy needs a man to make her happy. Is that right, Suzy?"

"The whole point of wanting a man in our lives is to make it better," she answered.

"Yet, you always end up disappointed. Probably even less happy than before you met the man."

"Of course, you're disappointed," said Felicity. "You're always meeting the wrong man."

"And why do you think that is so?" asked Campbell. "I mean why do you think you're always attracting the wrong man?"

"Unlucky. Being at the wrong place at the wrong time." Suzy gazed at the women with a sad smile. "I'm self-sufficient. I can take care of myself. Which is, in itself, the entire problem. Too many women are now able to take care of themselves. They've bought their own forty-inch TV screen, they hire handy men to fix things around the house, their mortgages are paid off, they had in vitro babies and go on exotic trips. What man can keep up with this? Their power has been stripped away; their roles are no longer clear. Open the car door or not? Pay the entire meal or go Dutch and pretend it doesn't take away some of the romance?"

"Maybe there's something more," said Campbell. "Maybe you don't believe you're worthy of being happy." Silence filled the room, as it always did whenever she mentioned this in her previous groups. "Here's what I think. If you succeed in a relationship with a man, you'll be jeopardizing your subconscious belief that you're not worthy of one. It's the typical pattern of daughters abandoned by fathers. She's looking for a man to make her happy, but her early experience with the first man in her life has shown her that it's impossible."

"Which is it?" asked Missi. "That we don't feel worthy, or that we think it's impossible to be happy with a man?"

"Both," said Campbell. "No man will ever make us happy. We need to find love within ourselves. Only then will we be able to love someone else."

"I don't agree," said Missi. "Max makes me happy and I'd love myself a whole lot more if he came back."

Chapter 16

It was drizzling when Campbell left the center. She hated the walk along the overpass in the dark, especially since she'd left her walking shoes at home. Her umbrella only partially opened because of its two bent wires; she had meant to replace it. There was no way to avoid getting wet. Still, she needed to think, and walking in the rain always helped to cleanse her thoughts.

The meeting this evening disturbed her. Was she compensating for a lack of Prince Charming through a successful career? Not that she had done phenomenally well in her work before getting this award. Fortunately, though, she'd inherited her mother's duplex mortgage free. But now that the upstairs tenants were going back to London, she needed to find new tenants to help cover her expenses. She hoped that the award she was about to receive for her research would launch her career into the stratosphere where she felt she belonged. She had paid her dues; it was time.

The March wind whipped her face as mini vans and trucks passed by. As she approached her home, she remembered a time when only a few scattered homes lined the street and she could play in the fields. The space she had loved as a child had been replaced with the brick walls of modern houses, stretches of asphalt and neglected back yards. Things changed without you even noticing them.

By the time she reached her front door, her wet pants clung to her after being splashed by a heartless motorist, and her feet ached from walking in her stilettos. She removed her coat and went into the bathroom, where she grabbed a towel to dry her hair. As she listened to the hum of the hairdryer, she wondered if she had not subconsciously chosen to become a counselor in order to better understand her own failed relationships with men. Hearing other women talk about their relationship problems reassured her. She was perfectly content to live her life as a single woman, free from the anguish that came with being part of a couple. But now a shift had taken place that made her wonder about her life choices. She had released her desire for Prince Charming years ago, so why was it coming back? Did she still consider fulfilling herself through a career her ultimate goal?

She changed into her pajamas and began to type notes for her speech. Her fingers raced on the keyboard as she documented, as accurately as she could, how this evening's support meeting had impacted her.

In striving to be accepted by the Women's Studies Community, had she set aside her own desires? Was her belief that she would never find Prince Charming rooted in wanting to protect herself from disappointment, from being hurt once more?

Her phone rang. When she heard Chand's voice, her whole body relaxed. She hadn't seen him for over a week, although they spoke to each other every day over the phone. She had come to anticipate these phone calls and they had swiftly gotten into the habit of recounting the day's events to each other.

She told him about her walk home in the rain.

"Why didn't you call me?" he said. "I would have gone to meet you." So many guys she'd dated would have never even considered picking her up at work. Chand was so sweet.

"Have you eaten?" he asked. She told him she hadn't. "Then let's have a bite together. I'll be over in forty minutes and we can go to that brasserie near your place. I'll meet you inside."

Chand was spot on time as usual, looking irresistible in a brown leather jacket and a pair of khaki pants. His warm hug lasted longer than it normally did.

"You look lovely," he said as he led her past the crowd and towards a candle lit table. He reached over to pull a chair out for her and helped her get seated. His fingers lingered on her shoulders, giving them a gentle squeeze.

Campbell always enjoyed coming to this brasserie where an experimental band often played here or poets did readings. This evening, a young woman played the piano, filling the room with her soft, melodic notes.

They each ordered beers and shared a platter of fried calamari as well as a plate of steamed vegetables. They talked about the rain, a recent senate scandal, and a problem Chand had with an employee at the hotel he managed. At a lull in the conversation, he reached out to caress her cheek; she stroked his hand.

"So, how's work?" he asked her.

She shrugged. "The women have decided to call my research The Dating Club, of all things."

"And...?"

"And it's just the opposite. All of them are so keen on talking about Prince Charming and how to meet him that I feel guilty about trying to convince them not to. What started out as case study material for my speech has turned into a dating club."

"Have you considered telling the group how you feel?" he said.

"I can't do that," she said.

"You mean you can't be honest with them." His eyes challenged her now.

She didn't know what to say. The truth was, she didn't want to look like a fool.

"Tell them the truth," he said. "I'm sure they'll understand. And likely be happy as well."

"Oh, they'll be happy alright. But what about my research and my talk at the conference?"

"You still have time to figure it out. Just trust that things will turn out."

After a waiter picked up their empty plates, she finished her beer. Her career had always been her passion but now she wondered if she'd let it replace the sensual passion of an intimate relationship.

Chand moved his chair closer and reached for her hands across the table. Holding them in his, he looked directly into her eyes and said, "I don't want to invest in us if eight months down the road, I realize that we want different things. What do you expect from a relationship?"

Was that what they had? "Define relationship," she said.

"Every interaction with someone is a relationship. I can't tell you what others expect or want from their partners. I can only tell you what I want from you."

"And what is that?" she asked.

"To be with you; make a life together. You brighten my life, Campbell. But I'm not certain I brighten yours."

A chill ran through her. "I don't know, Chand. I really like being with you, but things are moving so fast."

Chand stared at her, and then finally said, "Can you trust your feelings and see who I am. Someone who cares deeply for you and will be there for you? Or would you rather pretend to the world that I don't exist?"

She wanted to say, *You're everything I ever wanted in a man. You do exist.* But she couldn't speak.

"Every day with you enriches my life," he said. "I want you to give us a chance. Can you do that?"

"Part of me wants to say yes. I like you a lot. I enjoy being with you. Give me some time, Chand."

At the look in his eyes, she knew that he would only be so patient. She needed to be as much a part of this relationship as he was, if she wanted him to stay.

Chapter 17

Felicity turned on the shower to rinse out the coloring in her hair. She had put in a few more purple streaks. As she massaged her head under the warm water, she thought about the last fashion exhibit she'd been to. It was a tribute to Yves Saint Laurent. That was years ago when she had just graduated from business school. She remembered walking through the rooms of the museum, admiring the designs with a heavy heart. As she watched purple-colored water stream in rivulets down her body, she thought about how much she'd lost by casting her dream aside. She missed the energy of the art world.

She stepped out of the shower, toweled herself, and slipped on a pair of jeans with a cozy woolen sweater. As she dried her hair, she decided to speak to her father that very day about her need for a change in her life.

Since she had moved out of his house eight years ago, Felicity went there every Sunday for lunch. After sharing a meal together, they settled in his library for an hour or so. This ritual had been established after her mother left.

At first, she had found solace in their weekly ritual. As the years wore on, though, it felt like more of a duty. She liked spending time with her father in a personal setting, but his imposing presence became harder and harder to accept.

She clicked off the dryer and combed her hair. She admired the daring purple streaks she had added in the front, feeling that they suited her.

After popping two anti-anxiety pills into her mouth, she swallowed them with a glass of juice. Then she put on her ski jacket and headed out the door.

It was a thirty-minute drive to her father's house along the lake shore. A house, Felicity thought, that was far too large for him now that he lived alone. She had tried to convince him to sell it and buy one of the luxurious condos facing the lake. But a big house symbolized his success, just as his Jaguar and his monogrammed tailor-made shirts.

Instead of the bumper-to-bumper traffic that occurred on weekdays, the drive off the island on Sunday morning was quick and smooth. She felt like an actress auditioning for a role she was unprepared for. She knew that she would disappoint him when she told him that she didn't want to work at Starr Transport anymore. And how much he counted on her to fulfill his dream. As she drove unto the ramp to the West Island, her father's words resounded in her mind.

"I don't know what I'd do without you," he had told her about a month after her mother deserted them.

Felicity had taken his words to heart, happy that he needed her. She had always been there for him and always would be. The only thing she could no longer do was to work in his company, feeding his dream of her one day taking over Starr Transport.

As she drove along the Lakeshore, she noticed how the sun sparkled on the iced-over lake. Winters here seemed to last forever. She slowed down, suddenly nervous about confronting her father. Then she turned up a cul-de-sac, heading for his house at the end. It was a white brick building hidden behind a row of tall evergreens. Felicity parked her car along the circular driveway and reached into her bag for another pill, which she popped into her mouth.

Her father, a rather short man with a full head of blonde hair, greeted her in his customary manner. "My lovely Princess," he said, giving her a fierce hug.

She followed him into his kitchen, where an array of sushi lay on the counter along with a chilled bottle of white wine. They filled their plates and glasses and went into the den, where they sat on wingback armchairs, with their meals placed on trays in front of them. Outside the window, the skies had clouded over and tiny flakes of snow floated past the glass.

"I checked out The Sports Club the other day," Felicity said.

"It's quite impressive, isn't it?"

"It's very state of the art," she said. "It's just not for me."

"Oh, you'll get used to it. It's good for you to be surrounded by such a fine class of people. Good for business contacts. It's all about networking." He helped himself to some pickled ginger on his plate before reaching for a piece of maki sushi.

Felicity picked up a sushi roll and then put it back down. "I don't feel like I belong there."

"In time you will," said her father. He reached for *The Economist* on a side table and flipped through its pages as he continued to eat.

"Daddy, I ... I need to talk to you." The tremor in her voice alarmed her. She closed her eyes and pulled in a long, calming breath.

Her father's eyes remained fixed on the pages of his magazine. "What is it, Princess?"

Felicity swallowed hard. "It's about your company. Actually, my job in your company."

"*Our* company," he corrected her. "One day my Princess is going to become queen of the Starr Transport Company. Knowing that my efforts and hard work will be continued by you is what keeps me going." He put down the magazine, picked up the remote and turned on the television. "So, what's bothering you?" he asked.

Spit it out, she thought; there was no other way. Otherwise, the words would stay stuck inside forever. "My job isn't fulfilling me."

"Why's that, Princess?" He flipped through a few channels.

"I feel so useless," she told him. "You don't really need a marketing department." Why couldn't she come out with the whole truth, that she hated her job and felt suffocated by it?

His eyes still on the TV he said, "Maybe you need a change. I'll see which department you haven't worked in yet. It's good for you to know every aspect of the company."

Regardless of which department she worked in, she would never feel at home there. And she most decidedly did not want to be queen of Starr Transport. She squared her shoulders and leaned forward in the armchair. "It's just that I don't think..." she began.

"Sshh. I want to watch this," he said, turning the volume up.

Felicity glanced at the screen. The tenseness in her chest now transformed into anger as she realized that her father was watching a documentary on oil - its political, economic and religious impact on the world. Not that she didn't care about world events – the problem was how he'd so effectively silenced her. She couldn't stomach the way she had again allowed herself to be controlled.

She gathered the empty plates and glasses and carried them into the kitchen. Then she shoved her arms into the sleeves of her jacket, grabbed her handbag and strode back into the den. When he looked up at her, she couldn't find the words to express what she was feeling. Her habit of deferring to him had taken over. In a tight voice, she said, "I'm leaving,"

Returning his attention to the TV, he said, "First thing Monday morning, I'll see what I can do about having you train in a different department."

A soft snow had begun to fall as Felicity made her way back to the city. She had calmed down, her anger turning to sadness as she realized how weak she was when it came to her father. She wished now that she had confronted him, turned off the television and told him that the last thing she wanted was to become queen of Starr Transport.

Chapter 18

Campbell started slowly counting to ten as she pressed her father's doorbell, in an effort to remain calm. Her stomach churned. She would have been better off lying on her sofa at home reading the current issue of *Neurosis*, she thought.

Her time with Chand and "The Dating Club," as the women now referred to their Tuesday meetings, made her question her relationship with her father and filled her with uncertainty.

Tina answered the door. "Campbell," she said. "I'm so glad you made it." She gave her a warm hug, which Campbell returned with equal strength. She removed her boots and coat.

"Here, let me take that for you," As Tina hung Campbell's coat in the closet, she said, "So how's your research coming along?"

Campbell wished she could tell her that it wasn't going as she had planned. That she now doubted her underlying premise that women like her – women who'd been abandoned by their fathers – were doomed to unsuccessful relationships with men. But it was neither the time nor the place for such revelations.

"It's coming along fine," she said.

"I was hoping you'd changed your mind about bringing along your young man."

"He's hardly young," Campbell said. "He's a few years older than I am."

"For your father, anyone under sixty is young. Come, everybody is already here." Tina linked arms with her and led her into the living room.

"Everybody" was her father's four other children. There was Abigail, who was twenty-eight, four years younger than Campbell, and who looked like she had just stepped off the front cover of ELLE Magazine. Which she probably had. Then Jonathan, who was in his early twenties, and his brother Mark, seventeen. And finally, Tina's three-year-old, Cooper. Five children, four different mothers.

They all said an unenthusiastic "hi" to her and she greeted them back just as unenthusiastically. None of them, except for Cooper, had ever shown any interest in her. But then neither had Campbell. Sometimes she learned what they were up to by their Facebook pages. It was difficult keeping track of her father's different girlfriends and households throughout the years. He never stayed with anyone for very long and she wondered how long it would last with Tina. Although she supposed, now that he was sixty, he might settle down.

Campbell acted as if she were glad to be there, asking her step-sister and brothers what they were up to. Jonathan was working up the ladder in his banking career, while Mitch was too occupied text messaging to answer, and little Cooper was playing some game on an iPad. Abigail, dressed in a cute black tulle skirt with a shimmering top, bragged about her recent trip to Paris for a fashion shoot. Her outfit reminded Campbell of her own black dress that no longer quite fit.

"There you are, Cambie," her father said, placing an arm around her as he led towards the bar set up on the other side of the room. "What can I get you?"

"I'll have one of those," she said, pointing to his drink. Although she wasn't a scotch drinker and barely touched the hard stuff, her taut nerves made her feel the need for something strong.

She watched Abigail prance around her father, complimenting his skills as a bartender and how young he looked. Campbell had to admit that her father still looked handsome. He'd lost a bit of belly lard and although he was now semi bald, it suited him in a Bruce Willis type of way. And she had been right when she met him with Chand. He'd had his teeth whitened. Too white, she thought, against his tanned face.

192

Tina glided into the living room, carrying a tray of appetizers fit for a Martha Stewart magazine layout.

"Tina got a job testing recipes for a gourmet magazine," said her father.

Campbell's mother had always despised cooking. Although she liked Tina, she hated that her father now had this Martha Stewart wife. It just didn't seem fair. But life wasn't fair, was it? She thought of how her mother had given up her studies in accounting to work as a waitress in a fast-food restaurant to support him through law school. And how, after passing his bar exams, he had gotten Abigail's mother – a lawyer in the same firm he articled in – pregnant.

"Cheers," her father said, lifting his glass to hers. "Are you still seeing that gentleman from India?"

"Chand," she said.

"You should have brought him over. I liked him. Extremely polite."

"He's just a friend," she said.

She had to admit to herself that he was more than a friend. She realized that she missed him and wished he were here with her. Chand was the only man whom she could absolutely count on for support. She could explain the situation with her step-siblings to him and why she didn't fit into this family. Afterwards, they could talk about why she felt so alienated whenever she came here. In such a short time, she had become attached to him, and his talk the other day of being in a relationship both frightened and excited her. The scotch burned her throat as she took another sip.

"Your friends are always welcome here," her father said.

She tensed at the notion of inviting friends to his home. Except for Missi, she hadn't made any real friends. So much of her time had been taken up with her research and maintaining her duplex. She did enjoy her Tuesday evenings, though, and was beginning to consider Felicity and Suzy as friends rather than subjects for her research.

"Tina went all out decorating," she said, changing the subject. "This room could be a runner-up for the best birthday-decorated room in the country."

Strings of balloons floated over the stone fireplace; vibrant happy birthday cocktail napkins were artistically laid out on the coffee table. White lights in the shape of hearts glittered all over the room and gifts piled on the table were all perfectly wrapped in silver and gold. Campbell had brought a box of Cuban cigars, neither knowing nor caring whether her father smoked them.

"Actually, Abigail did most of the decorations. A mixture of Valentine and birthday rolled into one. And you did a wonderful job, darling," he told his younger daughter, who now held onto his arm.

"Leave it to Daddy to have his birthday close to the most love-filled day of the year, even though we are celebrating it rather late. But that's only because I was tied up in Paris," Abigail said. She held out an empty wine glass to him. "Can you give me a refill?'

"Red?"

"Daddy, you know I only drink white. Red wine stains my teeth."

"I know. I was just teasing you," her father said.

Campbell's jaw clenched at their affectionate exchange. She brought the scotch to her lips, this time taking a gulp rather than a sip.

"Tina told me that you're going to give a presentation in New York in May. What's it about?" her father asked as he handed Abigail a glass of white wine.

She would have loved to mention her subtopic of the father/daughter relationship, but then he would brag about what a super father he was. And he'd have Abigail's full support. Campbell wasn't about to give him that opportunity. "On Prince Charming," she said. "Actually, the Prince Charming myth."

"Oh, that sounds interesting," said Abigail. "Most men I meet believe they're Prince Charming although I have to admit, in my line of work a lot of them are gay." Her cell phone rang and she turned away to answer it in a kittenish voice.

"These machines certainly break up conversations, don't they?" said her father as Abigail stepped away from them.

Thank God, thought Campbell.

"I heard you mention Prince Charming," Tina said, wrapping her arms around her husband's waist. He turned to kiss her.

Campbell thought of her conversation with Chand and his assertion that her research could be a shield to protect her from getting involved with men. Although she had denied it to his face, she knew that she was afraid of being hurt. She feared being treated like her mother —cast aside, traded in. And she wasn't sure she could take it. It was better to abandon men before they abandoned her. She took another gulp of scotch. But Chand was not like her father, was he? He was reliable and steady; the opposite, in fact.

Cooper came running up to his parents and her father swooped him into his arms.

Campbell reached for his tiny arm and said, "Hey, Cooper, you've grown so much. How old are you now?"

"Three," he said, holding up three fingers.

A wave of sadness passed through her. She realized that her biological clock was ticking and that she had put aside having children for the sake of her career. So much of her life was invested in her career.

"Come," Tina said to everyone there, "before the food gets cold."

The meal was festive, with roast leg of lamb, French string beans, potatoes roasted in fresh rosemary and olive oil and bottles of expensive wine. Campbell listened as everyone talked about their accomplishments. Abigail had signed a contract with a perfume company. Jonathan had just received an impressive promotion at the bank, while Mitch, in his last year of high school, had become the star athlete of his school.

Campbell felt like a failure. The award she was about to receive for her work on the father/daughter relationship and the Prince Charming myth would give her the recognition she had longed for. But now that Chand had come into her life, she was filled with doubt about her research. Maybe Prince Charming wasn't such a myth after all.

It was a little after nine when Campbell left. "Keep in touch," everybody said. She knew that it was just a formality. She really didn't feel like she belonged in this family. Deep down, she yearned for a family of her own. It shocked her to realize that that family might be with Chand. She wondered what it would be like to move into Chand's pristine apartment or to live with him in her duplex, and then what their children would look like. The thought sent a warm glow through her body.

Her father walked her to the door and handed her an envelope.

"This is for you, Cambie darling, to treat yourself to something special." His voice was drawn out and he swayed a bit as he stood before her. "We didn't get to see each other at Christmas or your birthday, so it's a late Happy Birthday/Merry Christmas."

She didn't have to open the envelope to know that it contained a generous check. Money had always been her father's way of compensating for his absence in her life, for having walked out on her when she was only a child. Plus, his calling her "darling" didn't mean a thing. He used that term of endearment for everybody. The bank teller, the waitress, the dog catcher, female cops, and of course Abigail.

As soon as she reached home, she called Chand. When he asked how it was going, she said, "alright."

"Just alright?"

"I just got back from my father's," she said.

"That explains it," he said.

"It never goes well with my father," she said. "He gave me my birthday card and Christmas card all at once."

"And that offended you?"

"My birthday was in January and Christmas was in December. He only gives me the envelope in February. It doesn't make me feel that important."

"Did he give you a gift?"

"Just money."

"That's always better than a pair of slippers that don't fit you," Chand pointed out. "So, you took the money in spite of your anger."

"What would be the point of refusing it? He wouldn't get it."

"What is he supposed to get?"

What exactly was he supposed to get? That his walking out on her had ruined her life? That before he left to build other families, he'd been her hero? And that now she could never again believe in heroes? That he had forced her to abandon her dreams of romance and having a family of her own? "He just doesn't get it," she repeated.

"Maybe it's you that doesn't get it."

It infuriated her that Chand would think that. Wasn't he supposed to be on her side? "What don't I get?" she snapped.

She roamed around the rooms of her apartment, tripping over an oversized potted house tree that almost reached the ceiling, and then stubbed her toe on the edge of a terracotta pot housing a large cactus. Although her plants demanded attention, she loved them all. She had grown fond of African violets whose colorful blooms now adorned every sunlit window ledge in her lower duplex. She traced the huge double blooms of a violet with an index finger.

"Have you ever thought that it's you and not him who keeps this wall up? Why don't you just let it go? Let go of whatever it is that keeps you from seeing how much your father cares for you."

"Cares for me? You don't even know him. That time you met him, all he did was brag about himself. He was so busy impressing you that he barely noticed me. My father is unreliable, fickle and incapable of real caring."

"Or maybe he cares for you in the only way he knows how," he said in a low voice.

The muscles in her neck stiffened as she paced around her living room. What if Chand was right? What if she needed her father to reject her? Otherwise, her entire career would be based on a falsehood.

She swallowed hard before saying, "I don't want to talk about this."

"Campbell, honey, you have to talk about this. You of all people should know that."

"Yes, well, I also know that you shouldn't force anyone to talk about what they aren't prepared to discuss."

"There is a saying in India that if you shut off one love, you shut off all loves. You see, as long as you don't trust your father with your love, you won't be able to open your heart for me."

"You and your Guru philosophy," said Campbell. "It's so damn self-serving."

"Does that mean you want me to come over?" he asked.

"Yes," she said weakly, reaching for the watering can next to her. As she began watering the plants, she wondered which underwear she should wear for Chand's first visit here. She continued towards her bedroom, watering the plants along the way.

From her dresser drawer, she pulled out a pink and black lacy bra and panties, an electric blue tiger print bra with black panties, and a little red lacy bra with a pair of thongs that she seldom wore because she found the thongs just too uncomfortable. Finally, she decided on the pink and black lingerie, under a sexy black top and short skirt. She needed to know if what Chand felt for her was just sexual. If he lost interest in her afterwards, or treated her differently, she'd have her answer.

While showering, she thought of her feelings for Chand. And that maybe – just maybe – she could have a healthy relationship with him even if she'd been abandoned by her father. But wasn't the purpose of her research to prove just the opposite? And what about her research group? Could she risk telling these women about her feelings for Chand? What if she was wrong? What if her entire research was wrong?

Chapter 19

It was well past midnight, but Suzy couldn't sleep. The pitter-patter of rain against her windowpane brought memories of other nights, other times. Feeling restless, she slipped into a pair of jeans and a sweat shirt before shrugging into her rain coat. She didn't bother with makeup and her hair hung straight and loose past her shoulders.

Before heading out into the night, she grabbed a fuchsia umbrella with a decorative trim. Holding it as she stepped into the quiet street reminded her of Hong Kong, where the umbrella had protected her from the hot sun.

She thought of the time she'd spent there with Kevin on their way to Vietnam.

At night, they strolled through the narrow streets to the Hong Kong waterfront, where they watched skyscrapers light up the sky. In the day time, they roamed around the shops and museums in Tsim Sha Tsui and again feasted on the harbor view. They lunched at the Lock Cha Tea Shop in Hong Kong Park. Even after all these years, Suzy remembered it as the most exquisite lunch she had ever had. Was it because it had been with Kevin? Their last meal together?

Suzy thought of Campbell's research group and why she'd decided to join. She had hoped to find answers to her repetitive failures with men. But then Campbell had asked them to fill out that questionnaire on father/daughter relationships and the hatred for her father which she had all but forgotten resurfaced. Acknowledging to herself that he had abandoned her sometimes filled her with despair. But she'd never connected it with her relationships with men. Then to complicate matters, there was Kevin's death. Perhaps the women in the group could help her sort out her feelings, but not now. The pain was still too raw.

In a few weeks, it would be the anniversary of Kevin's death. Ten years already since her son had died. While in Ho Chi Minh, they had made friends with the people living across the hall from their rented apartment. The couple invited them to the five-year death anniversary of the wife's grandfather. They travelled across the city until they reached a huge house painted pale blue. Tents were set up outside and a live band played. There were more than a hundred people present. There was even a place set in honor of the dead man. It intrigued Suzy how people from other cultures celebrated death. Perhaps, she thought, she should have a celebration for Kevin. That was the kind of thing he would find amusing. But who would she invite? No one here knew about Kevin.

She recalled how, in the months after his death, she had given away almost all his books, his clothing, and his collection of CDs. She had been so angry that she smashed his guitar against the wall. He was gone and she didn't want any of his possessions in her space. But no matter how fierce, her anger couldn't bring him back. When she realized this, she decided to move away from Vancouver so that she wouldn't have to look at the places that reminded her of him. She had chosen Montreal for two reasons: she could teach French and she had never been there with Kevin.

As she kept walking, tears began to stream down her face. She was grateful that it was dark and rainy. When a man passed her, she lowered her head under the umbrella to hide her tears. Waiting at a red light, she recalled how Kevin had held her arm in Vietnam whenever they crossed the street, because she was so terrified of the traffic. The pain of missing him ripped through her heart.

Marguerite Duras' novel, *The Lover*, had sparked Suzy's desire to travel to Saigon. She wanted to see the district of Cholon, where the young girl had her affair with the older Chinaman. On the plane ride over, Suzy read Kevin passages from the book.

When the traffic light turned green, she crossed the street and headed home. She passed a bank, a stationary store and a pastry shop. At this hour, the pastry shop was closed and its display window empty. Suzy imagined her chocolate éclairs, her macaroons and carrot cake filling the space. Soon she turned a corner that led to the street where she lived.

She wished her mother had gotten to know Kevin. Once home, she sat down at her kitchen table, her head on her arms, and wept. Perhaps, she thought, it was time to tell the women in The Dating Club about her son.

Chapter 20

"I've never wanted a woman as much as I want you," Chand said, as he started to unbutton Campbell's cardigan. Lowering his head, he planted a trail of butterfly kisses on her forehead, eyelids, cheeks, neck and collar bone.

She slipped out of his embrace, reached for the lamp and turned it off. She had always felt uncomfortable about showing her naked body. It wasn't that she felt ashamed; she took good care of herself. Her body was muscled and well-toned. Even as a child, she had been physically active. She did gymnastics and played on the soccer team, and later enrolled in aerobics classes. For the last three years, she did Pilates. Yet, after showering at home, she always covered up when she went from bathroom to bedroom; feeling shy even with herself.

"You are extremely beautiful, Ms. Jones," Chand said. When he gently led her towards the bed, she felt the firmness of his arm around her shoulder. Her eyes met his as he positioned her on the mattress. In the dimness of her room, she could only make out his silhouette as he removed his t-shirt, then slipped out of his jeans and boxer shorts. A surge of desire coursed through her. It had been a long time since she had experienced such an intense feeling of anticipation.

He kissed her slowly, almost playfully, nipping at her lips until she opened her mouth to his. When he caressed her breasts, she felt her senses quicken. They lay together, their legs entwined and their hands roaming each other's bodies like explorers discovering foreign lands. As he reached between her thighs, he continued stroking her, trying to find the rhythm that brought her the most pleasure. The intensity quickly became unbearable. She leaned over to extract a condom from a drawer in her night table and helped him slip it on.

After they had made love, Chand fell asleep and she curled naked next to him, listening to his breathing. She kissed him lightly on his shoulder. His skin emitted a faint spicy scent, more intoxicating to her than any men's cologne. She had never felt more satiated. The sexual release they had experienced together was likely the culmination of their attraction to each other and nothing more, she told herself. How could anything this perfect last? In time, something would happen to break them apart, again proving the validity of the premise of her research.

Yet, she couldn't deny how wonderful it felt to sleep with Chand next to her. As she awakened the following morning, she was happy to see him stretched out in her bed.

"How did you sleep?" he asked her.

"I'm not used to sleeping with someone else. I drifted in and out. What about you?"

"I slept like a rock. It's so nice to wake up with you next to me," Chand said. "Maybe we should live together."

She couldn't tell if he were teasing her or not.

"I don't want to live with you unless I'm married." What she had meant to say was that she could only live with a man if she loved him enough to marry him. Not that she wanted to get married. That certainly wasn't in her plans.

"I'll have to speak to my father about that."

"Do they still do that in India? Have the parents approve of marriage?" She knew enough about Indian culture to know that the parents' approval of a marriage was customary.

"Some do. How about if I made you breakfast in bed? Do you have any eggs?"

While Chand was busy making breakfast, Campbell threw on a bathrobe and went into the washroom to shower and brush her teeth. Looking at herself in the mirror, she liked what she saw. Her skin had that distinctive glow that only came after good sex.

She returned to her room, took off her bathrobe and slid between the sheets. Chand returned with a tray holding coffee and scrambled eggs on toast.

"Did you have any trouble finding everything?" she asked.

"No, although you do have a messy kitchen."

Their hips touched as they ate their breakfast.

"I really like you, Campbell," he said. "The more I'm with you, the more I long to be with you. I want us to get better acquainted. Please come to India with me. I'd love for you to meet my parents."

"I can't," she said. "I have to prepare for my conference. Besides, I'm afraid of flying."

Chand placed the breakfast tray on the floor and began to caress her. After brushing her hair back, he tenderly kissed her forehead. Then he drew her against his muscular body. She smelled coffee and egg on his breath. His warmth radiated through her, as if all her pores had opened to welcome him. The warmth of his body felt good against hers. She stiffened in excitement as he began to nibble at her breasts. It was wonderful to feel so desired.

"I could stay like this all day," Chand said.

"Me, too. But I have so much to do today. A Pilates class, and then laundry. I should be getting ready."

They both slid out of bed and Chand began to straighten out the sheets.

"Just leave it," said Campbell. "Actually, can you help me flip the mattress over?"

She took one end of the mattress while Chand took the other. As they lifted one side up, a few papers went flying and landed next to Chand's bare feet. He picked up the pages and began reading.

The list! She remembered now that she'd placed it under her mattress years ago, hoping that somehow the criteria she'd written on it would magically seep into her subconscious while she slept and get the universe to fulfill her wishes.

"Give me that," she demanded, lunging at him.

Chand held the pages above his head so she couldn't reach them.

"This is very interesting," he said. "When did you write it?"

"Years ago."

He began to recite the list to her: *intellectual; unselfish in bed; unselfish, period; has a career; nice teeth; doesn't have other girlfriends on the side; generous; affectionate...* Her list contained more than fifty criteria, including such contradictory statements as *not religious but spiritual* followed by *not too spiritual.*

Campbell covered her face with her hands. "Stop it," she said. "It doesn't mean anything. None of it does."

Chand began to laugh.

"What's so funny?" she asked.

"This list. Look at it. Three pages long. It's like a golfer who always expects to make a hole in one. You know how impossible that is?"

"Maybe the list is a bit long," she said, glancing over the sheets. There were so many things on it that didn't matter to her anymore. "I wrote this list a long time ago. A lot of it is no longer relevant. I realize that I was looking for the perfect man. The man with no flaws. I get that. But I don't want to settle, either." Her eyes fixed on his.

"Is that what you believe you're doing with me? Settling?"

She shook her head. "I don't know, Chand. It's all so confusing for me. All these years that I've spent researching the Prince Charming myth; I can't discount them."

"You're very stubborn," he said. "I always thought that counselors should have an open mind."

"It's just that I've devoted so much time to my study. Every paper that I've published has been to support the Prince Charming myth. All my groups have been about that."

She thought of The Dating Club. How could she keep lying to her group, trying to convince them that finding a man would not make them happy?

And if she admitted the truth, it would be admitting failure.

Chapter 21

Missi opened her mailbox, hoping to find the check for a story she'd sold to Real Romance Magazine. Instead, she found a pile of bills. It wasn't that she desperately needed the money right now. Max continued to pay for the condo as well as living expenses for her and Randy, but she knew that wouldn't last forever.

She set the bills aside and got ready for her weekly meeting at the Women's Center. Already running late, she pulled a coat on over her gym outfit. Missi had meant to go to the gym today. She began every day with good intentions, pulling on her leggings and t-shirt, but by the time the gym class rolled around, she felt too exhausted or depressed to go. Instead, she spent her afternoons in front of her television set, watching soap operas and munching on junk food while thinking of ways to lure Max back into her life.

At first, Missi called Max once a week to come over and repair something in the house. After a pattern was established, once a week turned into twice a week. Her last call had been about the bathroom sink. There was always some problem only he could fix and each time he came over, they ended up having sex.

Sometimes, she asked questions about the house. *How do you program the heating system? Where is the fuse box located? How can we stop losing heat when the front door won't close properly?* Of course, the "we" implied Randy and her, but in her heart, Max was still included. Mostly though, she would call just to tell him that she missed him.

As weeks rolled by, her sexual encounters with Max became filled with passion and eroticism, curiosity and discovery. Using sex in an attempt to reel him back to her had an interesting side effect. Missi was becoming less inhibited with her body, exploring sides to her sexuality she'd never known. Her heightened sex drive, along with her hope that Max would return, became the focus of her life.

As she was about to leave the lobby, she came face to face with Max. He told her he was just dropping by. Missi's heart fluttered. This was the first time he'd come without her calling him on some pretext.

"I'm off to a meeting," she told him.

"You look great," he said. "What time does your meeting end?" When she told him, he asked if he could come over then.

"What about Sheri?" she asked.

"She's in Toronto visiting her mother," he said.

She knew that she should stop having sex with him. Every time Max left, she felt depressed. Like a cocaine addict on a high, who came down as the buzz wore off, she felt worse when it was all over. But knowing and doing were two different things. Besides, Max looked so darn sexy.

By the time she reached the subway station, she realized that she hadn't put on any makeup. When she'd been married to Max, she'd always gotten up early to apply her makeup, wanting him to see her at her best. Now, he had seen her *au naturel* and complimented her appearance. His words made her glow for a moment before the reality of their situation sank in once more. Why did she keep wanting him? In the two months since he'd moved out, they had sex twelve times. Not that she was counting.

She stepped out of the subway station into a soft snowfall. Even her boots were more sensible now – thick soled boots with traction to keep her from slipping. With Max by her side to hold on to, she'd have worn her leather boots with heels.

If only she could stop lying to herself about needing him in her life. The truth was that she no longer knew whether she wanted Max back. Sex was her last stronghold, and although she enjoyed it, she knew that she would soon need something more. A steady relationship with a devoted man – exactly what she thought she had before her illusions were shattered. That man wasn't Max, she realized with a pang.

Only the fear of being on her own kept her from letting go.

"Hey, Missi," she heard someone call out. She turned and spotted Suzy. Now here was a woman who wasn't afraid of being on her own. She walked towards her in a pair of high-heeled boots, long hair swaying, as she carried her pretty pastry box.

"You look sad," Suzy said. "Is it because of Max?"

Missi sighed. "It's always Max, although I don't think of him as much as I used to."

By now, Missi phoned him only three or four times a week instead of every day, which itself was an improvement from every hour in the first chaotic days of his leaving.

"Well, that's progress," said Suzy as she linked arms with Missi. The wind had picked up, driving the snowflakes into their eyes. Suzy pulled her fur-trimmed hood over her head as they headed towards the faded brick building that housed the Women's Center.

"Not the kind of progress I'd like. I want Max to come back. I still have visions of him telling me what a fool he was and asking for my forgiveness."

"And would you forgive him?" Suzy asked as she opened the door to the building. A gust of wind pushed them inside.

"I'm not sure," Missi said. "Of course, it was much easier when I was married to him. I didn't have any money problems. Things are okay for now, but eventually I'll have to manage on my own."

"What about your romance stories?"

"They're cutting back. Online magazines seem to be taking over." Because of the shift in the publishing industry, print sales for Real Romance Magazine had dropped tremendously. Although they still liked her stories, they had other writers to consider.

Their conversation continued in the elevator and inside the Center, where Campbell had already placed the mugs, box of teas, milk and sugar on the table. After the two women had removed their coats and boots, Suzy opened her pastry box. Inside nestled a tempting sampling of her baked goods, including gooey pecan tarts, miniature brownies with basil and mint, orange peels dipped in dark chocolate, carrot-topped cupcakes and tiny mille-feuilles.

"Why don't you try a different angle?" asked Felicity, who had joined in their conversation.

"Like what?" asked Missi. "I've been writing romance stories for ages. That's all I know."

"I mean go with the trends. What about writing a novel on mid-life dating?"

"Like I have lots of experience in that area."

"No, but I do," said Suzy as she delicately transferred the pastries from the box to a platter which Campbell had put on the table. "I've kept print-outs of all my notes on men I've dated. Some of them are truly unbelievable. You're more than welcome to use them."

The kettle whistled. "There's nobody more qualified than Suzy to act as your mentor," said Campbell as she stepped towards the back of the room. "I think it's a great idea."

"Who would want to read it?" asked Missi.

"Lots of women," said Suzy. "The dating sites are filled with middle-aged women frustrated about meeting the right person."

"And you can go on the sites yourself," added Felicity while nibbling at a brownie.

"The way you've been talking about those sites, I'm not sure I want to go on them," Missi told Suzy. "What if I run into a psychopath? Or someone who's been in jail? Or terrorists looking for a place to build their bombs?"

"You really do have a writer's imagination." Campbell laughed. "The men on those systems are just ordinary people. You have to be more trusting of human nature," she said as she started to fill the cups with the boiling water.

"No, Missi's right," Suzy said. "There are a lot of weirdoes out there. People lie." As soon as she said this, she thought of her own lie. Well, it wasn't exactly a lie but the omission of an important part of her life. She wanted to tell these women about Kevin, but it never seemed the right time. "This guy I met online wanted to know if I had a webcam so that he could show me his penis."

"That's what I mean," said Missi. She reached for a pecan tart and placed it on a napkin in front of her.

"At least he's up front about it," said Campbell, lighting the candle before reaching for a cupcake. "Men have always tried to manipulate me into bed. *I've never felt the way I feel about you* clearly means *I'm horny as hell and can't control myself because I haven't had sex for a long time.*"

Felicity lifted a mille-feuille from the platter and took a bite. "My conversations usually go like this: *How long have you been on the dating site? How many men have you met?* So boring. I'm glad that I met Theo."

"You should have seen the photo of webcam guy," Suzy said. "He had this jaded look, like he's seen it all."

"You can't count on the accuracy of a photo," said Felicity. "Not everyone is photogenic and some people look better in a picture than in real life."

"Especially now, with all the Photoshop techniques, you can easily turn a frog into a prince," said Suzy.

"Isn't what's inside the package what counts?" Missi said. "You know, don't judge a book by its cover? And you want me to go on these sites? I hope you gave webcam guy a lesson in savoir vivre."

Suzy told them how her fingers had raced across the key board as she replied to his message. "There was no stopping me. I told him he was a pig and that I'm not an escort service. There are sites for that, I said. Paying sites."

The women all laughed.

"Sounds totally depressing," said Missi.

"I like Suzy's idea that you write a book about mid-life dating. You could go online and who knows — you just might meet someone interesting," said Felicity. "Consider it as a project for your writing. Maybe you can write a book on disastrous dates. Women would love that."

"Besides, if you dated, it might help you get over Max," Suzy said.

Missi started to cry. Both Felicity and Suzy sat in silence while Campbell gave Missi a comforting hug.

"Oh, honey," said Campbell. "It's hard to let go of him, isn't it?"

"The worst part is that I finally signed the damn divorce papers," Missi said as she dabbed at her nose and eyes with a tissue. "I get to keep the condo and Max keeps his business. And now I don't want to live there anymore. I don't want any memories of him. It's so confusing. I want Max back and then I don't want anything to do with him."

"It's normal," said Campbell. "You're still adjusting to the changes in your life."

"You could sell your condo," said Suzy. "I've seen it. It must be worth a fortune."

"We can help you. I'll hire my father's transport company, so you won't have to do a thing. I also know a real estate agent who can get a good price for your condo. She specializes in selling to companies who want an apartment for their out-of-town clients. Yours is in an area that's also an important business hub."

"But where will I go?" asked Missi.

"Talk about serendipity," said Campbell, reaching for another cupcake with the remainder of the last one still in her mouth. "You know my tenants ... well, it just so happens that they're going back to London at the end of the month. I've been looking for someone to replace them. You can move in upstairs. You can try it for awhile and if it doesn't work out, I'll help you find another place. It would be fun having you there."

"What about Randy? He might not want to move."

"It's your condo, and Randy won't be with you forever," Suzy pointed out. "I think it's a wonderful opportunity for you to start over."

By the look on Missi's face, it was obvious that she wasn't going for it. "I just want Max back. That's all I think about. To move out of my condo makes it so final."

The room went quiet as the women sipped their tea, not sure what to say next.

"I had a terrible conversation with my father the other day. If you can call it that," Felicity said.

"Oh?" said Campbell.

Felicity chewed on her lower lip. "I went there to tell him how dissatisfied I am with my job. That I no longer want to work for him."

"How did he react?" asked Missi.

"He was so engrossed in what he was watching on TV that I left without telling him. How could a program on oil prices be more important to him than talking to me? He solves every problem with money. As far back as I can remember, whenever I complain about something, he gives me a gift. Each time the gift gets larger and more expensive."

My father too, thought Campbell. "And you get smaller and thinner," she said as she popped a butterscotch square into her mouth.

"I'm seeing a nutritionist. And I'm working on it," Felicity said, picking up a chocolate-dipped orange peel. "Anyway, he's always dangled the prospect of my becoming president of his company in front of me. It excited me at first but not any longer."

"Nice gift," said Suzy. "I wish someone would offer me my own company on a silver platter." She took a bite of one of her éclairs and judged its quality as it melted in her mouth. The texture was fluffy and the inside creamy, but not too sweet. Perfection.

"I'd like to hear more about your relationship with your father," Campbell said to Felicity.

"I've never rocked the boat. I thought that to get people to love you, you need to be what they want you to be."

"So, you lost yourself," Campbell offered. "Or never got in touch with who you really are."

"I'm tired of doing what others expect of me," said Felicity, still nibbling on the orange peel. "My dream was to study fashion design in Italy."

"Florence, especially, is a great place to study art," Suzy said as she licked chocolate off a well-manicured finger. "When are you going?"

"It would break my father's heart if I left. He's counting on me to take over the company. I can't let him down, not after all he's done for me."

"Done for you?" said Suzy. "You mean ruined your life?"

Chapter 22

When Missi got home, Max was waiting for her with a bottle of Silver Oak Cabernet Sauvignon, one of her favorite wines.

She removed her coat and boots in the foyer, but he kept his coat on as he followed her into the living room. As she turned on her electric fireplace and then the sound system, Max uncorked the wine. Like he usually did, he poured a glass for each of them, with a bit more for her.

"I want you to know that I've made a decision. I'm not going to have sex with you anymore," Missi said after her second glass.

In his eyes, she saw him rise to the challenge; this was not a man who took "no" for an answer. She had upped the game and she saw that excited him.

"I'm serious, Max," she said. "It's not good for me to keep sleeping with you."

"Why make such a big deal of it? I still love you, Missi. I always will," he said, finally taking off his coat. The top of his shirt was already unbuttoned, revealing a spattering of chest hair. She tried not to think of how she loved running her fingers across his chest, still taut and firm for a man his age.

"Love me? What does love mean to you?" she asked.

"It means I care about you."

"Oh, really? If you cared about me, you'd come back home."

"I thought you were cool with this. Just because I'm with Sheri doesn't mean that I love you less," he said.

The artificial flames in the fireplace glowed red. She longed for real logs and the smell of burning wood. Why did she always settle for what she could get? "I don't want to play second fiddle."

"You're not," he said. "We have different relationships with different people. Ours is special. It always will be, Missi."

"I want to be important to you, Max. I thought that by having sex with you, I'd get you back."

He slid his hand from the top of her head down to her neck, where it rested lightly. Then he began to kiss her. Slowly. Sweetly.

Gazing into her eyes, he said, "You think all I want is sex? You're the mother of my child. I'm forever grateful to you for giving me a son. We're in the twenty-first century, Missi. You need to lighten up."

By now, his other hand was fondling her breast. She pressed tightly against him, the blood rushing through her veins. Walking backwards, he led her to the bedroom, where they stood kissing in the doorway, their arms locked around each other, their breathing labored.

His words rolled around in her head. Maybe she should lighten up. After all, Max didn't belong to her. And maybe Sheri was just a fling – his reaction to a mid-life crisis. If she were living in Paris, wouldn't his having a mistress be normal?

Except Max is no longer living with me, she thought, and now I'm the other woman. As Max tugged off her t-shirt and nuzzled her breasts, she pushed the thought away.

Soon they stood naked before each other, as they had hundreds of times before. She pretended that nothing had changed between them, that he was still hers. Except this excitement was new for both of them, a heady rush that came from breaking the rules and doing what was forbidden.

They fell on the bed together, skin against skin, arms and legs entwined. When he thrust himself into her, she moaned with intense pleasure. Afterwards, she held on to him, not wanting the moment to end.

She was about to say, "Max, do you still love me?" but he placed a finger on her lips and said, "I really should get going. It's getting late."

It reminded her of the last time she'd asked him this question. She had interpreted his silence then as an indication of his uncertainty, but with time and distance, she saw things differently. She was discovering a different side to the man she thought she knew – and it disturbed her. Could a man who cheated on both his wife and his girlfriend be capable of love?

Chapter 23

The phone rang in the president's office at Starr Transport. Felicity assumed it was her father calling from Chicago. He had only been away for half a day and yet she knew that he was checking up on her. Or rather on the work she was doing for his company. No matter how long his business trips lasted, he liked to stay in control. As much as she disliked her job, the feeling of having him constantly look over her shoulder was even worse.

"How's my Princess doing?" he asked.

"Fine so far," she said. She glanced around his office. It was spacious, with a polished mahogany desk and rented paintings – abstracts – on its walls. Something twisted in her chest. Of course, her fashion designs would be out of place here, in a transport company, but knowing they were stashed away, hidden from the world and even from herself, bothered her. She repeatedly tapped her pencil on the desk as she listened to her father.

"I left you instructions regarding some new contracts that are coming in," he said. "Oh, and there's a surprise for you, Princess. Look in my top right-hand drawer."

Felicity opened the top drawer and found a small envelope, longer in length than width, with her name written across it. Tucked inside were two front-row seats for the Mariinsky Ballet. Felicity smiled. It was one of the most important ballet companies in the world. Going to the ballet was her favorite form of entertainment. She had taken lessons as a young girl, followed by a special ballet program in high school. But although she loved dancing, she loved fashion design even more.

She thanked him for the tickets before they both hung up. Whenever she started to chafe under his tight control, he would buy something to please her. She knew he cared; that was what made leaving her job so hard.

Felicity thought of inviting Theo to the ballet. She looked at the date on the ticket. It was in three weeks. Would she still be with him then? Things had been heating up between them. Although they had not yet slept together, they were growing very fond of each other. Each time he spoke of Valerie, Theo reassured her that he wouldn't take her back, not after the way she'd hurt him. Felicity slid the tickets back into the envelope and placed them in the drawer. As she did so, her gaze fell upon a pile of invoices for diesel fuel.

She took them out and spread them on the desk. The invoices dated back five years. Several of them had a code name instead of the name of a recognized supplier. These still indicated the amount of fuel received, only with a much smaller amount paid. This puzzled Felicity, as the price of fuel had certainly increased in the last five years. Something wasn't right. The closer she got to the present date, the less expensive the fuel. How could that be? Her father's company had increased their business, adding more trucks and expanding outside the country. The gas bills should have gone up.

Why hadn't they?

Chapter 24

"Can I come in?" Missi asked. Just looking at her son filled her with warmth and made her want to hug him, even though he was almost an adult.

Randy swiveled his computer chair away from his desk to face his mother. "How did your meeting go?" he asked. His hair was disheveled and faint stubble shadowed his chin. He wore a polo shirt loosely tucked into a pair of jogging pants, with nothing on his feet; his comfort always came first.

"That's what I want to talk to you about." She sat on the edge of his bed. There was no easy way to say this. After taking a deep breath, she blurted, "I'm thinking of selling the condo."

"Cool." When she stared at him in disbelief, he said, "It's your life, Mom. You have to think about yourself and what you want."

"You wouldn't mind moving? Campbell's upper duplex will be free at the end of the month and we could move in there."

"Mom, I don't have to move with you."

His cell phone rang. "Hey, babe. Listen, I can't talk right now. I'll call you back, okay?"

"You have a girlfriend?" Missi asked, feeling glad for him. She had assumed he had no time for girls with his busy schedule; he studied during the day and worked nights at the Jazz Bar.

Randy shrugged. "I guess you could call her that," he said.

"Why didn't you tell me about her? Bring her over. I want to meet her."

"Mom," Randy said in a tone of voice that made Missi wince. "I don't think you'll like her."

"Why not?"

"She's old. I don't mean old, but she's about your age."

"You're dating a cougar?" Missi said. She thought of what it would be like to date a boy her son's age. It felt ridiculous.

"Don't call her that, Mom. I knew you'd be angry; that's why I didn't tell you."

"So, what's her name?"

"Angie."

"Is she married?" She didn't know why she asked, except that the woman was so much older than him.

Randy lowered his eyes. "It's not going well with her husband," he said. "It's been like that for years."

"You're having an affair with a married woman. Does she have children?" Missi knew her questions bothered him but she had to know the truth. Her son was naïve when it came to the harsh realities of life.

"No," Randy said.

"What does she do?"

"She's an entertainment lawyer. I don't want to talk about her anymore. I feel like I'm on trial here."

Her baby. What could she do to protect him? "I just don't want you to get hurt," she said.

"Mom! I'm eighteen. I don't need anybody to tell me what to do."

She felt like her world was collapsing. Maybe she had lost Max, but she wasn't about to lose her son over some cheap woman. "So, you don't mind moving?"

Frowning, he said, "I don't want to move to the north end of the city. It's too far from school and work."

"Then I'll just stay here."

"You don't have to." He glanced past her, as if he knew how much his words would hurt her. "I already discussed it with Dad, and he said I could move in with him."

She stormed out of her son's room and, as she passed the mantle, picked up the mail she'd left there. Then she saw it. A letter from her an agent. She tore open the envelope and began to read the contents.

Just when she thought her heart couldn't sink any lower, it dropped another level.

Chapter 25

"I find it odd that there's such a big drop in the company's fuel bill even from last year," said Felicity.

It was the club's fifth meeting and Campbell had brought in a bouquet of daffodils to mark the beginning of April. As she put the flowers in water and centered the vase on the table, she said, "The other evening at Chand's, we were listening to an Indian broadband about oil thieves who had been caught in Delhi. The entire oil industry is tainted by corruption and violence. Do you think your father's company might be involved in buying illegal petrol?" Campbell asked.

"What do you mean? How?"

"The modern oil industry is shady business. It's filled with gangsters, dictators and multinationals wanting to get their finger in the pie. Certain gangs specialize in stealing crude oil from the pipelines and then sell it to companies," Campbell said, moving her cup closer to her. With their mugs and napkins and Suzy's pastry box, they really needed a bigger table.

Felicity couldn't believe that her father would be involved in criminal business deals. Besides, there was no pipeline close by.

"I've heard something similar," said Suzy. "Only the thieves stole their diesel from private gas stations. Put the gas stations out of business."

Felicity gasped. Surely her father wouldn't allow that to happen. He was returning home from Chicago this evening. Tomorrow, she would ask him about the invoices. Surely, he would have a good explanation.

"Who's Chand?" she asked, veering the subject away from her father.

Campbell finished her tea, stalling for time. Should she tell them about her romance with Chand? "Oh, some guy I met," she finally said.

The three other women stared at her.

"Is it a friend type of guy or is this more serious?" asked Missi.

"Well, to tell you the truth, I'm not sure."

"And all along, you've been telling us not to get involved with a man." Anger sharpened Felicity's voice, although it was hard to tell whether she was upset with her father or reacting to Campbell's news.

"I feel awful about it. I mean, here I am discouraging you from pursuing your Prince Charming, when I'm having doubts of my own," Campbell said.

"I knew it," said Missi as she helped herself to a leftover cupcake. "A man does make our lives happier."

Light from the evening sun streamed through the window, highlighting a carpet of dust on the wooden floor. All the floors at the Center needed cleaning; it wouldn't take long to make them gleam. Campbell's dilemma, though, could not so easily be resolved.

"All these years I've been disappointed in love. My research shows that a failed father/daughter relationship leads to problems in forming close relationships with men. Now I'm afraid of falling in love with Chand."

"That's an odd name," said Suzy.

"His real name is Chandrashekar. He's from India."

"Hmm," said Felicity. "This kind of screws up your research, doesn't it?"

"It does. I'm getting this award in a little over a month. How can I accept it? I feel like such a fake."

"Have you slept with him?" asked Suzy, brushing her hair back from her face.

"Yes." Campbell felt the heat rise in her neck.

"How was it?" asked Felicity.

"It was wonderful. Except that he mentioned something about us living together and I said that I wouldn't live with anyone unless I was married."

"You said that?" said Missi.

"I don't know why. It was only a general statement, which he took personally. God, I don't ever want to get married."

"What did he say?" Suzy wanted to know.

"He needs to ask his father for permission. What forty-year-old man needs his father's approval to get married?"

The women laughed.

"Well, it is a different culture," said Suzy. "I mean, don't they still have arranged marriages in India?"

"He's been living here for over ten years. You'd think he would have adapted by now." Campbell reached for one of Suzy's chocolate éclairs and bit into it. Some whipped cream spilled on her chin and she wiped it with her finger. "Can't he decide on his own?

"Maybe you do want to marry him," said Missi.

Campbell considered her statement. Maybe she did. "I always told myself that I'd never get married, but now I'm having second thoughts. Part of me does and another part doesn't. What about my research? How can I accept an award for the Prince Charming myth when maybe Chand is my Prince Charming? I'd feel like such a fraud."

"Isn't finding your Prince Charming more important than an award?" asked Missi as she wiped the crumbs off the table and into her napkin.

"The award means just as much to me," Campbell said, licking her fingers. "What if things don't work out with him? Don't fairy tales always end badly?"

"But what if they do?" said Suzy.

Chapter 26

When Randy was nine, Missi had saved his life at the lake. Although he often swam distance, he had developed a severe leg cramp and was panicking in the water. Sensing danger as only a mother could, she looked up from her rowboat and instantly tossed him a rubber ring.

Missi knew she had to do something to help protect him now.

She Googled *entertainment lawyers* in Montreal and quickly found Angie's office number. When the receptionist asked who was calling, she said, "Just tell her Randy's mother."

Angie agreed to meet her for lunch that afternoon at the Sofitel Hotel. When Missi arrived, the other woman waved to her from a table by the window.

She was not at all as Missi had imagined her. She had pictured a woman in heavy makeup and tight-fitting clothes. Instead, Angie had delicate features and round, innocent eyes. She wore a pale grey business suit with a rose-colored blouse and her soft brown hair fell in waves to her shoulders. She appeared to be in her thirties rather than forties. It flattered Missi that her son had compared Angie to her.

As Missi approached and introduced herself, the lawyer got to her feet. She grasped her hand between both of hers. "I'm so glad to meet you. Randy talks so much about you."

Missi noticed that she still wore a wedding ring.

As they both seated themselves, Angie continued, "He told me that you're trying to write a novel."

Missi squirmed in her chair. Trying? She hadn't come here to discuss her frustrations with her novel. It was bad enough that she didn't know where it was going and that she was beginning to lose faith that she would ever make it as a novelist. She could hardly admit this to herself, let alone to Ms. Lollipop, who not only oozed success but had stolen her son from her.

All the same, she wanted to know what else her son had said about her. This was not the time to get distracted. Focus, she scolded herself. She glared at the glass of mineral water on the table. She needed something stronger if she was going to get through this.

As the waiter appeared, she noticed two elderly women sitting across from them with flutes of champagne. A little champagne would be nice, along with some chips. But champagne was for celebrating and this was definitely not a happy occasion.

She asked the waiter for a glass of chardonnay.

"I would join you," Angie said, "but I need a clear mind. I have an important court case this afternoon."

Missi stiffened. Angie's involvement in the outside world highlighted the emptiness of her own life, where no one cared what she did or how long it took her to do it. A feeling of uselessness settled in her stomach like a stone.

She ought to ask Angie about her case, for wasn't that how social niceties went? But she wasn't here for casual chit-chat. Although she'd never liked confrontations, that was how she had to categorize this conversation.

"You're married," Missi blurted out.

Angie lowered her eyes, looking at the diamond solitaire in her ring. An almost imperceptible line ran across her eyelids in dark blue, expertly drawn. When she looked up at Missi, her eyes glistened. "Yes, I am."

The waiter arrived with Missi's wine. She took a long gulp before saying, "I want you to break off with Randy."

If Angie was surprised, she hid it well. "Why would you want me to do that?"

How could Missi admit that she felt she was losing her son? She also couldn't tell her that she'd been terribly hurt by a woman breaking up her own marriage and would never condone such behavior, especially coming from her son. It felt like a betrayal to her. "Do you have a son?" she asked Angie.

"No," she said. "I don't have any children."

There was a long, drawn-out pause. Angie finally said, "You don't think it's possible that I'm in love with Randy?" she asked.

Missi shook her head. She signaled the waiter for another glass of wine.

"What's really bothering you?" asked Angie. "That I'm married or that I'm older?"

"Both," said Missi. "I don't want him to get hurt."

"Neither do I. If anyone risks getting hurt here, it's me. I know that Randy will eventually meet someone his own age. I'm well aware of that. But there are no guarantees in love."

It was easy for Missi to understand Randy's attraction to Angie. But don't call it love, she thought, when it's only an eighteen-year-old's testosterone.

"But you already have a husband."

Angie's eyes misted over. Missi couldn't decide if they were hazel or green. "I do. And I love him dearly. I wouldn't hurt him for the world."

Missi's jaw dropped open but she clamped it shut. She couldn't believe what she was hearing.

The waiter arrived with her chardonnay and removed her empty glass. She thought of Max. If she had never loved him, she wouldn't have endured the pain that constantly gnawed at her. Then again, she never would have had Randy. But without Randy, she wouldn't be facing Angie now with this problem. Oh, why was her life so complicated?

"Don't you think this would hurt your husband, if he knew that you're having an affair with my son?"

Angie nodded slowly. "I'm certain it would." After taking a sip of her mineral water, she said, "It's possible to love more than one person, but in different ways."

Missi thought about Max's statement that he loved her and Sheri. She closed her eyes. This was not how she defined love. To her, love was sacred. It was to be shared between one man and one woman.

After Missi finished her wine, the room started to swirl around her. She had lost count of the number of glasses she'd consumed. She should have eaten before coming. There was nothing worse than drinking in the early afternoon on an empty stomach. When she spoke, she pronounced the words carefully, knowing they would otherwise run into each other.

"I don't care for your values. That's not the way I raised my son. And if you don't leave Randy alone, I'm going to tell your husband."

Angie stared at her; her lips drawn into a tight line.

Missi suddenly realized what she had said. She felt like a ten-year-old in a school yard. *I'm going to tell your mother.* What kind of person was she becoming? It was Max's fault, for leaving her as he had. Without him and the stability he provided, she was off kilter.

"What do you think that will achieve?" Angie asked in a cold voice.

Damn Angie. She made it sound like Missi was out of line, not her.

"I'm not the one who started this." The words came out slurred. Missi began to gather her belongings, called the waiter over and asked for her check.

"Did you come by car?" asked Angie.

"No, by taxi," said Missi.

"I'll ask someone at the front desk to call you a taxi," Angie said, adding, "Don't worry about the check. I've got it covered."

Eventually, Missi tumbled into her apartment, tossed off her coat, and fell onto her bright orange couch. An hour later, she awoke with a pounding headache and remembered her meeting with Angie.

What had she done? She'd made a complete fool of herself.

During the next twenty-four hours, Missi called Randy repeatedly but always got his voicemail. There had to be a logical explanation. His courses in architecture, working at Max's bar, and his cougar took all his time. Deep down, though, she knew she was losing her baby.

Each time she got his voicemail, she apologized for what she'd done. It was one thing to sneak into Max's apartment, acting from her pain and fury. That was excusable. But to have snuck behind Randy's back to protect him? He wasn't a child anymore and had to learn from his mistakes.

She felt ashamed of how she'd behaved with Angie. The whole situation depressed and saddened her.

As bad as it had been losing Max, losing her son's trust was worse.

Chapter 27

Felicity stormed into her father's office. He was busy with the company accountant, but she didn't care. She had hardly slept last night. The truth of her father's illegal business deals had finally dawned on her. She could no longer accept the luxuries her father gave her, knowing that others had suffered because of them.

"I need to talk to you," she said.

Anger sparked from her father's eyes. He hated being disturbed in the middle of a discussion. "Drew and I will be through in about an hour."

She wasn't going to let him get his way.

"No. I need to talk to you now. Alone."

Felicity had never spoken to him so forcefully. And never in front of his associates. She saw the stunned look on his face, but she had to confront him.

Her father looked at Drew and said, "Just give us a few moments. I'll call you when I'm through."

The sharpness in her father's voice showed his displeasure. But she wasn't going to allow anything to deter her from saying what needed to be said. Her fury shifted to sadness. All these years she had admired him, seen qualities in her father which she sought in a prospective suitor. Integrity, sincerity, kindness, honor.

Her stomach churned.

"So, Princess," he said after Drew had left. "What's so urgent? I told you that I'd look into getting you a different position in the company."

"It's not about that," she said as she marched around her father's desk and opened his top drawer. She pulled out the packet of invoices.

"It's about these." She waved the packet in front of his face.

"What do you mean?"

Her heart pounded as she glared at him. "You know perfectly well what I mean! These invoices are for only half our fuel costs. I want to know about the other half."

Her father's face turned pale for a moment but he swiftly recovered.

"Oh, that," he said. "We can't let the oil companies get away with murder."

"But that's illegal," she pointed out.

"It's beating the crooks."

"By cheating?"

"That's business," he said, drumming his fingers on the desk. "Everybody does it."

"So, the oil company sells you fuel without an invoice? Why's that, Daddy?"

He remained silent. Until now, Felicity had never understood why her mother had left him.

He was successful. Handsome. Talented. But maybe his dishonesty had undermined her love for him.

Felicity knew she would always love her father. What she had lost was her respect for him. She didn't wait for him to answer. Although she had promised herself that she would remain calm, anger swept through her. The fake invoices trembled in her hands and her voice wavered. "It's because half of the supply for your trucks comes from stolen fuel."

"Oh, Princess, you don't understand."

"What I understand is that small companies have to go out of business because someone steals their diesel," Felicity said.

"This is business," he repeated in a heavier voice. "We can go crazy if we worry about everyone else's problems."

"And I suppose you paid off the auditors as well," she said.

He leaned back in his chair, massaging his temples. "It's just business, Princess."

"You're a thief, Daddy," she said before striding out of his office.

Alone at home that evening, Felicity watched the drizzle fall on the seaway. Everything she had, all the luxuries and comforts she took for granted, had come through illegal means. Knowing that she had enjoyed these perks at the expense of someone else's suffering, she felt deeply ashamed. She also knew that she could no longer work at her father's company.

Felicity dug into her purse for her bottle of Clonazepam. As she shook it in her hand, she listened to the tiny tablets rattling inside. She opened the lid and tapped out two of the pills into her hand. She was about to pop them into her mouth, when she realized that she didn't want to do this anymore.

Although the pills had calmed her anxiety, they'd also cut her off from her emotions. She overturned the bottle over the toilet and watched the pills swirl away from her.

For the first time, she felt free to live the life she'd always dreamed of.

Chapter 28

A few days later, Felicity told the women at The Dating Club about her confrontation with her father regarding his criminal behavior. The others listened sympathetically and when she'd finished, Campbell handed her a tissue to wipe away her tears.

"Oh, sweetie," she said. "I know it's hard, but maybe it's the best thing that could happen to you."

"How could it be?" asked Felicity, dabbing at her eyes. "It's bad enough that I can't possibly continue working there, but I've lost respect for my father. How can that be good?" The purple streaks in her hair had widened since their last meeting, Campbell realized.

"It's a big adjustment when your Prince Charming tumbles off his horse," said Suzy. There was something different about her, too. Her eyes seemed sadder than usual and her earlier antagonism was completely gone.

"But a necessary one," Campbell said, following Suzy's remark. "It's time for you to stop comparing every man you meet to your father. And to stop needing his approval for every move you make."

"Maybe I was searching for Prince Charming because I wanted someone who Daddy would approve of. I let a lot of good men slip by."

"Oh?" Campbell leaned away from the table now.

"When I was in second year university, I met a guy from California who wanted to marry me. He wanted me to move there. My father threatened me then. He told me, if I married the guy, to never come home again."

"So, what happened?"

"Nothing. I couldn't hurt my father over a man I wasn't in love with." Felicity reached for another tissue and blew her nose. "I'm wondering if my father threatened me because he wanted me in his company. He probably hated the idea of outsiders running his business. With me at the helm eventually, he could still be in control. How could I have been so blind?"

"Don't be so hard on yourself," said Campbell. "How were you to know?"

"What are you going to do now?" Suzy asked.

"I've already told him that I no longer want to work for him. He thinks I'm a fool. And that I'll change my mind. But how can I? I can't stand knowing that the car I drive and the apartment I live in were bought with someone's misfortunes."

"Maybe this is an opportunity for you to do what you really want," said Campbell. "Move to Italy and study fashion design."

"Oh," said Suzy, clapping her hands and folding them to her heart. "We could all go visit you there."

"I love Italy," said Missi. "Especially Rome. Max and I..."

"No memories of the good old times with Max. Save those for your old age," scolded Campbell. "Focus on his cheating and betrayal."

Missi drew in a deep breath and nodded.

"So, what do you think?" Campbell turned her attention to Felicity. "Florence. Art. A change might be just what you need."

Felicity's face lit up. "Yes, I could do that. I've saved enough money to last me at least a year." Then she frowned. "What about Theo? What if he's The One?"

"You don't have to give him up just because you're going to study in Italy. He can visit you there," Campbell pointed out.

Felicity looked doubtful.

"Don't give up your dream." As soon as Campbell said that, she wondered if this was what she was doing with Chand. All this talk about Felicity's father made her consider her own father. Perhaps Chand had been right - that she'd placed a barrier between her father and herself.

Maybe it was time for her to test her own theory on herself. So far, she had blamed her unsuccessful relationships with men on her relationship with her father.

She didn't doubt that failed father/daughter relationships affected a woman's sense of self and her capacity to develop a warm, intimate adult relationship. But now she was starting to question whether it always had to be this way. Whether such a woman was doomed to a series of unfulfilling relationships.

Was she trying to sabotage her relationship with Chand because of a self-fulfilling prophecy?

The next evening, Campbell and Chand were on their way to a concert. Free tickets to popular shows in town was one of the perks of his job – managing a hotel where a band's out-of-town members stayed.

"I spoke to my father," Chand told Campbell as they queued up for the concert.

Although it was a warm evening, a chill passed through her.

"About what?" she asked.

"Our getting married."

Had she heard correctly? It had really been a joke on her part. Or had it? She was curious about what his father had said. "What did he say?"

"He agrees with you. He thinks it's time I settled down. He would have preferred me marrying an Indian girl, but I think at this point he's desperate."

"Thanks," she said.

"Of course, he wants to meet you first."

"He's coming to Montreal?"

"Good God, no! He hates the cold."

"You know this entire idea is preposterous," she said. "We hardly know each other."

"There have been worse ideas," he said, slipping an arm around her waist as they inched forward in the line.

She didn't know whether to take him seriously. His culture did put great emphasis on marriage and family life. And although they had met only a few months ago, they spent every available moment with each other. The amount of time she had spent with Chand during this short period was probably equivalent to dating someone once a week for an entire year. She really missed him when they were apart. "You're not just agreeing because you don't like waking up alone. Or need someone to share the rent."

He leaned closer and kissed her. "Of course not," he said. "I just want to see you with a *bindi* between your eyebrows. What other reason would I have?" he asked.

She poked him with her elbow.

"It's to show that you're taken. My mother said she'd pick out a few Indian dresses for you and my sister suggested that you die your hair darker to fit in." He laughed.

"They'll just have to accept me as I am," she said. "And what about you? How are you going to show you're taken?"

"Indian men don't need to do that."

"That's not fair," she said.

He drew her closer. "Who said that life was fair?" As he began to laugh, she remembered why she liked him so much. She had never laughed as much as she did when she was with him. Also, she adored the way he smiled at her. He had a sweet, Hallmark smile that said *I'm so happy to be with you*. Chand was fun, smart, and good to her. Sex with him was also extremely satisfying. How could she say no?

"You know, of course, that we'll have to go to India now to get married," he said.

Campbell didn't know what to say. She knew that in such circumstances, it was better to say nothing. Instead of heeding her own advice, she said, "Can't we do it on Skype? I hate flying."

Chapter 29

Missi shook her head at the pile of boxes lining her kitchen floor. It had been a week since she'd moved into Campbell's upper duplex and she hadn't had the strength or the willpower to make herself a meal, let alone unpack her kitchenware. Everything had gone so fast. Max's moving out. And then Randy moving in with Max while she was still living in their condo in Old Montreal. Getting the divorce attorney to insert that clause, whereby Max had to provide financial support as long as Randy lived with her, had been for nothing. Even worse, since her meltdown with Angie, her son was giving her the silent treatment. And now to add insult to injury, she found herself having to start her life over. Alone.

Her regret mixed with the heaviness of defeat. The condo had sold even before it was put on the market, thanks to Felicity's real estate contacts. Picking up a box marked *dishes*, she carried it over to a table facing a window. The oak table was an antique belonging to her grandmother. It featured flaps to widen it, if need be. As if she would ever entertain company here, she gloomily thought.

She pushed aside her laptop, notes, piles of books, pens and a stack of post-its to make room

for the box of dishes, which the movers had so
neatly and securely packed. The first thing she'd
done when moving into her new home was to
make an office for herself. Although she could
have used one of the two bedrooms as an office,
she preferred the kitchen table because of its
garden view. Besides, she had earmarked one of
the bedrooms for Randy, in the hope that he
would decide to come and live with her. She'd
even made the bed with his Star Wars sheets from
when he was a little boy. She missed her son and
now she'd messed everything up.

What if he never spoke to her again? What if
he and Angie got married, she thought, and he
didn't invite her to the wedding? She had so often
dreamt of being the mother of the groom, going
so far as to Google *bridal wear* for ideas of
dresses she might wear. It was just as well,
because she'd only feel awkward at the wedding.
Max would be standing with Sheri by his side and
she'd be all by herself, sitting among the coupled
guests. She'd have to endure the pitying looks
from her mother and sister, as well as their fake
reassurance that she was better off without Max.

She looked through the patio doors to the
garden below. Most of the snow had melted,
leaving patches of hardened earth and dried-out
flower beds. The thought that spring was just
around the corner almost lifted her spirits. But

then, spring brought thoughts of love, which led her once more to Max. A few tears gathered in the corners of her eyes before turning into a deluge that rolled down her cheeks. She had never felt so lonely. Wiping her face with a tissue, she forced herself to begin unpacking her kitchenware. She was determined to focus on her new life. At least here in this new place, there were no memories of Max; no echoes of their lovemaking within these walls.

When lunch time rolled around, everything was neatly stashed away in drawers and cupboards. Although she still felt bereft, Missi enjoyed the freedom of knowing that this apartment was hers to live in as she pleased. She made herself a lunch of grilled vegetables and pieces of left-over chicken from last night's take-out. Along with a cup of mint tea, she brought her lunch to her writing space. As she ate, she glanced at the query letter she was working on. Writing the query was proving to be much more difficult than she had anticipated. She spent the remainder of the afternoon writing and rewriting. After several cups of tea and over ten versions of her query, Missi finally e-mailed it to Lydia Ferrell, a literary agent whom her editor at Real Romance had recommended. Her query, along with a sample chapter, gave the impression that her novel was completed. What was the point of investing more time and energy in this book if nobody wanted it? Attracting an agent's interest would motivate her to zip through the rest of it. All she had to do was incorporate Suzy's box of notes on her own disastrous dates.

After pressing the *send* button, she looked at the mess on the table. It felt liberating to know that she could leave her papers out and not have to pick them up, as she had when writing stories for Real Romance Magazine, with Max on his way home.

Her phone rang. It was Campbell, inviting her down for a cocktail.

Missi quickly washed up and changed into a pair of clean jeans and a sweat shirt. This was something else she liked about living alone. She didn't have to put as much time and effort on her appearance. She cringed as she recalled how she'd forced herself to get up fifteen minutes earlier than Max every morning so that he wouldn't see her without makeup.

The duplex had a common entrance, so Missi didn't even need to go out into the cold.

Campbell popped open a bottle of wine. She poured them each a glass and raised hers to Missi. "I'm going to India," she said. "Chand wants me to meet his parents."

"Wow. That's serious."

"It's not like that. We're going as friends."

"Didn't Chand ask his father for permission to marry you?" Missi said.

They stood in Campbell's living room. Missi loved all the plants in this room; it felt like being in a greenhouse.

"Who does that in this day and age? Anyway, it's not up to them whether or not I decide to marry their son. Of course, they have an important say in the matter. Oh, Missi, this is so confusing for me. I don't know what to think anymore. Go in my place; I'll send you by proxy to meet his parents. You know how I hate flying. By the time I get to India, I'll be so stressed out that my skin will break out in hives. Why couldn't I fall in love with someone whose parents lived within driving distance?"

"So, you're letting Prince Charming into your life, after all?"

Campbell shrugged. "I want to cook for him. That's never happened before. It was always the other way around; I wanted a man to cook for me. I was so afraid of making a mistake."

"Think of the bright side. If you do decide to marry Chand, you won't have to see his parents that often."

Campbell smiled. "I'm thinking of wearing a bindi. What do you think?"

"Does it replace a wedding ring?"

"I don't think so. I just think it's neat. And besides, when I'm older and start getting creases between my eyebrows, the bindi will camouflage them."

Missi took a sip of wine and immediately placed her glass on the end table next to her. Campbell might know her psychology, but she certainly didn't know her wines. "What about your award?"

Campbell's shoulders slumped. "I'll figure something out. The award's only at the end of May; by then, I'll be back from India. Who knows, maybe things won't work out with Chand. I don't want to give up on my dream."

"Which dream – Prince Charming or the award?" asked Missi. When Campbell shrugged, she went on, "I know what my choice would be. I envy you. Going to India. Finding a man who's crazy about you."

"You still wish Max would come back?" Campbell removed a fallen leaf from the jade plant near the window.

Missi sighed. "Do you think I'll ever get over him? I think it has more to do with my pride than anything else; I feel humiliated."

"What you're feeling is betrayed."

Missi joined her at the window. They both watched cars passing each other on the street. "You know, I sometimes wonder if what I miss most about Max is the lifestyle he gave me. But I also resent him for keeping me from my dreams."

"Nobody keeps us from our dreams," said Campbell. "We all have choices to make."

"Easy for you to say, with Prince Charming hanging on your arm and an award around the corner. I miss Max. Isn't it crazy? I'm not even that attracted to him anymore, but I still don't want him to be with another woman. If I really loved him, wouldn't I want him to be happy?"

"You're not a saint, Missi."

Missi began to cry. "What's wrong with me?"

Campbell began to refill her wine glass. When she reached for Missi's, the other woman placed her hand over the glass. "I don't feel like drinking right now."

"Your behavior is typical, you know," Campbell said as she sipped more wine. "Daughters abandoned by their fathers grow up assuming they're flawed. No wonder you feel there's something wrong with you. Did you ever think that there might be something wrong with Max instead?"

"The only thing wrong with him is that he stopped loving me," Missi said.

"And he stopped you from pursuing your writing."

Missi thought of her afternoon spent revising the query letter and polishing the first chapter of her novel. While immersed in her writing, she had not entertained one unhappy thought. But now that she was filled with doubts about her writing, thinking that the agent, Lydia Ferrell would hate it, her mind once more entertained thoughts of Max. "So, why can't I get him out of my head? He's stuck to my brain cells."

"You've got to give it time, Missi. It's been less than two months since he left you."

"Am I doomed to be alone the rest of my life?" she whimpered before sinking into Campbell's leather couch. She propped her feet up on the coffee table. That was when she noticed the vase of yellow roses and the florist's card placed in front of it. "Who sent you the flowers?" she asked.

"Chand."

Missi leaned forward. "Can I read it?" When Campbell nodded, she read out aloud: *I hope these flowers bring you as much joy as you bring to me. Will you marry me?*

Campbell laughed. "Now that marriage is on the table, he's always finding different ways to propose."

"That's so romantic. I wish I was going to India to get enlightened by a guru."

"I'm not going to be seeing any gurus," Campbell said, looking puzzled at her statement.

Missi gazed past her, her imagination carrying her to a foreign land. "Well, I would. A guru could help me clear my thoughts of Max."

Chapter 30

As Missi drove through the Vermont mountains, their faint greening reminded her of an Impressionist painting, only hinting of the foliage to come. The idea of enlightenment felt just as unreal to her. Campbell had found the meditation retreat center for her and convinced her to go. It offered a weekend seminar on The Art of Letting Go.

As she continued down the Interstate, Missi thought of the few yoga classes she had attended. She remembered trying to focus on her breath and instead wondering where the woman next to her had bought her adorable yoga bag and whether sitting so long on the mat would expand her buttocks.

She brightened at a billboard advertising factory outlet a little farther on.

At the Lululemon outlet, she asked the sales girl if they had any meditation clothes. Although her suitcase was already filled with fairly new yoga outfits, she yearned for some retail therapy. Besides, she reasoned, except for a pair of black flared yoga slacks, her clothing was too colorful. As far as she knew, meditators usually wore pure white tunics with wide flowing sleeves to let in the vibes of the Universe. She bought a couple of pants with matching tops as well as a jacket, in case it would be cool in the mountains. Buying something new always comforted her and in the past, it had temporarily relieved her of boredom when Max worked long hours at the Jazz Bar.

She also bought a sweet little cushion with bead trimming. It was really meant for decoration, but if she flipped it over, she could sit on it. Besides, the tag said *made in India*. How appropriate was that? In pictures she'd seen of women from the East, they all wore jewelry. Wanting to fit in at the retreat, she picked out a ring, then a pair of dangling earrings. And two necklaces.

She knew that she was again spending excessively, but it was for her spiritual enlightenment. How could you put a price tag on that?

As she handed the cashier her credit card, her elation at trying on the clothes became shadowed by a feeling of guilt. To counteract it, she focused on the retreat and how she would learn to let go of Max and finally find peace of mind.

Once she was on the road again, an idea struck her. Why not put out a line of meditation clothes? With all this interest in Eastern religions, how could she fail? For the next half hour, she fantasized about travelling around the world, visiting the stores and retreats that were buying her line of clothing. If people were willing to fork out hundreds of dollars just to sit in silence, they would certainly purchase clothing they could take home with them. Reality sank in. What about finances? With the little money she earned from her romance stories and her dwindling funds from the condo sale, how would she find the funds to manufacture clothing? Maybe Max. No, she had to let go of him. Wasn't this the whole purpose of the retreat?

It was after five o'clock when she reached the center, a dark monastery surrounded by thickets of trees. As she registered, she noticed a store at the end of the hallway. Inside the shop, she discovered meditation tapes and books on purification, wisdom, and reincarnation, as well as adorable statues of Tara (whoever she was) and Buddha. Him, at least, she recognized. As she was about to leave the shop, she noticed a shelf filled with Dr. Hauschka products. Had the Universe placed them in her pathway for a reason? She touched her cheek, it felt a bit dry. Definitely in need of moisturizer. Since the retreat center endorsed these products, she decided to invest in a few items in spite of her over-stretched budget.

Her room was sparse. A single bed. A few shelves to place her clothes. It was like the magazine, *Simple Living*. Of course, this furniture was not in any way as glamorous or high-tech.

She lined up her new Dr. Hauschka products on a shelf: face cleanser, exfoliant, aromatherapy bath kit, deep cleansing face mask and, of course, the deep nourishing cream to match. Oh, and some nail polish remover. She looked at herself in the mirror. Did anyone else notice the tiny lines beginning to take shape around her eyes when she smiled? Or those tiny, spidery lines on her upper lip?

Missi could hardly turn around in this space. What was she doing here? She recalled the lavish hotel suites she and Max had slept in. Vienna. Paris. Venice. The expensive bottles of wine ordered in restaurants. Even before she had met Max, she had been a big spender. Hairstyling for over a hundred dollars, Chanel makeup and watches by Gucci and Mira. Thousand-dollar handbags. And the shoes! But none of these things had helped her attract a man she could fall in love with. So, when Max came along, possessing all the qualities she wanted in a man, she clung to him like a burr.

Now here she was at a retreat, trying to learn how to let go of him. The excitement she had felt in the Lululemon shop had faded, replaced by disappointment in her lack of restraint. Max had often complained that she spent too much. Maybe if she learned to be more frugal, she thought, Max would come back.

Straightening her spine, she went down to the lobby. She followed a Welcome sign to a room down the hallway. Inside, a small group of women in identical orange-colored togas had shaved heads. If this was the price of attaining enlightenment, Missi wanted no part of it. Her thick, dark hair was her crowning glory.

Missi cleared her throat. "Hi there," she said in her friendliest voice.

"Sshh." One of the women walked over to her and whispered, "This is a silent retreat."

What? How could she be silent for an entire weekend? There had to be a mistake. Campbell had said that *The Act of Letting Go* was a workshop with exercises and inspirational guidance from a well-known guru named Swami Adi Rahim. How could it be silent?

Someone had put out snacks on one of the tables. Since she was starving, Missi went over to examine the food. Apples. Some kind of squares. Tea. That was it? She thought of the refreshments Max would order with room service: champagne, caviar. A bowl of exotic fruit and a variety of cheeses. She picked up a square and a cup of tea and headed for the balcony, where several women had gathered.

Missi took a bite of her square. Dog biscuits probably had more flavor. All the same, she shoved the rest in her mouth and chewed. The muscles in her throat contracted as she tried to swallow. Mixed with her saliva, the dough had expanded in her throat. She coughed, attracting attention to herself. Respecting their "silence" rule, she wrapped a hand around her own throat in a choking pantomime. One of the women quickly handed her a bottle of mineral water, which she guzzled down. Better. What was in that square anyway? Silly putty?

She headed for the door and spit out the contents into her hand. Instead of a garbage bin, she found a large garden that was still bare at this time of year. She followed a well-trod path, inhaling the crisp country air. The empty space around her suddenly overwhelmed her. She sat on a bench facing a pond, wondering what she was doing there.

"Are you here for *The Art of Letting Go* retreat?"

At the sound of a man's voice, she stuffed the glob of dough into the pocket of her leather jacket. Before her stood a man with white hair flowing past his shoulders. His countenance looked peaceful and untroubled.

"Yes. But aren't we supposed to be silent?"

"You must have run into the group doing the silent retreat. We have different types of retreats going on at the same time." He told her that he was leading the group she had registered for.

Missi's mouth dropped open. She hadn't expected the Swami to look so Western.

He extended his hand to her. "I'm Swami Adi Rahim."

As she took it and introduced herself, she glanced at his left hand for signs of a ring or tan line. She found none. Was he gay? His dusky, unlined features, flowing hair and calm presence inexplicably drew her.

When he asked why she'd signed up for the retreat, she told him about Max. "I don't know if it's the sex or what he represented to me, but I can't seem to let go."

Something flickered in the Swami's dark eyes before he responded. For a moment, she wondered if he ever got personally involved with his participants.

"Ah, sensual pleasures are the greatest obstacle to self-actualization," he said. "To rise above temptation and release our attachments, we need to create a new paradigm. A new way of being."

A lump formed in Missi's throat. Did this mean she would never have sex again?

"In the end, everyone must follow their own path," he said, as if he could read her thoughts. "We should be inside. I'm giving a welcoming speech in ten minutes."

His welcoming speech was about letting go of the illusion of love. It sounded to Missi a lot like what Campbell had been telling them at The Dating Club.

A forty-minute meditation ensued. With her eyes closed and every part of her body relaxed, Missi kept thinking of Max and whether she should continue to have sex with him.

Alone in her room that evening, she again thought about him. What was happening? She had come here to let him go and now her mind was coming up with ways to get him back. The voices in her head kept her awake, stronger and more persistent in these quiet surroundings.

At around one-thirty in the morning, she finally drifted off, only to be awakened at five-thirty for morning meditation. The woman next to her kept prodding her to stay awake. By six o'clock, they went into a room with large windows to do salutations to the rising sun. Everything felt grey and shadowy to her until she saw a radiant, pink-hued sun emerge in the sky.

They all headed into the dining room for a silent breakfast. This time she stayed away from anything that might contain flour. Just plain fruit for her. And tea.

In the bright, sun-filled room, Swami Adi Rahim gave them a pep talk. "We need discipline and focus to achieve Clear Mind and leave our confusion behind. And those sincerely interested in helping others will find peace and joy in their hearts." He then went on about equanimity. "Imagine you are surrounded by three people. One of them is someone you love dearly. The second, your worst enemy and the third, a stranger."

Max. Sheri. And the woman sitting next to me, thought Missi.

"Now," the Swami said, "I want you to feel love for all these people and see if you have any resistance."

Suddenly Missi felt guilty about choosing Max instead of Randy. And what about Sheri? How could she bring love into her heart for her? All she could think of was how much she hated her, and the more she told herself not to hate her, the more she did.

A little bell tinkled and she returned to the reality of being in this sunny room with a group of strangers. She glanced at her watch. Had she really been seething over Sheri for almost fifteen minutes? She was exhausted. Wasn't meditation supposed to make you feel relaxed and calm?

Instead, she felt all jittery inside. By seven-thirty, she felt like she could use a stiff drink.

Swami Adi then asked them to write down their fears and share them with the group. Missi had thirty-six fears on her list. Among them was her fear of cats, spiders, snakes, being caught alone in an elevator, not ever again being happy, Randy never speaking to her again, missing his wedding, never seeing her grandchildren.

As Missi read her list to the group, she felt embarrassed at the number of fears she had. When the Swami asked them to pick out their greatest fear, she thought about adding one more fear: of not being able to choose her greatest fear. This made her so anxious that, when it was her turn to speak, she blurted out, "Of not finding the right dress to wear to my son's wedding." That is, she thought, if I'm invited at all.

"When is your son getting married?" the Swami asked.

She stared at him. Why, oh why did she say this? Now she would have to admit to the group that Randy was having an affair with a married woman her age, and because of her meltdown with Angie, he would probably never to speak to her again. Now there was another fear to add to her list: the fear of growing old alone.

On her way home from the retreat the next day, she decided that she needed to be less materialistic. Like a true alkie or junkie, she gave herself one last fix at the outlets and splurged on a brand-new wardrobe.

"How are you going to pay for all of this?" Campbell asked when she later showed her what she had bought.

"I think of it as an investment," Missi told her. "With all these new clothes, I'll be better able to attract a guy."

"Wasn't the whole purpose of your retreat to detach?"

"It was a waste of money," she said. "I still want Max back. I feel like such a failure."

Campbell frowned at her. "Missi, the fact that you're a survivor is proof that you're not a failure."

"I don't want to be a survivor. I want to be one of those women who have lovers fighting over them, women who meet their husbands at cocktail parties with celebrities and models, someone whose husband calls in the middle of the day to say *I miss you*. I don't want to grow old alone."

Chapter 31

Missi was stunned by Lydia Ferrell's quick response. Oddly, the e-mail made no reference to her recent query. Instead, the literary agent asked whether she would have lunch with her when she came to Montreal for the Blue Metropolis Writers' Festival. Since the theme of this year's festival was *romance*, it made sense for Lydia Ferrell to attend. Festival or no festival, Missi thought, Lydia Ferrell must have been intrigued by her query and sample chapter to invite her to lunch.

On her way to their meeting, Missi enjoyed the sidewalk fashion show as she ambled along St Denis Street. In her pink Chanel coat, she felt an intrinsic part of the moving kaleidoscope of colors, textures and styles. Montreal women took such care with their appearance, and Missi felt it her duty to fit right in.

Why would a literary agent ask to meet her unless something promising loomed on the horizon? Missi pictured herself attending the Oscars for a screenplay nominated for best picture based on her novel. She ignored the fact that it was still in the conceptual stage, without even a completed first draft. In her mind, she was flying to London, Berlin, and Hong Kong for book tours and attending cocktail parties with Georgette Heyer, Helen Fielding and Nora Roberts. As she approached the restaurant, Missi imagined herself moving from Campbell's upper duplex on Mozart Street to a beach front cottage in Bali or maybe a mountain-top villa on the Amalfi Coast where she could hobnob with other residents like George Clooney, Elton John or Mick Jagger's latest girlfriend.

At Le Continental, she spotted Lydia Ferrell at a corner table, sipping coffee and studying the menu.

The woman removed her red reading glasses as she approached. "Call me Lydia," she said when Missi addressed her by her last name. "I'm so glad you could join me."

She appeared to be in her mid-forties, with spiked hair that had prematurely turned white except for a wide black streak. *The Devil Wears Prada* flashed through Missi's mind.

"I was coming to the Writers' Fest and asked myself who I could meet in Montreal. Then I got your email and here you are." She indicated that Missi take the seat opposite her.

Missi's heart sank. Maybe this had more to do with Lydia's desire for company than any excitement about her query.

All the same, she pulled out the chair facing Lydia and began to make small talk, covering the weather, Lydia's plane ride from New York, and the hotel she was staying at.

A few moments later, the waiter arrived to take their orders. Le Continental was one of Missi's favorite places; she went with her standard Salade Nicoise along with a glass of Aligote. Lydia ordered another coffee and their lunch special of broiled salmon.

When the waiter left, Missi said, "What did you think about my query?"

Lydia looked puzzled. "Your query? What was it about again?"

Be zen, Missi told herself although she didn't quite know what that meant. If only she had gone to more yoga classes or paid attention at that retreat instead of spending money on yoga clothes that she would probably never get to wear. She would have to go on a strict budget now that she was on her own.

She took a long, deep breath and began to summarize the plot of her novel. Halfway through, she became flustered. She'd written so many versions of her query that she couldn't remember which one she'd sent Lydia. There was a version describing her novel as a series of linked disaster dates, most of which she'd lifted from Suzy's notes and dating blog. Then a version based on the fears and frustrations of a middle-aged woman having to start dating again. These vignettes were drawn from her own unsuccessful dating experiences and the many, many evenings she'd spent chatting with men living on other continents, knowing that they'd never meet. And, lastly, she had written a query for a novel in which she ranted about women stealing husbands. Surely, she hadn't mistakenly sent her that one?

Missi paused as the waiter appeared with her wine and refilled Lydia's cup with fresh coffee. She watched Lydia pour two packets of sugar into her coffee.

The literary agent looked up at her and said, "It all seems confusing and unclear. A series of vignettes? Sounds more like a collection of short stories. That's not what we handle. We represent authors who provide readers with a dream, usually a damsel in distress who is eventually saved by her Prince Charming."

"You don't believe in that fantasy, do you?" asked Missi. Her writing, she realized, could never be marketed in the niche which Lydia had just described.

"What I believe doesn't matter. We sell to publishers that provide readers with the illusion," Lydia said in a clipped voice. "Escape. A vicarious romance. This is what our agency represents." She popped a chunk of salmon into her mouth. "This is delicious."

Realizing this was her only chance to convince Lydia to take her on as a client, Missi began to describe her protagonist in great detail. "She's got a combination of Daphne Blake's fashion sense and willingness to venture into the unknown in Scooby-Doo, and Betty Boop's wide-eyed innocence."

"A cartoon character," Lydia said, spearing another piece of salmon on her fork. "Is that what you're creating? Nothing wrong with that, of course. It's perfectly alright for an agent or publisher that handles that kind of writing. But you shouldn't be wasting your time or mine with your proposal."

"She's nothing like a cartoon," argued Missi. "I'm just saying that she has the traits of..."

Lydia cut her off. "Readers of romance fiction want real-life heroines to identify with. Not cartoons. Here's a suggestion for you. You can have your character, what's her name again?"

"Brenda," Missi said, her fork hung suspended over her salad.

Lydia frowned as she repeated the name. "Right. So, she's having trouble making ends meet and has these horrendous dates with men. Nothing comes of it but at least she gets free meals. That could be her whole purpose."

Missi exhaled before slumping in her chair. "But my character's not like that."

"Well then," Lydia said. "You have to make up your mind. Do you want to sell or do you just want your novel to sit on a shelf? You have to make it interesting."

Still, when the meal was over, Lydia agreed to read more of Missi's work. "If you e-mail me what you've got, I'll read it on my iPhone on the plane home."

As she lay in bed that evening, Missi felt the heaviness in her body. After going through her notes and pulling a complete story together, she had sent Lydia a detailed summary of her novel. Knowing that she would be reading her work on the short plane ride home discouraged her. Especially on an iPhone. How could Lydia give it the attention it deserved with flight attendants interrupting with drinks and little beeping signals to fasten your seatbelt? Thinking of the agent's lack of interest reminded her of Max, who had told her not to waste her time writing. *Why wasn't I stronger*, she thought? *Why did I give more importance to Max's opinions than to my own? And why did I allow Lydia Ferrell to say such awful things about my book when she hasn't even read it?*

She turned the light off her bedside table and thought about what she had learned in The Dating Club. Failed relationships with fathers led to failures in love relationships. But could it also,

Missi wondered, convince a woman that she is doomed to failure in her professional life?

Her thoughts went back to when she had met her father for lunch. She recalled how jittery she had felt inside when she saw him waiting for her at the restaurant – a fairly tall man in a business suit. She had hoped to sense something familiar about him, something that would tell her they were related, and found it for a moment in his smile.

For some reason, she could still remember what they had ordered: hamburgers and a milkshake. She had forgotten their entire conversation except for one part. The part where she asked him if he had other children.

"Step-children," he answered.

"Do they know about me and Emily?"

"Missi, I think you're old enough to understand. I didn't tell my wife that I was meeting you today. When I got remarried, I agreed to walk away from my past. I failed at one marriage and I don't want to fail at another. I'm too old to start over."

Too old to start over. She fell asleep with her father's words looping in her head, wondering if she, too, was too old to start over.

Chapter 32

Felicity met Theo on campus after his mid-afternoon class. They walked past the library and bookstore, where groups of students milled around. Their energy was palpable and revitalizing. She realized how much she missed being a student.

"Valerie got in touch with me again," Theo said as they cut across the soccer field. "She's back from Spain."

"That's great," said Felicity, filled with fresh hope. How many times had he complained about not being able to set things up the way he wanted in his apartment? "Just think of all the room you'll have with her stuff cleared out."

She linked her arm into his as they continued walking, dreamily recalling their first meeting, when he had predicted that they would fall in love. With Valerie out of the picture, she felt that she could safely allow her feelings for him to blossom and grow.

Theo raised the collar of his jacket against the stiff breeze and said, "Let's go for a drink somewhere."

It was mid-afternoon and Felicity thought of all the work awaiting her. She needed to empty out her office today. "I'm busy this afternoon," she said. "Maybe we can get together later on."

They continued to walk in silence. Felicity drew on Theo's solidity as she held onto him. Although he seemed rather subdued this afternoon, his banter and wit had entertained her these past few weeks. She looked forward to deepening their relationship and becoming more intimate.

"I don't only mean she's back from Spain. I mean she's coming back," he said.

Felicity stopped walking and dropped her arm from his. "What do you mean?"

"She wants us to try again," Theo said. Felicity glanced at his face to see if this could be his idea of a joke. His expression looked pained. "When she called me last night, we spoke for a long time. I agreed to give us another chance."

She found herself at a loss for words. What about his swearing that he would never take her back?

"Really, if it wasn't for Valerie, you would be the woman I'd want to be with. You're so much fun."

"Oh," she managed to say. "We did have a good time, didn't we?"

Theo took her hand before she snatched it back. "We can still be friends."

Friends? How could he say that? Trying to keep her voice steady, she said, "Why don't we all get together then? I'd love to meet Valerie."

He started to chuckle but then stopped. She couldn't help herself; tears began to roll down her cheeks.

"I didn't mean to hurt you," he said, awkwardly trying to fold her into his arms.

"Don't." She stepped back from him and reached into her handbag for a tissue to wipe her eyes. She glanced at her watch. "I better get back to the office. I have packing to do."

Although not as large as her father's room, Felicity's office held a wide mahogany desk and a couple of chairs for visitors; it also led to a private bathroom. From the tenth floor, it had an unobstructed view of the mountain on one side and the St. Lawrence River on the other.

Was she making a mistake giving this up? Then she thought of her father. How could she ever trust him again? All he cared about was his transport business; everything was a means to an end. Fairness and integrity meant nothing to him. She had blindly looked up to him, honoring his wishes and believing that he only wanted the best for her.

Turning her back on the promise of continued ease and a stable future as CEO of this company wasn't the difficult part. Her problem was knowing that her father had no regrets about his business decisions. To see him as a hard, callous man was painful, but not as painful as the feelings of betrayal that now swept through her.

She emptied a drawer filled with her personal items into a tote bag. There wasn't that much - a tube of hand cream, a manicure set, some tampons, two pairs of sunglasses, and cards she'd received a few months ago, acknowledging her thirty-second birthday.

At first Felicity had considered visiting her mother in Mexico, but then she shoved that idea aside. It would only postpone what she needed to do. She needed to face her future head on.

In one of the drawers, she found a half-empty bottle of Clonazepam. She checked the expiry date and then shook the bottle, rattling the tiny pills inside. It had been almost two weeks since she'd stopped taking her anti-anxiety medication. She hated breaking her promise to herself, but today she didn't feel she could survive without them. She twisted the cap and flipped the top open. Her hand trembled as she reached into the bottle and slid up a pill. She then swallowed it with some left-over tea on her desk.

With her drawers now as stark as birds' nests in late November, she switched on her computer and Googled *art schools* in Milan. She spent the next half hour requesting information from various schools on their programs, tuition fees and the possibility of living with a family abroad. When she was finished, she looked around her office for the last time. Her eyes filled with tears as she stood at the threshold to her office, with her tote bag in one hand and her handbag in the other.

She had known that her father would be away at meetings this afternoon; his presence would have only made this more complicated.

In only a few hours, she had said goodbye to a lucrative lifestyle and to a man whom she had believed loved her. She had once read that great growth came through seemingly insurmountable loss, but she had also read that, if not handled properly, the upheaval could destroy a life.

Aware that she was closing a chapter of her life, she gently closed the door to her office and made her way to the elevator, her high heels click-clacking on the tiled floors. When she drove out of the building, her hands tightly gripped the steering wheel as she realized the uncertainties that lay ahead for her.

Felicity spent the remainder of the week lying in bed. She lacked the energy to even check her e-mails to see if any of the schools in Milan had responded.

Theo had called a few times but she soon cut their conversations short because all he wanted to talk about was Valerie. He seemed to forget that they had almost become lovers, and now treated her as a friend.

Her father had also called her, trying to convince her that all she needed was a holiday. Felicity had agreed with him to get him off her back, but she knew that she could never go back to working at Starr Transport.

She stared out the window of her living room. Below her, mothers strolled with baby carriages; people walked their dogs. Everyone had a life except her. She had received some e-mails from a few art schools in Milan with the names of families willing to take in students, but had not yet responded to any of them. The idea of going to Italy both excited and intimidated her.

In her bedroom, she pulled out the artwork from the back of her closet and from under her bed. She unwrapped her paintings, one by one, and leaned them against the wall. This was her series of watercolors from the summer she had rented a cottage with other painters in Cape Cod. She loved how the bright turquoise of the sea contrasted with the warm beige of the sand and the orangey sunset. The vividness of the colors cheered her up.

She selected her favorite paintings. Two landscapes which she'd painted while visiting her mother in Mexico before she started college, along with her only painting of fashion outerwear. Before she could change her mind, she packed the artwork in her car and drove to Eduardo's art gallery.

"These are fantastic," he said in his heavy Southern European accent. "When did you paint them?"

"Years ago. I travelled a bit before and after university. That was before I started working at my father's company."

"*Bravo*! Such magnificent colors! Just magnificent." He moved to the other side of the paintings to see them from another angle. "You certainly have talent. Of course, you could improve your style, but a little time in a studio would help."

Felicity realized that she had been holding her breath, waiting for his reaction. She expelled it in a rush.

"I'm thinking of going to Milan to study fashion design. It's something I've dreamt of ever since I was a student in the art program at university." She told him how she wondered where she would be now in her artwork had she not gone into her father's business.

Eduardo thoughtfully rubbed his beard as he listened to her. "Maybe that was not such a mistake after all. Only life experience can make one a great artist."

He leaned her watercolor of a fashion model in outerwear against the wall before stepping back to study it. "This is a delightful painting," he said. "So unique. I love the lines and colors. Do you have a series of these?"

Felicity shook her head. "It's the only one I did. I have lots of sketches but abandoned everything to work at my father's company."

Eduardo straightened his shoulders and looked directly at her. "If you can produce a collection of fashion paintings as good as this one, I'll definitely exhibit them in my gallery."

Felicity beamed. She hadn't felt this happy in a long time. Although she had enjoyed being with Theo, it had also been stressful, not knowing whether Valerie would one day return. As more time went on, she had somehow convinced herself it would never happen. Now she wondered if staying with him would have held her back.

"*Cara mia*, come over to my house this evening. I'll introduce you to my wife. Her sister teaches art at one of the art schools in Italy. It's not Milan, but Rome." His dark eyes twinkled at her, filled with warmth.

Sometimes, Felicity thought as she made her way home, Prince Charming comes in the shape of Eduardos with bushy beards. And sometimes break-ups have silver linings.

Once home, she took out her paints and canvases, and set up an easel by the window overlooking the seaway. The late afternoon light was perfect. She dipped her brush into the soft pastel palette. Her medication had worn off but her anxiety had mysteriously disappeared.

Her phone rang. Glancing at the display, she saw that it was Theo. She didn't pick up.

Chapter 33

"So, who wants to start this evening?" Campbell asked the group. Her hair was still damp from walking to the Women's Center in the rain; a slight chill ran through her. She warmed her hands around her mug of ginger tea.

"Theo went back to his wife," Felicity announced. "I was his insurance policy in case Valerie didn't come back. The worst part is that I knew the risk going in. And he was the first man that I didn't introduce to my father. He wouldn't have survived Daddy's scrutiny, and for good reason this time. I feel so stupid."

"You're making Theo responsible for your happiness. That can only be a recipe for disaster," Campbell said. "Right now, you see him as this wonderful man who can bring magic into your life, when the truth is, you're the only one who can do that. You'll soon come to see him as the egocentric and shallow person he is. Placing so much emphasis on a relationship paralyzes us. Keeps us from our own achievements, which are a much more satisfying source of fulfillment."

Felicity let out a heavy sigh.

"But what else is there?" Missi said. Even after all these meetings of The Dating Club and listening to Campbell go on about the Prince

Charming myth, she still yearned to be rescued from her loneliness and her fear that she would never love another man as much as she had loved Max. "Isn't love supposed to help us discover the person we're meant to be? Doesn't it make us stronger?"

"What about learning to stand on your own two feet? Being creative? Taking the initiative?" Campbell asked. "Depending on a man's appreciation of who we are only leads to a feeling of unworthiness when the relationship ends." She turned to Felicity and said in a softer voice, "Try not to put too much importance on Theo." How easy it was, Campbell thought, for her to dish out advice. It was much more difficult for her to follow it herself.

"I shouldn't let this overshadow the good things that are happening in my life," Felicity said.

"Like what?" asked Missi.

"I've emptied out my office and I'm going to Italy."

"That's wonderful news," said Campbell. "When are you leaving?"

"I contacted a few schools in Rome and..."

"Rome!" Missi broke in. "I thought you wanted to go to Milan?"

Felicity told them about Eduardo's sister-in-law, who was willing to have her stay at her home until she settled in. "I've scheduled a flight in May to check out the art schools."

"That's so exciting," said Missi. "Oh, wait until Suzy hears."

"Where is she, anyway?" asked Felicity. "I really miss her pastries."

"She called me to say she would be late. She sounded upset," Campbell said.

At that moment, Suzy walked into the room, carrying her pink tin box. Before she even had a chance to take her coat off, Missi opened the box of pastries and the other women reached inside.

"Sorry I'm late," she said. "It was parents' night and the school I substitute at asked me to be there. I don't know why; not a single parent came to see me. Substitute teaching is really unsatisfying, except for one thing."

"What's that?" Campbell asked.

"The children – they love me." Suzy helped herself to one of her own squares. "The real reason I'm late, though, is because I was chatting online with a married man. Well, I didn't know he was married at first. We were having a nice conversation before he said something banal. He said I was beautiful."

"And you have a problem with that?" said Missi, chomping into a pecan tart.

"I've heard it a million times, but it's so superficial, isn't it? I happen to have good genes, that's all. Both my parents were extremely attractive."

From her years of professional training, Campbell sensed an undercurrent in Suzy's voice, especially when she used the word "parents." Something was bothering her.

"You said they were attractive," she said. "Have they passed on?"

"Just my mother. Should I tell you about them?" When Campbell nodded, Suzy described her father as a man obsessed with his looks, a narcissist who needed to be constantly reassured. Her mother, she said, tried to be the perfect trophy wife but never quite measured up.

"I'm sure she knew about his mistresses, but turned a blind eye because she didn't want to give up her lifestyle. It was pathetic, the way she catered to him."

"And what does this have to do with your reaction to being called beautiful?" Campbell asked. She saw the startled look in Suzy's eyes and knew she had struck a nerve.

The statuesque blonde glanced at the women around the table before the next words tumbled out. "You really want to know? My father used to sneak into my bedroom at night and tell me that I was beautiful." The women waited for her to continue. "That was when he slipped under my sheets and fondled me. It was our secret." Suzy closed her eyes, as if she were travelling back in time. "It was confusing for me. On the one hand, I hated being awakened, for I was always tired at school the next day; on the other hand, I liked being special to him." She stopped suddenly, then started again in a halting voice. "Then he wanted me to ... fondle him. He even tried to penetrate me once but it hurt me too much. When a man calls me beautiful, I can't help but feel disgust."

"Did your mother know?"

Suzy's shoulders slumped. "Eventually she found out. One day the school nurse came into our class to talk about sexual abuse and incest. I told her about my father. I just wanted to know if what he was doing to me was okay. I didn't mean to cause such turmoil in my family." Tears filled her eyes. "I never told anybody about this," she said. "I was too ashamed."

"But it's not your fault. You were young," said Campbell. "How old were you?"

"Ten. Well, ten when I told the nurse but it had been going on since I was eight."

"Wow," said Felicity.

"It must have killed your mother when she found out," said Missi.

"Killed her? She was in total denial. She called me a troublemaker and accused me of making it all up."

Afterwards, Suzy explained, her family life became strained. Her father kept his distance and her mother tiptoed around her as if she expected her to say something else to upset them. They sent her away to a boarding school in Switzerland.

"Oh, Suzy, that's horrible. And to think that you kept it to yourself all these years. There are groups that can help you with this," said Campbell.

"When I lived in Vancouver, I thought of getting help. But by then I was embarrassed at having waited so long."

"If you want, I can find a group for you," offered Campbell. "Or maybe you prefer an individual therapist. I have some colleagues who specialize in sexual abuse. It would do you good to talk this through."

Suzy nodded. "So, what were you ladies talking about before I came in?"

"I'm going to Italy," said Felicity, her eyes shining.

Chapter 34

Missi stood in line at the butcher shop. A cloth bag filled with fresh leeks, bright orange organic carrots, two heads of bib lettuce, and pearl onions lay at her feet. She welcomed the challenge of preparing a full-course meal for her new friends. The women from The Dating Club were coming to her house this evening to celebrate Suzy's fiftieth birthday.

Why couldn't it be as easy to pick a man, she thought, as it was selecting fresh vegetables from market stalls? As far as men were concerned, the truth –at least her truth – was that she rarely got what she saw. Those who showed up in her life tended to be like potatoes that were firm to the touch when you bought them, but once sliced open, had thick black streaks through their flesh.

As she made her way home from the market, she wondered how Randy was doing. Her son still hadn't returned her calls and, last night, in another of her meltdowns, she had left a series of text messages on his cell phone, asking for forgiveness. Then, when she still received no reply, she'd ranted about his disrespect for his mother.

In her kitchen, she cut mini x's through the roots of the pearl onions before dropping them, skin still on, into a pot of boiling salted water for five minutes. She set the portable timer which Randy had given her as a gift, after she'd burned too many pots on the stove. The gifts she'd received from Max were much less selfless: a weekend with him in New York (his favorite city), or tickets to some sport event he wanted to see.

Missi, now on better talking terms with Max, phoned him for advice on what kind of wine to serve at her dinner party.

"What are you serving as appetizer?" he asked.

"A simple salad," she said. The lettuce which she had chosen that morning had tender, delicate leaves that needed no cutting. "A champagne vinegar with olive oil and some champagne mustard as dressing."

"Sourire de Reims will go well," Max said. "What's your main course?"

"Lamb navarin."

"Remember when we had that in Paris?" The rhapsody in his voice made Missi wish they were back in the *City of Love*. It had been such a wonderful time for them and she felt a tinge of sorrow that it was over. "Are you making those carrots to go with it?"

She smiled. "I am," she said. "With the leaves still on them." She had learned the recipe from

Guy Savoie when they'd eaten at his restaurant in Paris.

"Hmm." Max considered. "I suggest a Morgan for your meal. What are you serving for dessert?"

Missi told him that she had a cheese platter and nectarines, peaches and apricots.

"Poach the fruit in Sauternes for ten minutes. It will be fantastic."

She had both a bottle of champagne and a Morgan. "Damn," she said. "Can I use something else? I don't have time to go to the liquor store."

"I'll send one of my workers over with a bottle," he said.

He sounded more like the man she had fallen in love with so long ago. Max can be so sweet, she thought as she placed her cell on the counter.

Later that afternoon, one of his employees showed up with a box full of wines: One Sourire de Reims, two bottles of a fine Morgan and a bottle of Sauternes for dessert.

Missi shut her eyes. If only he hadn't left her. She poured bubble bath into her tub and, lying back in the sudsy water, recalled the last time she had seen him, less than two weeks ago. Max had shown up at her doorstep, drunk and in tears. Sheri was threatening to leave him because he had slept with another woman.

"Oh, Max," she sighed. "When are you going to grow up?"

Although he wanted to sleep with her then, Missi had made a bed for him on the couch. Even in his inebriated state, part of her longed to feel him next to her; she was proud of herself for resisting.

She stepped out of the tub, wrapped a fluffy towel around herself and went into her bedroom, where she selected her favorite black silk dress from her closet. There were so many dresses that she'd worn only once and would likely never wear again. She ought to give them away to charity.

Although the black dress was a simple sheath, she felt comfortable in it. She accessorized with a silver necklace and matching earrings and finally slid into her silver ballerina shoes.

Missi was putting the finishing touches to her makeup when the doorbell rang. Her reflection in the mirror showed flushed cheeks; even her eyes sparkled. This was the first time she entertained in her new apartment. She had imagined bringing a date home one night, just to hear a man's voice in these rooms, someone who was not Max.

This, though, was far better – a real celebration with friends. Unable to contain her excitement, she pressed the buzzer to open the door downstairs and prepared to greet her guests.

Chapter 35

Suzy carried a huge bouquet of red and yellow tulips as she climbed the flight of stairs to Missi's apartment. The florist shop had sold her all they had and she still felt it wasn't enough. How could Missi possibly know how much this birthday dinner meant to her? She couldn't get over how supportive these women had been after she revealed the secret that had tormented her for years.

"Oh, I love tulips," Missi said, taking the flowers from her. "I know that protocol says you shouldn't have, but I'm really glad you did."

The doorbell rang. "Will you press the buzzer for me, while I find a vase for the flowers?"

Campbell came up the stairs, holding a bottle of wine in one hand and Suzy's birthday gift in the other. The two women hugged and then joined Missi in her kitchen, where she was filling a pretty blue vase with ice cold water. After embracing Missi, Campbell set the wine bottle beside the others already on the counter.

Suzy glanced at the expensive-looking bottles of Morgan and Sourire de Reims and was glad she had brought flowers. Her roommate at the Swiss boarding school, Fleur, had told her never to offer wine as a hostess gift. Fleur, a Parisian, had often invited her home on weekends. Her parents lived in a large, modern apartment near the Eiffel Tower. Although they weren't wealthy by American standards, they possessed class and sophistication. To bring a bottle of wine to a French home when you were invited for a meal implied a lack of trust in the host's ability to choose a good wine.

"These tulips are gorgeous," said Campbell, removing them from their cellophane paper and gently separating them. When the doorbell rang again, she nudged Missi away with her hip. "Let me take care of the flowers while you get that." Her fingers moved deftly as she alternated the red and yellow tulips.

"You're really good at flower arranging," said Suzy.

"I would have enjoyed working in a florist shop. All those fragrances and so many vibrant colors," Campbell said. With a sigh, she stepped back to study the arrangement.

"But you like counseling?"

"I do. I always knew that's what I wanted to be."

"You're lucky," said Suzy. "It took me a lot longer to figure things out."

"You had a lot to deal with. Any more thoughts about your past since the other night?"

Campbell casually asked, still fussing with the stems.

"I'm getting flashbacks," Suzy said. "Things I haven't thought about for a while. Like the social worker's visit after my parents were called." She repeated what her father had said: that he sometimes went into her bedroom to calm her from her nightmares. He had only been comforting her, he claimed.

"Perpetrators of sexual abuse rarely admit to their behavior," Campbell said, shaking her head. "Unfortunately, their victims can take years to pick up the pieces of their lives. Even longer to have normal relationships with the opposite sex."

"That explains a lot." Suzy thought of her early sexual experiences. At fifteen, she had slept with a French teen with a pimply face and greasy hair, whose name she no longer recalled. After that, she had sexual relations with many different boys. She had hoped that physical intimacy would make her feel good about herself, but instead it left her feeling hollow.

After Kevin was born, she no longer felt that emptiness; her life was magically restored. And then he was gone. Since his death, she had been desperately searching for a man to give her life meaning and fill the void inside. Now she realized how futile that was.

"Hey," Felicity said as she entered the kitchen with Missi. She carried two identical packages with large silver bows, one wrapped in pale blue tissue paper and the other in pink. "This one's for the hostess," she said, handing Missi the package wrapped in pink, "and this one's for the birthday girl."

When Missi received the go-ahead to open hers, she carefully unwrapped her present – a beautiful painting of cherry blossoms. "This is stunning," she said, showing it to the other women.

"You painted this?" asked Campbell.

Felicity nodded. "Years ago, before I got interested in fashion design. It's from a trip I took to Washington in the spring."

"No wonder you weren't happy working at the transport company," Suzy said. "Your talent was calling you."

"I know the perfect place for it too," said Missi. "I haven't done much decorating since I moved in, but this is going in my entranceway. It will inspire me every time I walk through the door." She leaned it gently against the wall before saying, "Let's go into the living room for a drink and some appetizers."

They followed her into the other room, where she carried a tray of crystal wineglasses and an ice bucket with a bottle of champagne. Suzy brought the appetizers.

"Excuse the mess," Missi said, indicating the boxes still lining the walls. "I need to put up some shelves before I can unpack my books." She pointed to a large package on the floor. "I don't know what possessed me to buy a do-it-yourself bookshelf. I'm so not a handyman."

"I know what you mean," said Suzy. "I used to dream about meeting a man who could help me renovate my kitchen. Meanwhile, years went by."

"Years when you missed out on having the kitchen you wanted," said Campbell.

Suzy nodded. "Only now I've hired a contractor who's going to do all the work. It might be more expensive this way, but once it's done and I've paid him, I won't owe anyone anything."

The women laughed.

"And something else. I went to the bank yesterday and they're willing to give me a loan to open a pastry shop," Suzy said.

Oohs and aahs filled the room.

"That's so exciting," said Felicity.

"I'm so happy for you," said Missi.

"Where is it?" asked Campbell.

"Actually, it's a franchise for Patisserie Lyse. Every Saturday when I deliver my pastries, we talk for awhile. I told her how dissatisfied I am with substitute teaching. Lyse suggested that we become business partners. She had been thinking about expanding."

"Oh, Suzy," Campbell said. "That's wonderful news."

"I know. It's a little scary, too. Lyse and I went hunting for a location and found a vacant store right in Griffintown."

"That's a great place to start a commerce," said Felicity, her business sense kicking in. "Everything there is still under development. It's expected to be the new Plateau."

She frowned. "Oh, my God. I just realized that I've always wanted to live in Le Plateau." She loved the area's brightly-colored houses, cafes, and book shops as well as its artsy feel. "My father convinced me to move to Nun's Island so that he could claim the condo as a business expense. I never even asked myself what I wanted."

The three other women gave her a sympathetic look.

"Let's stay with Suzy's news," Felicity said, her face brightening again. "Griffintown's great. The industrial area is being converted into residential space, with parks, bicycle paths and neighborhood cafes."

"Here's to Suzy's new business," said Missi, lifting her glass to the other women.

"To enormous success," said Felicity.

"And happiness," Campbell added.

Missi slid a platter of canapés on the glass coffee table. "Help yourselves," she said as she filled their champagne flutes.

Felicity reached for a canapé of smoked oysters on cream cheese and popped it into her mouth. "Hmm, this is delicious," she said, reaching for another one before sliding the platter across the coffee table to Suzy.

When the champagne bottle was empty and the canapés eaten, Missi invited them into the kitchen for the meal she had so carefully prepared.

Her kitchen table had been transformed from a working space to a beautiful dining area. A starched white linen tablecloth ran its length, along with equally starched white napkins neatly folded into wineglasses, silverware inherited in the divorce settlement, and small candles floating in a bowl of water.

"Everything is so lovely," whispered Felicity.

"And smells wonderful," said Suzy.

Missi placed platters on the table of steaming lamb navarin, carrots with their tails still on, and rosemary roasted potatoes, as well as a basketful of warm bread rolls.

They all took second helpings and when it was time for dessert, Missi said, "I didn't bake a cake. How could I compete with Suzy? Instead, I have peaches and apricots soaked in Sauternes."

"I didn't know you were such an accomplished cook," said Suzy.

"I'm not. My repertoire consists of just a few great dishes. And how much skill does it take to soak some fruit in wine?"

"Well, I know it takes a lot of work," Suzy pointed out. "Thank you and," she looked across the table at the other two women, "thank you all for helping me celebrate my fiftieth. I appreciate your being here."

"Open your presents," said Missi. She placed the packages in front of Suzy before filling their glasses with Sauternes to go with the dessert.

The first gift she opened was from Campbell – a watch with a silver bracelet and a photograph of a cupcake on its face. "How original I love it!" Suzy said, passing the watch around. "Thank you so much, Campbell." She leaned over to hug her and kissed her on both cheeks.

"Here's a little something from me," said Missi.

"Oh, Missi, just this party is enough," said Suzy as she began to unwrap her gift. In a moment, she held up a blue and pink polka-dot vintage apron.

"This is so pretty." Suzy immediately fastened it around her. "I'm going to wear this to the opening of my pastry shop. It will be my "good luck" apron."

"Here's my gift," said Felicity, handing Suzy the package wrapped in pale blue tissue paper. "It has nothing to do with baking."

Beneath the tissue paper was a painting of four women sitting around a table.

"Why, it's The Dating Club!" said Suzy. "You made us all so beautiful."

"But we are beautiful," protested Felicity.

"Isn't it wonderful how life brought us together?" said Campbell.

She noticed a shadow cross Missi's face. "You don't look too happy about the painting."

"I think it's lovely. Really, Felicity, you have a lot of talent," Missi said. "It's just that you made me look so young in this painting and these days I feel so old."

"I should be the one complaining. You're only forty-one, and look ten years younger," said Suzy.

"I certainly don't feel it," said Missi.

"Something else is bothering you," said Campbell. "Spit it out."

"Is it that obvious?"

"Yes," the three other women chorused.

Missi's shoulders slumped. "It's Randy. He's dating a cougar," she said as she poured more Sauternes into her guests' glasses.

"I hate that word," said Suzy.

"Have you met her?" asked Felicity.

"Yes. I told her that I didn't want her to date my son." Missi took a few gulps of her wine.

"You didn't!" Felicity's eyes widened as she swiveled in her chair to face her.

"What's she like?" Campbell asked.

"Married. That's what she's like." The tension which Missi had felt when Randy first told her about his girlfriend now squeezed her chest, making it difficult to breathe.

"Oh, my. That must hurt."

"I hate the idea of my son dating a married woman. But I also feel like I need to protect him."

"Protect him from what?" snapped Suzy.

"I don't want Angie dating him." The sound of the woman's name made Missi clench her teeth. "She's too worldly, too experienced. He's only eighteen, for God's sake. He should be dating girls his own age."

"I'm sure she can teach him a few things, especially in the bedroom," Felicity said with a wicked smile.

"I don't even want to go there. I just don't like to think of my Randy being used."

"I doubt very much that he feels like he's being used," said Suzy.

"Maybe you're being too possessive," Felicity said as she spooned an apricot into her mouth.

"Age has nothing to do with love," said Campbell.

"Nor sex," said Suzy. "I can't say I loved the younger men I dated. Or was in love with them."

"Now that's encouraging. How can you expect me to feel good about this?" Missi's fingers curled around her wine glass before she lifted it for another swallow.

"I wouldn't worry about Randy. Some pretty young thing will come along and blow his socks off," said Suzy. "He still has his whole life ahead of him."

They were all feeling buzzed and light-headed from the champagne and wine. Thankful she had worn ballerina shoes and not stilettos. Missi somehow managed to keep her balance as she carried another platter to the table. This time she offered a selection of soft and hard cheeses, along with Clementine wedges and small bunches of red grapes.

"Stop being such a control freak," Suzy said.

"I'm not." Birthday girl or not, Missi felt herself bristle towards her.

"You are. Let Randy be; he needs to learn from his own experiences. You're only driving him into her arms," said Campbell, as she served herself some gooey Brillat-Savarin cheese.

Was she really a control freak? Was that why Max had left her? Why Randy had moved in with his father? Perhaps they were right. Randy needed his own life. What happened to him was his responsibility. Missi took another sip of wine, more slowly this time. "I guess you have a point. Randy has to make his own way."

And so did she.

Chapter 36

As the jetliner began to taxi for its take-off position, Campbell's stomach tensed. Adrenaline pumped through her, making her forget her exhaustion from the last ten days in India.

Chand's father had managed to get them business class seats, and Campbell was thankful for the extra leg room. She had been looking forward to a good sleep as soon as they were in the air. But the same fear that had overtaken her on their plane ride to India gripped her now.

"You alright, honey?" Chand asked, taking her hand. As he interlocked his fingers into hers, the engines revved and the plane started down the runway. When they lifted into the air, Campbell reached for his arm with her other hand, clutching him like a frightened bird as they gained altitude.

"I'm fine now. Thanks for being so understanding," she finally said. He was really sweet. In spite of her doubts, whenever she was with him, she felt a heady mixture of physical attraction, mental stimulation and pure joy.

She leaned over him to view Mumbai from their tiny window as the city began to wake up. A wave of sadness passed through her. "Thank you," she said. "Thank you for bringing me here."

Chand lifted her hand to his lips and gently kissed each of her knuckles. "I'm glad you enjoyed it," he said, giving her hand one last squeeze before releasing it.

She reclined her seat and then leaned back into it with a sigh. Every bone and muscle in her body ached. While her stay in India had surpassed all her dreams, she was utterly exhausted. It wasn't only visiting his family, the tourist spots and other charming areas that had drained her energy, but the constant doubt that woke her up in the middle of the night, making her wonder if she was sabotaging her career.

"I really like your family." Campbell had felt so at home with them. Was everything which she had done before, especially her research into the Prince Charming myth, preparing her to be Chand's wife? Part of her had hoped they wouldn't be able to accept her into their midst, thus making it impossible for her to keep seeing Chand. Part of her wanted to end this budding relationship, while the rest of her thirsted for more.

She closed her eyes and went over her stay in India. The two of them had been on the go the whole time. Chand had taken her to the Ganges as promised, and although he hadn't changed his mind about its pollution, she had stood before it in awe. It was easy for her to understand why it was considered such a holy river.

Chand had rented a hotel along the banks of the Ganges in Varanasi, one of the holiest cities for Hindus. From their hotel room, she watched hundreds of pilgrims along the levee, some bathing, others simply dipping their hands or feet into the holy waters. At dusk, they had witnessed a worshipping to the Ganges.

"This is so beautiful," she had whispered into Chand's ear, not wanting to disturb the worshippers.

"It's called *aarti*," Chand had whispered back. He draped his arm around her as they listened to Hindus singing hymns and watched them place little candles made of clay into the river. The lights of the candles flickered as they drifted on the water.

Aarti. Even the word itself felt sacred on her tongue.

In the morning, she and Chand had walked along a footpath skirting small houses with pretty gardens. Flowers bloomed everywhere and everything was green.

Later they had wandered through an older area of Varanasi, where Chand bought her several dangling bracelets. As they wound their way back to the banks of the river, Campbell had slipped on the delicate bracelets and then worn them during the remainder of their trip, removing them only for sleep.

"Too bad you didn't have a chance to meet Smriti Mehra," Chand said as the plane reached its cruising height and all they could see from the window were clouds.

Campbell smiled at him. "Playing a game with her would have been awesome. But my trip was perfect."

Chand leaned over to kiss her. A kiss, she thought, that tasted faintly of cardamom and curry.

"Your mother and your sister, Sarla, were so kind to me. I really like them."

"They're also fond of you," Chand said. "My mother's glad that we found each other."

As she finally drifted to sleep, she remembered how Chand's mother had treated her like a daughter, lavishing her with gifts of jewelry and handwoven silk saris.

"These are special saris," she had told Campbell, her eyes filled with tenderness. "They're made from Banarasi silk and are to be worn on special occasions."

Campbell had held a glittering pink sari in her hands and imagined herself wearing it at the award ceremony for her research.

She awoke a few hours later to find Chand's arm around her, a set of headphones in his ears. She glanced up at him. "I fell asleep, didn't I?"

Chand removed his headphones and turned off his iPod. "You missed the meal. Would you like some tea to go with these?" he said, handing her cellophane-wrapped cookies which he'd saved for her.

The flight attendant brought her a tea with milk and she dipped her cookies into it.

"While you were sleeping, I was thinking about your research," he said.

"What about it?"

"You really want to know?" His eyes looked grave. When she nodded, he went on, "I think you find it convenient to keep a distance between you and your father."

"Oh, since when did you become a therapist?"

He squeezed her arm. "It's just so obvious to me. You need someone to blame for your unhappiness."

"I'm not unhappy," she said.

He lifted an eyebrow. "Maybe *unhappy* is not the right word. What I meant is that blaming your father rather suits your research, doesn't it? Did you ever think that your research is more about seeking outside validation?"

"Of course, it's about validation. Doesn't everybody want to have their work recognized?"

She handed her empty cup to the attendant and reached for the in-flight magazine in the seat pocket in front of her.

"We all want to do something meaningful," Chand insisted, "but not everyone is willing to give up their own happiness in order to prove to the world that they're special."

"I'm not doing that." She flipped through the pages of the magazine, pausing periodically to pretend she was reading.

He squeezed her arm again. "Now that you've found me - your Prince Charming - your whole father-blaming theory is kind of down the drain, isn't it?"

She reached for his hand and linked her fingers through his. "Nothing's down the drain," she wanted to say. Surprisingly, though, not one word came out.

Chapter 37

Back in Montreal, Campbell decided to see her father. Chand's comment on the plane had plagued her since her return from India. Was she purposely distancing herself from her father in order to prove her research? Chand had to be mistaken. Years on her research proved that she had spent most of her life trying to get a superficial, self-centered and disinterested father to be there for her. Today she would put her doubts at rest.

She suggested meeting her father at the Museum of Contemporary Art. The museum was hosting a photo exhibit by the Brazilian artist, Vik Muniz, and if things went badly with her father, at least she'd see the exhibit.

On her way to the museum, Campbell stepped into the Notre-Dame Basilica. There, she sat on a pew in the incense-scented interior, asking God for clarity and the courage to see her own truth. Except in desperate situations, such as when her mother was dying, Campbell rarely called upon God. It wasn't that she doubted the existence of a Divine Deity; it was just that she couldn't envision Him, Her or even It. All the same, she felt the need for spiritual guidance this afternoon.

Aside from groups of tourists speaking in hushed tones as they wandered around, admiring the ornate architecture and stained-glass windows, the church was empty. Campbell sat in a dark corner, thinking about her evening by the Ganges. She wished she were as devout as those Hindus, with the kind of faith that made you feel safe and loved, something her father had never made her feel. Still in a pensive mood, she got up from the church bench and made her way to the museum.

She saw her father standing by the fountain where they had agreed to meet. The area around the museum bustled with people strolling in the spring sunshine, sitting on outdoor terraces as well as kids on skateboards and bikes.

Campbell's breathing quickened as she walked up to her father. Although she knew what she wanted to say, she needed their conversation to begin casually. "Nice hat," she said, referring to the grey fedora on his head.

He wore a pair of tight black jeans and a grey leather jacket. It looked like he was trying too hard.

Something Chand told her the day he met her father popped into her head: *don't confuse me with your father*.

They were as different as night and day. Chand listened to her, while her father wanted others to listen to him. Chand cared about her feelings; her father cared only about himself.

"Your call was a nice surprise, Cambie," he said. "I hope nothing is wrong."

"Not at all," she said, as he leaned over to kiss her cheek. She asked him about Tina and baby Cooper as they went up to the ticket counter. As he paid the entrance fees, he brought her up to date on Cooper's development and then boasted about Tina's online cookbook.

A sour taste filled her mouth. She wanted to say, *I guess you hit the jackpot, finally finding a wife who can cook as well as admire you.* Instead, she remained silent. It had taken a lot of courage to ask him to meet her and she wasn't about to waste this opportunity on a past resentment.

The first photo they came to was of Jacqueline Onassis.

"Notice how clever Muniz is," said her father, "the way he uses different media to create his own version of Warhol's Jackie."

How like him, she thought, to tell her what she ought to think. Seeing the photographs through someone else's eyes, especially her father's, defeated the whole purpose.

"Art is meant to be a personal relationship between the artist and the viewer," she said, tucking her hair behind her ears.

"Of course," he said. "But there's a specific way of looking at it." As they moved towards Marilyn Monroe's photo, her father told her how his third wife had talked him into taking an art appreciation course.

Campbell felt anger simmering inside her. She hadn't come here to listen to him brag about what he'd learned in his course, especially since she'd heard it all before. She sank on a bench facing the photo. Tears stung her eyes as she thought of the times she had stood by the living room window waiting for him to show up. Over and over again, he had disappointed her until she lost all hope, left with only the sense that she wasn't good enough.

Sitting there, she became a girl of nine or ten again, feeling the weight of rejection. "Why didn't you come all those times you said you would?" she blurted out before she lost her courage. When her father gave her a puzzled look, she continued, "When I was younger, you promised to take me out and never showed up. So many times."

Her father sat next to her and patted her knee. "I don't know why, Cambie. I guess I was too busy."

"You really hurt me," she said.

"I'm sorry," he said. "But let's put this behind us. It was such a long time ago." He patted her knee once more, as if that could pacify her.

She held back from saying, *You ruined my life,* unwilling to give him the satisfaction of knowing that he'd had that kind of power over her.

"Isn't that painting of Marilyn Monroe divine?"

Campbell clamped her lips together, took in several deep breaths and finally said, "Yes. It's divine."

In the remainder of their time together, her father continued to explain the artist's work. She felt like she was with one of the museum guides.

Once outside, Campbell glanced at the people gathered in the square between the museum and Place des Arts. Everyone seemed so joyous, and so in harmony with each other. She squeezed her eyes tight, wishing she could shut out her pain.

Chand was wrong. She had never distanced herself from her father; it was the other way around. All her life she'd struggled to show her father that she was worthy of his love. What about him? Was he worthy of hers? Had he ever given her the protection and support a daughter needed from her father?

It became clear to her. Maybe she had subconsciously wanted to validate the conclusions of her research. *Girls abandoned by their fathers have difficulty developing meaningful relationships as adults.* But she hadn't been wrong about her father. She had not imagined his disregard and lack of concern for her.

Maybe the research was right – that such a background kept women from fulfilling relationships. But did that doom them to a dismal future? There was a missing link. *What do you do once you realize you lack your father's love and support?*

"I'm going to marry Chand," she said.

"Chand?"

"The man I introduced you to a few months ago while you were jogging with your friends." They walked along the promenade leading to the subway and different bus stops. With a sense of longing, Campbell watched young and old couples holding hands as well as fathers carrying infants in baby carriers.

"Does marrying him feel right to you?" asked her father, as they swerved around a group of teenagers tossing a Frisbee.

She caught herself reverting to her old behavioral pattern of following his line of thought. What did he care whether or not it felt right to her? His words were only platitudes.

"You're hesitating," her father said.

"Am I?" She realized that she didn't want to share the intimacies of her private life with him. They weren't close enough for that.

At times like this, she wished her mother were still alive. Campbell would have told her about her conflict in marrying Chand. Her mother would have understood. She would have guided her in the right direction. Was she making a mistake marrying Chand?

She picked her words carefully. "He's good to me," she said. "He listens to me. He cares about what I think." She thought about the conversations she had with Chand. Unlike many of the other men she'd dated, whose conversations revolved around the latest baseball score or the power of their car's motor, Chand had informed opinions about music, art, politics, religion. About everything. He was well read and his selection of reading material ranged from the classics to pop culture. He was interesting, bright and lively. He made her laugh and, though it was a cliché, he made her feel better about herself.

"I never told you about my research," Campbell said.

"How Prince Charming doesn't exist?"

"There's more to it than that." They headed towards the bus stop for the No. 80 that would take Campbell home. She wanted to get this out before it was too late. "My research concerns the effects of fathers who abandon their daughters. I always believed that the reason I couldn't have a relationship with a man was because you'd abandoned me."

He adjusted his fedora, tilting it forward. "Well, it all makes sense now."

"What does?"

"Why you avoided me all these years. Now I understand your anger towards me. You know, in all this time, I never blamed you."

Blamed her! The blood rushed in Campbell's ears and her hands curled into fists. She waited for her fury to subside before turning to face him once more.

She saw her father so much more clearly now. No longer would she allow him to control her life – this man, whose ego was so large that he couldn't accept responsibility for his actions. "I have to go," she said. "My bus is coming."

"You sure you don't want me to give you a lift home?" he asked.

"No." She needed to get away from him; needed to be alone.

"Keep in touch," he called out as she ran for her bus.

She sat next to a window at the back of the bus. They passed Fletcher's Field, where a group of boys played hockey and others rode their bikes. When the bus finally reached her stop at Park Avenue and Jean Talon, she decided to walk the five blocks home instead of transferring to another bus. It was still light out after five o'clock and she felt a surge of joy at the realization that days were now getting longer.

Yes, she thought as she turned down her street, she had shut men out of her life to avoid being hurt. There was no guarantee that love wouldn't leave her broken-hearted. But she preferred to risk a broken heart rather than live with an empty one.

Chapter 38

It was past ten o'clock when Missi woke up. She slipped into an old pair of Levis and a T-shirt and made herself a pot of Lady Grey tea before turning on her computer to check her e-mails. There was one from that literary agent, Lydia Ferrell.

She chewed on her lower lip as she opened the e-mail. She had worked hard on the summary of her manuscript after their lunch at Le Continental, knowing that Lydia would read it when she flew back to New York. Although three weeks had already elapsed since she sent it to her, she knew that agents often took three months and more before responding. This had to be good news.

Dear Missi -

This is to let you know that there have been layoffs and I decided to take the publisher's offer of a severance pay package. I'm sorry that I will not be able to work with you on your novel. However, I passed your proposal on to Yolanda Lovejoy. You can reach her at my old number. I'm sure you'll be happy working with her if she decides to take you on.

All the best.

Lydia

Missi dialed Miss Lovejoy's number, introduced herself and then in her cheeriest voice said, "Lydia said that you'd be working with me."

"About that," said Miss Lovejoy. "I had a chance to glance over your synopsis, and although your premise is delightful, I prefer taking on more serious projects."

Missi felt her heart shrink. Just because her project didn't meet Nobel Prize standards didn't mean that it wasn't to be taken seriously. "*Glance over*," she blurted out. "So, you haven't really read the summary or the opening chapter?"

"We receive hundreds of queries a week," Yolanda Lovejoy said. "I'm not saying that your work is not worthy or that you don't have talent. I just think that it's not the kind of project that I feel comfortable handling right now."

Missi hung on to Miss Lovejoy's last words: *right now*. She swallowed her disappointment and said, "So, can I send you more chapters in a month's time?" As soon as the words emerged from her mouth, she felt like one of those pesky telemarketers asking when they could call back.

A heavy sigh came over the line. "Feel free to query your manuscript elsewhere. You may want to have a look at Writer's Market for a list of literary agents."

At The Dating Club the following Tuesday, Missi complained to the other women,

"Elsewhere? Where else can I send it? I was counting on her. You don't know how much I hate having to look for an agent. Worse, being rejected by one. My entire life is about rejection. First my father. Then Max and now this Miss Lovejoy. What a misnomer that is!" She put her face between her hands. "I hate being single. At least if I had someone, I wouldn't feel so alone."

"But you have us," said Campbell. "You had Max and he wasn't any support."

"You know what's worse?" Suzy said as she slid her pastry box to the center of the table. "A boring man. So many men complain about their bosses or the women they dated. And I'm fed-up hearing about how they eat blueberries with their oatmeal or that their grandchild is taking piano lessons. The silent types are even more frustrating. I'm happy seeing a movie by myself or reading a good cook book. Or going to concerts with friends."

"At first, I thought Theo could be The One," said Felicity, reaching for a lemon tart. "He made me feel that with a little more time, I could really fall in love."

"Maybe you wanted to prove that you could still be in love with someone. Or that someone could be in love with you," said Campbell. She glanced at her notes and read, "Women who suffer from abandonment issues tend to be overwhelmed by the belief that they don't deserve success, happiness or love in their lives. Their ability to trust in others and themselves has been compromised. Or they feel the need to prove that they're still desirable."

"At least I learned to stop waiting for a man in order to begin my life," said Suzy, tossing back a sheaf of long, blonde hair.

Campbell smiled. Suzy's words reassured her of the value of her work. Women needed to build their own lives before they could start building a life with someone else. "I know it's scary being on your own," she said, directing her words to Missi. "It's a big adjustment for you."

"I should be elated that my dream of opening a pastry shop is finally coming true. And I am," Suzy said. "It's unnerving, though. What if I don't succeed? And what if, after all that, I still don't feel fulfilled?"

Suzy's chin quivered with emotion but her eyes were evasive, as if she were struggling with an inner conflict. Campbell had seen that look before. What could she be feeling guilty about? she wondered.

Chapter 39

After weeks of not hearing from Randy, Missi was surprised to see him at her doorstep, toting a bottle of wine as well as a bag from The Sushi Shop.

"Hey," he said. "I was in the neighborhood and thought I'd stop by."

She gave him a big please-forgive-me hug. She loved that about Randy. He'd never minded her hugging him, not even in front of his friends. He was dressed in his usual attire – a pair of worn jeans, a T-shirt underneath a hooded sweatshirt, ankle-high runners and a baseball cap which Missi swore he slept in. He had this beautiful head of golden hair that was still a mystery to her. Both she and Max were dark haired; they had produced a son so fair that, if it weren't for the fact that he came out of her womb and looked just like Max, she'd wonder if he was really theirs.

"How's your novel coming along?" he asked as he opened the bottle of wine.

Missi's shoulders fell. "Not so great. I've lost my motivation." She told him about the rejection from Yolanda Lovejoy. "I'm sure my story would appeal to a lot of middle-aged women, but finding a literary agent seems so impossible." Missi took out a platter for Randy to place the sushi on.

"I'd offer my table," Missi said, "but, as you can see, it's a mess."

"Your work?"

She nodded. "I guess we'll have to eat off my counter."

"And pretend that we're in a tapas bar in Spain," said Randy. His broad grin warmed her.

"One of Angie's clients is an editor for a big New York publishing house. I talked to Angie about your novel and she asked her client if he'd have a look at it. He agreed. So, if you e-mail Angie a copy, she'll send it off to him."

"I don't want to go through the back door. I want my writing published because it's good, not because I know somebody." She stuffed a shrimp sashimi into her mouth.

"Mom, you just said you're tired of being rejected. What you need is someone to help you take your novel to the next level." He paused. "If it were anyone other than Angie, you'd jump at the opportunity."

She could see why Angie was attracted to him; he had such earnest features, seemed unaware of his natural good looks and kindness shone from his eyes. He was right. To go through Angie to get her book in the hands of a publisher would be endorsing their relationship.

"Isn't it better for you to go directly to a publisher instead of through an agent?" Randy asked.

Right again. Even if she found an agent who loved her novel, there was no guarantee that he or she would be able to sell it. Here a door had opened wide for her but she hesitated to go through it because of her pride and personal biases.

"I think you're afraid," her son said.

She thought of what Campbell had said at their last meeting about how early abandonment by a father could erode a woman's ability to trust. Was this what was happening? "Maybe I am. What if the publisher doesn't like my book? That would be a blow to my ego, wouldn't it?"

"That's not what I meant. I think you're afraid to like Angie." Randy dropped a sliver of pickled ginger on his tempura roll.

She stared at him for a few uncomfortable moments. "I don't like the idea of you having an affair with a married woman. Why doesn't she leave her husband?"

A heavy silence fell between them. "It would hurt him too much," Randy finally said. "He's a lot older than she is and he's in the advanced stages of Parkinson's. She placed him in a special care facility. She goes to see him every day. I don't know anyone who's more unselfish. And she deserves a life of her own."

Evidently, she was the one being selfish. Missi thought of what Suzy had said the evening of her birthday celebration. Now, apart from being *controlling*, she was selfish. What kind of a mother disregarded her son's happiness to maintain her own old-fashioned values? "I'm so sorry, Randy," she said. "I wish I had known this sooner."

"You were so stubborn, Mom, that I didn't think it would make a difference. I didn't want you to accept Angie because you feel sorry for her but because we love each other."

"Are you really in love with her?"

"I really like being with her. She appreciates who I am and encourages me to expand my horizons. Plus she's a lot of fun in bed."

"That I don't need to know," Missi said with a scowl.

It felt good to hear Randy laugh. Their relationship had become so tense in the last few weeks.

"She seems like a lovely person," Missi said as she popped a piece of sushi into her mouth and then washed it down with wine. "And I will contact her."

Chapter 40

Before sending Angie her book proposal, Missi had reworked her synopsis and written five more chapters. Now that she had sent the whole thing off to her, Missi's initial excitement faded. Of course, she was happy that there was still hope for her book. If anything, she wanted readers to get to know her main character, Brenda. She just didn't want to build up any false expectations.

Writing the novel had also motivated her to go on internet dating sites. Apart from her chats with men living abroad, she'd been on a dozen dates, all of them leaving her terribly disappointed. She wondered now whether she had subconsciously created Brenda in order to allow herself to prowl these sites night after night. There was no doubt in her mind that each time she went on these sites or met men to research her book, she secretly hoped that she would meet her own Mr. Right.

Missi heard the knock at her door. It was Campbell.

"You ready to go?" she asked. Since Missi's move into Campbell's upper duplex, the two women went for power walks twice a week.

"Just let me get my jacket," said Missi. She pulled on a light four-season jacket over her T-shirt and yoga pants.

They walked along Mozart Avenue, then turned right on St. Laurent until they reached the park where the Rogers Cup tennis tournament was held every year. It was exceptionally warm for April and sunshine flooded the streets. A few sparrows chirped overhead as they walked with their jackets open.

"I finally decided to quit online dating," Missi said. "Now that I've gathered all my anecdotes for my novel, there's no need for me to keep going online."

"Really?" Campbell said skeptically.

"I hate having to lie so that I don't hurt people's feelings. How can you tell someone you don't want to see them again because of bad breath? Or bad teeth?"

Campbell laughed. "I believe in honesty."

"You would tell someone that they smell bad?"

Again, Campbell laughed. "Maybe not that."

"I'm also tired of being disappointed. These men think that we're meant for each other just because we're both lonely. It's pathetic."

"You have to learn to tolerate the loneliness without turning on your computer."

"I know," Missi said, "but it's still scary."

"Life is scary. The problem with you, Missi, is that you're looking for an Adonis and keep meeting men who want more from you than you're willing to give."

Missi stopped to catch her breath. "All I want is to fall in love with a man who will say *marry me*. A normal guy. You think they still exist?"

"Look at me and Chand," said Campbell as she picked up her pace, her arms and legs moving in perfect rhythm.

"What are you going to tell those people when you accept your award?" Missi asked.

"I don't know yet. I also haven't decided if I can accept the award."

They cut through the park until they reached Jarry Street and then turned around. "It's coming home to an empty house that makes me anxious," said Missi, changing the topic.

"Why don't you get yourself a roommate?" suggested Campbell as they stopped at a red light. "Maybe a student. The spring semester is going to start soon, so there may be out-of-town students looking for a place to stay."

When she got home, Missi showered and changed into a nightshirt designed with tiny hearts on the collar. It was getting late; still, she wanted to delete all her profiles on Match.com, Plenty of Fish and Middle Aged Singles.com.

She had to do it quickly. Otherwise, she knew that she would change her mind and remain in this limbo state, addicted to the thrill of meeting new men in an endless crash-and-burn cycle. It was as futile as a romance writer who kept sending her work to science fiction publishers only to get rejected. Love would now have to find her and not the other way around.

Chapter 41

Suzy stood outside the Women's Center. She had arrived early for the Tuesday meeting of The Dating Club and the door was still locked. As she waited for the others, she reached into her handbag for *The Lover*, the novel that had inspired her to visit Marguerite Duras' Saigon ten years ago.

The book had coffee stains on some pages and what might have been jam on others; several passages were underlined. She turned to a page towards the back of the book and read: *The wild love I feel for him remains an unfathomable mystery to me. I don't know why I loved him so much to want to die of his death.*

She did not recall having read this before. Had she not finished the novel? Or perhaps she had only focused on the romance between the man and the girl. No matter; the intensity of these lines hit her now. They explained why she had become so obsessed with men who were the age Kevin would have been had he lived.

"I hope you haven't waited long." Campbell glanced at the novel as she unlocked the door. "Any good?"

Suzy felt a tightening in her chest. "I always knew it was unhealthy to date men so much younger than me, but I never understood my compulsion until now." As she slipped the novel back into her handbag, she said, "This book helped me to see it."

"What compulsion? What book?" Felicity asked as they all walked into the room. Since leaving Starr Transport, she had become more outspoken, with a liveliness that matched the purple streaks in her hair.

"I'll tell you later, once Missi joins us," said Suzy.

Spring jackets were hung on pegs, water set to boil, and pastries displayed. As Campbell opened the box of teas, Missi arrived. They all took their seats around the table.

When Campbell asked her to start, Suzy rubbed at the skin on the back of her neck, below the colorful scarf. She felt a rush of heat. Oh, God, she hoped it wasn't another of those hot flashes she'd started having.

"I was telling Campbell that I finally 'get' my attraction to younger men. It came to me when I was re-reading this novel." She held up her copy of *The Lover*. "It was a mother's quest for immortality. Part of it, anyway."

"A mother's quest?" asked Campbell, as she reached forward to light the candle in the center of the table.

The jingling of Campbell's bracelets annoyed Suzy. Since her return from India, she'd dressed differently. Her dangling Maharaja-like earrings and the Indian dress and pants were too much. She wasn't even Indian. Or in India. Didn't she know that less was more?

Suzy felt the muscles in her shoulders tense as she contemplated the three women. Could she trust them with the truth? Would they blame her for Kevin's death?

Her explanation came out jumbled and soon the women bombarded her with questions. *How did Kevin die? Who is Kevin?*

She heard the early evening traffic through the open windows. "In a car accident. I was driving."

"How did it happen?" asked Felicity.

"We had just returned from our trip to Asia and picked up my car at the airport. With the long flight ...I'd had a few drinks... hadn't eaten. It was late at night. I didn't see the other car as I pulled on to the highway." Suzy closed her eyes, wishing she could shut out the memory. "Kevin was only twenty; would have been thirty this month."

Missi, still preoccupied with thoughts of Randy and Angie, said, "You had a lover half your age?"

"Not a lover. He was my son," Suzy said.

"Your son!" Campbell said, almost spewing a mouthful of ginger tea.

Suzy told them that she had just turned twenty when she learned she was pregnant. "I fell in love with a handsome Princeton graduate from a political family, who later told me he was engaged to someone else. I was crushed." She took a deep breath. When I discovered I was pregnant, I was determined to keep the child." Her voice softened, almost to a whisper. "Finally, I'd have someone who would love me. Someone who would always be part of my life."

A long moment of silence followed as the other women absorbed what she had just told them. A sense of peacefulness seemed to envelop the room.

"How did your parents react?" asked Campbell.

Suzy's shoulders drooped. "I'd never seen my father so angry. When I said that I didn't know who the father was, he called me a whore. Said I couldn't stay in the town. I was a disgrace to him."

"A disgrace?" said Felicity.

"He was the mayor. We lived in a small city outside of Seattle."

"He might have wanted to cover up." Campbell said. "What if people started to gossip about what went on before and speculated that you were carrying his child?"

Suzy shook her head. "No one knew about the incest. When I got back from boarding school, my parents acted as if nothing had happened. I understood that it was a family secret that would not be mentioned again." She reached for a tissue from the box on the table and blew her nose.

"What about your mother?" asked Missi. "Did she disown you, too?"

"She wanted me to have an abortion."

"So, she didn't stand up for you when your father told you to leave?" asked Felicity.

"That's right." Suzy adjusted the silk scarf around her neck. After turning fifty, she had started wearing more casual, youthful clothes and took care to cover the almost imperceptible lines in her neck.

"She never contacted you all those years?" Campbell fiddled with her bracelets.

"No. I wrote to her but my father must have intercepted the mail. I moved to Vancouver because I didn't want my son to go to war. He was too important to me and I couldn't allow any harm to come to him. I was there to protect him." She stopped talking for a moment. Then, through the thickness in her throat, she said, "Only I didn't protect him, did I?" Her eyes filled with tears and she felt another surge of heat. Her voice cracked as she said, "After the accident ... after it happened, I left Vancouver. I couldn't bear living there anymore."

"Didn't your son ever ask about his grandparents?" said Missi.

"I told him the truth. That they couldn't accept my having him out of wedlock. He was fifteen when my mother died. My father contacted me after she was buried and I brought Kevin to her grave. He wanted to meet his grandfather, but my father was cold towards him. It was such a disappointment. I should never have brought him there."

"What about Kevin's father?" asked Campbell.

"Kevin started asking questions about him. I owed it to him, so I called up his father and told him about our son. He agreed to meet me and then offered me a large sum of money to keep quiet. He was a powerful politician by then and married as well. His offer was all about avoiding scandal. The money would have paid for Kevin's education, but it would have denied him the opportunity to get to know his father."

Suzy played with the knot in her scarf. Missi and Felicity shifted in their seats.

"What did you do?" asked Campbell.

"I talked it over with Kevin while we were in Asia. By then he was twenty. I didn't tell him who his father was, but I explained the situation."

"What did he say?"

"That we were better off taking the money, for he had gotten along fine without his father all those years. And why cause pain for other people? I loved Kevin for that. He was such a kind and generous soul. Then, just when I decided that I would take the money, we had the accident."

"So, you never got a penny."

"Of course not." Suzy's voice quivered as she said, "If only I hadn't been drinking on the plane."

Campbell cleared her throat in the silence that now filled the room. "Life is filled with *if only*'s. But we can't go back and change the past. Besides, it was dark and you were tired from a long flight."

"I know. But I wasn't alert enough to be on the road. If anyone had to be killed, it should have been me. He didn't deserve to die. I still have his ashes in an urn at home. I've been telling myself that I'm going to give him a proper funeral one of these days."

"Maybe that time has come," said Campbell. "You need to let him go. And to set yourself free."

Chapter 42

Suzy spent days preparing for Kevin's memorial. She filled her apartment with white candles and put a striking bouquet of white lilies in her living room. At the entrance, next to a bronze urn with his ashes, she placed a photograph of Kevin in a silver frame. The photo had been taken during their wonderful trip to Ho Chi Minh City. Such beautiful memories! She had not been able to enjoy them, though, because of her guilt over his death.

Cushions were arranged in a circle on the floor of her living room. In the center stood five votive candles, one for each of the women and one for Kevin. Suzy left a pile of photographs of Kevin on a sidebar – from sitting in a high chair or on Santa's lap to older images of him in a Little League baseball uniform and skiing at Banff during spring break. Her gaze lingered on his high school graduation photo. His eyes shone with the promise of a bright future; she knew he would have succeeded at a number of things had he lived.

On the crisp, pink-flowered tablecloth, she put out a variety of salads over bowls of ice, cheeses, fresh breads and, of course, her very best home-made pastries.

At last, it was time for the memorial to begin. Suzy wore an amethyst-colored dress with a single strand of pearls that matched her earrings. She only wished her son were here. He would have been proud of her.

The women arrived one after another and seated themselves on the cushions Suzy had laid out.

Suzy passed around his photos and lit the candles. "I'd like to say a few words about my son. Kevin was everything to me. In losing him, I lost the best part of myself. He was bright, personable and lots of fun. He was also very caring. Once he brought home a stray cat and cried all night because we couldn't keep it. I never understood why God took him from me. Or why I had to be the cause of his death."

"It was an accident," said Campbell.

"One that could have been avoided if I hadn't been drinking," Suzy said.

Felicity tucked her legs beneath her, trying to get comfortable on her cushion. "How much did you have to drink?"

"I had three glasses of wine on the flight over."

"A fifteen-hour flight," said Campbell. "You weren't drunk. What about the other driver?"

Suzy rubbed her eyes, then stared at her candle flame. "He was a middle-aged man."

"Had he been drinking?" asked Missi.

With a shrug, Suzy said, "They found alcohol in his blood. But also, in mine."

"And you carried the entire blame on your shoulders all these years? You never thought that maybe he was as much to blame?" asked Campbell.

Suzy shook her head. "What difference would it have made? Kevin died. It wouldn't have brought him back to life."

Felicity finished looking through the photos which Missi had handed her. "The difference is in how you feel about yourself."

"I couldn't be happy after what I'd done." As a heavy truck rolled by, Suzy got up to look out the window, feeling the weight of the past ten years.

"Don't you think it's time for you to forgive yourself? That you've punished yourself enough?" asked Campbell. She got to her feet, too, and stepped beside her. The two women stood there for a few moments, Campbell's arm around Suzy's shoulders.

Suzy wiped away a few tears. Then she turned back to the group and said, "Until now, I didn't realize how hard I've been on myself."

Campbell found her handbag and pulled out a pad of paper and some pens. "Here," she said, handing each of the women a sheet of paper and a pen. "I want us all to write down what we no longer need in our lives. What we need to let go of in order to find ourselves."

She also pulled out a book of matches and a stick of holy incense from her trip to India. Campbell lit the incense and waved it in a circle over their heads. "For peace and good luck."

They sat in silence, each thinking about what they wanted to let go of before jotting it down. The women then read their answers aloud to each other and burned their pieces of paper over their votive candle flame.

"I no longer need Max to love me in order to feel whole," Missi said. She reached for the candle and watched her paper disintegrate into ash.

One after the other, the women repeated the ritual.

Of all the women in the group, Felicity had changed the most, at least outwardly. Her hair was almost all purple now and she wore an ankle-length crocheted beige skirt with a tight black t-shirt. Around her neck hung a beaded Native American necklace. "I need to let go of my fear of doing what I really want to do," she said.

"I no longer need to feel guilty about my past," said Suzy.

"I no longer need to believe that a failed father/daughter relationship keeps us from a healthy adult relationship with a man," said Campbell.

There was a moment of silence and then the women hugged each other.

"Let's drink," said Suzy. She popped open a bottle of champagne.

They all drank a bit too much. And in their giddiness, they toasted the men they had dated. To Theo, who was Felicity's end-of-winter fling. To the good years Missi had with Max. To men who wanted to body paint them; men who used them for sex and men they used for sex. To the cheapskates and the chatterboxes who only wanted to hear themselves talk; to the doctors, lawyers and other professionals and to the many, many dysfunctional men whose paths had crossed their own. To the men whose profiles stated that they wanted younger women. To phone calls that never came. To the men they had cried over. To disappointments and heartbreaks. And above all, to Kevin.

"To love." They all clinked their flutes of champagne.

"And to Felicity's success in Rome."

"Are you ready?" asked Suzy.

"As ready as can be. I leave in three days. I managed to convince my father to keep some of my furniture and boxes of books in his company's storage."

"How is he coping with your going away?"

"He thinks I'll return in a month. That I'll come back to work for him. It's as if none of his oil thefts matter. Finding this out about my father doesn't make me love him less, but it sure makes me dislike him. It was tough seeing his faults. Especially since I'd put him on a pedestal."

"But now that you've seen that part of him...?" asked Campbell, her eyes meeting Felicity's over the rim of her champagne flute.

"I stopped idolizing him. I don't think I'll ever idolize another man again."

"How is your relationship with Randy now?" Suzy asked Missi.

"Better. It's been a rocky road. I always thought that the most difficult relationships were between mothers and daughters, or sons and fathers. I guess I resented Randy for leaving me right after Max did. Part of me wanted him to stay with me to punish Max. And then when he was with Angie, I felt he was replacing me with her. That I wasn't a good enough mother. Isn't that crazy?"

"Maybe not so crazy. After Kevin died, I became obsessed with men his age. For a long time, I dated men who were twenty, and then men who were whatever age he would have been. It's weird."

"It could have been your way of punishing yourself, by dating men that you knew would never lead to any real relationship," said Campbell as she took a sip of her champagne.

"I suppose I was searching for Kevin in those young men. Not sexually. I never associated those feelings with Kevin. It's taken me this long to accept his death."

"And have you?" Campbell wanted to know.

"I'm beginning to. Talking about him helps." Suzy felt grateful for the warmth and support of these women. For the first time in years, she could breathe a little easier as she let the past slip farther away. "And so does this memorial."

Chapter 43

Missi and Campbell sat by the window in Suzy's new pastry shop in Griffintown. Colorful balloons floated outside, announcing the grand opening. Inside, the aroma of chocolate, cinnamon and freshly baked dough mingled with the smell of coffee. A stream of customers waited in line, glancing at the chalkboard behind the pastry counter for the day's specials. Most of them left with boxes or bags of pastries. Others sat at the tables, enjoying dessert and cappuccino with their friends.

Suzy and two helpers worked swiftly, trying to keep up with the demand.

After the crowd finally thinned, Suzy came over to Missi and Campbell, wearing the frilly *good luck* apron Missi had given her for her birthday. She placed a tray of fresh coffee and a selection of mini pastries on the table before joining them.

When Missi asked how it was going, Suzy smiled. "It's been busy like this all day. I just hope they keep coming back."

"People always come back when pastries are this good," said Campbell, biting into a buttery chocolate croissant.

"Did you read Felicity's e-mail?" asked Missi. "She seems to be adapting well to Italy."

Campbell nodded. "She sounds so much happier. And the art school she's going to looks fabulous."

"I have no worries about Felicity," Suzy said. "All these paintings on my wall are hers. They're on consignment."

Missi and Campbell admired the paintings. "But they're not about fashion design at all."

"These are her early paintings. Her landscape period, when she spent the summer visiting her mother in Mexico."

"They're stunning," said Campbell.

"She's so talented," Suzy said.

"And so are you," said Missi . "I love how you decorated your pastry shop." Small glass tables bordered the front window and a banquette covered in a blue-and-yellow floral print ran along another wall. To add to the room's charm, the bright blue floor tiles created a Monet look.

"It was fun working with the contractor. And I'm really pleased with the results." A few customers came into the shop and then a few more. "I better get back to work," Suzy said.

"Opening her own business has really lifted her spirits," said Missi.

"When we find what we're good at, everything else falls into place," Campbell said. "What are you grinning about?"

"Remember how I sent my manuscript to Angie?" Missi said, still beaming. "Just before coming here, I got a phone call from Angie's publisher friend. He wants to publish my novel."

Campbell leaned over to squeeze her arm. "That's terrific news. But why didn't you say something earlier?"

"This is Suzy's parade," said Missi.

"It's all our parades."

Suzy joined them again with another fresh pot of espresso and more pastries. "What are you ladies talking about?"

"Missi's novel is going to be published."

"Oh, Missi, that's fantastic!" said Suzy, as she swiped a napkin across her forehead. "Damn menopause."

"And something else," said Missi. "I placed an ad on the University bulletin board. I've decided to rent out Randy's room to a student. It'll supplement my income and give me companionship. It was Campbell's idea. I just want to enjoy life without the pressure of dating and being constantly disappointed by the men I meet."

"That's the way I feel about my business. I'm so absorbed by it that I don't have time to even think of dating. And you know something? I used to be on dates where I wished I were a million miles away. But when I'm making pastry or taking care of my business, there's nowhere else I want to be."

"What about you, Campbell. Do you have your speech ready?" Suzy asked.

"I better. I'm flying to New York this weekend for the award. You two are coming, aren't you?"

"We wouldn't miss it for the world," they said in unison.

Chapter 44

The following morning, Missi received a text message from someone who wanted to see the room she had posted for rent.

"When can you come?" Missi texted back.

"Late this afternoon," the next message read.

Missi got busy tidying up, cleaning and dusting the apartment. With all the energy she'd expended on her manuscript in the past few weeks, there had been no time for housework. She spent most days writing in her new yoga clothes, figuring it was better to make some use of them.

At four o'clock, the doorbell rang. After she pressed the buzzer to release the door catch, she was surprised to see a man walking up her stairs. She had presumed that the message had been from a girl. As he stood before her on the landing, she had a closer look at him. From the lines around his eyes and the slight greying around his temples, he appeared to be around her age, early forties.

"I was expecting ..." she started to say.

"Someone younger," he finished. His clear hazel eyes gazed directly at her, seeming to assess her in one glance. She shifted in the doorway, wondering if she'd even combed her hair.

"Yes," she said. "But also a female."

"Ah, I must have missed that in the ad. I'm sorry for troubling you." Missi caught sight of the well-toned muscles below the sleeves of his polo shirt as he turned to go down the stairs.

"Wait," she said. She thought of her bookcase still dissembled in its box. "Maybe having a man around wouldn't be such a bad idea."

He told her that he was looking for a place to stay until he found his own apartment.

Something temporary, Missi thought. Even better.

As she showed him around her home, she learned that he came from Boston and was in Montreal as writer-in-residence at McGill. His daughter worked in Geneva as a translator.

"You and your wife must be very proud of her."

"We are. Except she's not my wife anymore."

"How long have you been divorced?" she said before she could stop herself. This was what she'd always asked her online dates. She had met a variety of divorced men. Men who were ready to jump into a new relationship after being divorced only one month; others who admitted they were still living with their wives for financial reasons; and still others who said they were not "technically divorced" but had not slept with their wives in years, as if that made them emotionally available.

Missi felt the heat rise in her cheeks after asking such a personal question.

He didn't seem to mind. "It'll be seven years in October. I was married for twelve."

She walked him through her living room and past her bedroom to the guest room, next to the kitchen, that she had painted blue for Randy when she had first moved in. "This is the room that I'm renting."

He stepped around the simple bed and dresser to gaze out the window. "You have a lovely space out there. I always loved gardening. Do you use it?"

"Actually, it belongs to the woman downstairs. It's her duplex, but we're good friends." She told him that he was welcome to use her kitchen and that internet and phone services were included. "But of course, not your long-distance calls."

Missi offered him a beer, which he accepted. She opened the back door and they stepped onto her balcony. It was a warm, sunny May afternoon and it made sense to continue their conversation outdoors. They sat on two kitchen chairs which he helped her carry outside. Considering that they had just met, she was surprised at how comfortable she felt talking with him.

"So, what kind of work do you do?" he asked her.

"I'm a writer."

"Oh. What do you write?"

"Women's fiction," she said.

He laughed. "One of the courses I teach is women's literature. At first nobody else wanted the post. Most of the professors are male and frankly, they have a double standard when it comes to literature written by women. They consider it light and fluffy. I have to admit that I was of the same opinion until I started teaching it. There are so many amazing and insightful women writers."

She offered him another beer as they sat on her deck discussing literature. Finally, he said, "What do you think? Do you want to rent to me?"

"That depends," she said. "How much of a clean freak are you?"

He looked around her deck. Her recycling bin was brimming with wine bottles, plastic containers, milk and juice cartoons, and paper.

"About as freaky as you're messy," he said.

Was he flirting with her? Something inside her wished that he was, but she forced herself to focus on business. He asked her how much she was charging and when she told him, he said, "That sounds very reasonable." He looked at her sheepishly. "I like your place and I never really enjoyed living alone. Maybe we can be roommates."

She almost expected him to say, "*and who knows ... maybe we'll fall in love*," but he remained silent. They looked at each other and then began to laugh.

Chapter 45

Campbell stood on the sidelines of the stage, waiting to be introduced at the Annual Women's Studies Convention. She felt her legs tremble as she looked over the audience – rows and rows of women ranging from their early twenties to eighties. They were all anticipating her speech, no doubt hoping to glean something from what she had to say. Campbell ran her clammy hands down the silk folds of her bright pink sari. She thought of how Chand's mother had introduced her to the man who sold her the material and then to the seamstress who made the sari for her. Though India was now thousands of miles away, Chand's mother and sister still lived in her heart.

Focus, she told herself. *This is your big moment.*

"It is now my pleasure to present this award to Campbell Jones for her contribution to the Prince Charming literature," said the president of the Women's Studies Association. "For years she's been giving workshops on the myth, helping women become stronger and take control of their lives."

Campbell took in the applause as she strode across the smooth, wooden floor to the woman at the podium. The vaulted ceilings of the great hall created a feeling of spaciousness, making her feel as if she were floating across the stage. She paused as she searched the audience for Missi and Suzy. She found them sitting five rows down, next to Chand. They all gave her a thumbs up. Campbell straightened her shoulders as she turned towards the president.

The woman handed her a gold plaque with her name engraved on it. As she blinked through her tears, Campbell barely made out the rest of the engraving. Below the date, she read the words, *for research on the Prince Charming Myth*. She grasped the award with both hands, savoring the moment. This was what she had dedicated years of her life for.

"Thank you. Thank you. I can't tell you how much this means to me," Campbell addressed first the president and then the audience. "My decision to accept this award has not been easy. And perhaps, after I finish speaking, you will think that I don't merit it."

Campbell inhaled deeply and held her breath in her stomach. She slowly let it out before continuing. "As you know, my career is founded on debunking the Prince Charming myth. I spent five years of my life telling women to stop searching for someone who doesn't exist. The premise of my research is that Prince Charming is dead." She released one end of the plaque to reach for the bracelets on her wrist, drawing reassurance from their energy. "I have since found out that this statement is as untrue as it is true."

As she gazed over the audience, she found Missi and Suzy at the edge of their seats, listening to every word. She had kept the content of her speech from them as well as from Chand.

"If you're waiting for some man in shining armor to save you from being responsible for your life, you're in trouble," she said. "Depending on a man's appreciation of who you are only leads to a deep feeling of unworthiness, especially when the relationship ends – as they so often do. Let me show you what my definition of Prince Charming once looked like."

The screen behind her lit up with the long list of criteria which Chand had found under her mattress. Campbell went through each item: Successful in what he does. Professional. Available physically, emotionally and spiritually. Intellectual. A generous man who wants to spoil me. Loves to travel in luxury. Sexy. Not too religious, but spiritual. Not too spiritual. Communicative. Good listener. Physically attracted to me. Likes to play sports but not a fanatic. Doesn't expect me to be good in sports. Honest. Reliable. Does not get angry easily. Will not cheat on me. Likes country music. Had a stable relationship in the past. Is between 5'9 and 6' tall. Has nice teeth/good oral hygiene. Interested in my work and will help me succeed. Confident but not arrogant. Likes hi-tech gadgets and knows how they work. Is handy around the house. Reads scientific magazines. Reads period.

The laughter from the audience reassured her. Campbell turned away from her list and faced the women again. "There's a lot more," she said. "Two full pages, in fact. But I don't need to waste your time with this. I'm sure many of you have your own lists."

Her eyes searched out Missi and Suzy; she found them shaking with laughter. She held back her own mirth that bubbled from a place deep inside her, as she turned to the screen again and clicked on a quote from E.M. Forster: *we must be willing to let go of the life we have planned, so as to have the life that is waiting for us.* She paused before releasing the next slide. *If we wish to find our Prince Charming, we must let go of the Prince Charming we have imagined and make room for the one waiting for us.*

As she gazed over the audience, she felt confident and at the top of her game. In the last three months, she'd learned so much about herself. "It's not so much that Prince Charming is a myth; our definitions of him are."

She clicked back to her list of Prince Charming criteria. "You'll notice that my list is all about the qualities of the potential prince. It lacks the most important consideration." She let her words sink in as she made eye contact with the women looking up at her. "What counts is how you feel with someone. How you love being with that person. You seem to have more energy, a feeling of well being, a sense of security ... whatever it is you're looking for. That is your Prince Charming." She stared directly at Chand, who gave her another thumbs up.

Campbell pulled back her shoulders to stand even taller. "As long as I believed that Prince Charming was a myth, I was blocking him from my energy field. Prince Charming does exist. Just as there is a Santa. Just as there's childhood, adolescence, college ... and friendship. Life is filled with millions of different experiences. Fulfilling a Prince Charming dream is one of them.

She paced the stage before pivoting back to her audience. "I haven't thrown the baby out with the bath water here. I still deeply believe that we are responsible for our own self-fulfilment. You can't be happy when your happiness is tied to being loved by a man. Until you can count on yourself, you'll always be searching for that illusive fairy tale. That is the myth."

370

She drew in another deep breath, allowing the air to expand her lungs before slowly letting it out. "Prince Charmings do come into our lives, but it is up to us to recognize them." The screen lit up again with: *If we wish to find our Prince Charming, we must let go of the Prince Charming we have imagined and make room for the one waiting for us.*

Campbell looked at Suzy and Missi. "The man that shows up on our path," she said with a wink at Missi, "that's the one we need to make room for." She turned her head to either side of her to encompass the entire audience and clasped her hands to her chest. "What I've learned through my research is that when a woman gives up finding the perfect man, usually after years of disappointment and disillusionment, when she stops idolizing the father who abandoned her, clearly seeing that it is not her who is unworthy of his love but he who is unworthy as a father, then she is truly open to love."

She let her hands drop and smiled at the women before her. "In doing this research, I found my own Prince Charming. He lacked a lot of the criteria on my list and at first, I resisted him. I thought that if I fell in love with him, then my entire research would be invalidated. But I was wrong. Once I let go of my pre-conceived ideas, my fears, and my insecurities, love was able to enter into my life." She fixed her gaze on Chand before returning to the audience.

"Finally, I'd like to thank all of you for not only being here this afternoon to share this special occasion with me, but also for encouraging me along the way. I am enormously grateful to all of you. Thank you." She bowed her head until the sound of people clapping filled the entire hall.

With the ripples of applause still in her ears, she stepped off the stage. Now that her speech was over, her legs trembled again and she thought she might trip on her sari. Chand, though, was there in the wings to catch her, along with Missi and Suzy.

"Terrific speech." Suzy gave Campbell a fierce hug. After the others had hugged and congratulated her, Suzy said, "We're heading into the streets of New York to take it all in."

"The Empire State Building, Museum Mile, Tonnie's Minis for cupcakes, and drinks in Greenwich Village. You guys want to join us?" asked Missi.

Chand met Campbell's eyes.

"You go ahead," said Campbell. "We'll meet up for dinner."

Campbell and Chand went back to their hotel room, where they spent the remainder of the afternoon locked in each other's arms.

"Are you ready now to become Mrs. Rajumar?" Chand said, his chest still heaving from their last bout of lovemaking.

"Hmm ... so I'll be Mrs. Rajumar. What exactly does your name mean?"

Chand trailed a finger across her forehead as he gazed into her face.

"Prince," he said. "It means prince."

Thank you for reading *Getting to Mr. Right*. If you enjoyed what you've read a comment on Amazon, Goodreads or other social media will be gratefully appreciated.

About the Getting to Mr. Right Series

The series starts off by focusing on Campbell Jones –an award-winning relationship-therapist at the peak of her career. Friendship and support shared between the characters of Campbell's focus group evolves as the novel progresses.

The underlying theme throughout the original *Getting to Mr. Right* and the four novellas which follow is "being true to oneself." The novellas are all expansions of the main story – dating adventures for Missi, a café for Suzy, dealing with an uprooted life for Felicity and an unexpected pregnancy on the edge of mid-life for Campbell.

The series has gone beyond the original premise of "Getting a man" and in true *women's fiction* style, deals with the issues that come after "happily ever after."

Although all these women are now in romantic relationships, it's more the by-product of living their lives fully than a pursuit for finding a partner.

Book 1: Getting to Mr. Right

Campbell's research into the father/daughter dynamic and how it affects a woman's personal choices proves that Prince Charming is nothing but a myth. In a few months, she will receive international recognition for her work.

As part of her study, Campbell gives workshops to help women still seeking Mr. Right. Her latest group is made up of three women: Missi Morgan, who can't seem to let go of a philandering spouse; Suzy Paradise, a self-proclaimed queen of online dating; and Felicity Starr, whose life and career are dictated by a controlling father. In the midst of her study, a charming and personable man enters Campbell's life, putting her theories in shambles. Not only does she now question the validity of her research, but she must choose between her career and having her own Prince Charming. This personal dilemma makes it difficult for Campbell to give these women advice, as she encourages them to find their own paths to happiness and helps them set themselves free.

Book 2: Missi's Dating Adventures

After learning to let go of Max, her husband who dumped her, Missi Morgan explores the world of online dating. Through one disastrous date after another Missi learns lessons that help her discover who she truly is. She may not find the perfect match but she finds the perfect self. A romantic comedy for anybody having to tackle online dating and letting go.

Book 3: Not by Design

Ever since she first appeared in *Getting To Mr. Right,* Felicity Starr has been struggling to find her own kind of contentment. Now, at thirty-five and living in Rome, Felicity is about to break into the world of fashion design, and caught in a flurry of plans for her wedding when calamity strikes. Her father's sudden death brings into question the whole meaning of success. Then Marco, the man she's about to marry, leaves her when he learns of her Multiple Sclerosis diagnosis. Forced to return to Montreal, Felicity finds her life thrust into unexpected turns. As she confronts the on-going challenges presented by her disease, she gains the strength to let go of old beliefs and face her inner truths. Love, friendship and rewarding work come in different forms and

Felicity finds it all in ways she never imagined –
in a life that's *not by design.*

Book 4: **Café Paradise**

Most of Suzy Paradise's dreams died along
with her son over twenty years ago.
One thing has re-ignited her passion for living -
running her own café, which specializes in home-
baked donuts. For Suzy, this is a long-cherished
dream come true. Her business is starting to
flounder when Donuts-A-Million, a giant chain,
opens across the street from her. Her unexpected
attraction to Coen Walsh, a regular customer at
her café, creates more tension when she learns of
his affiliation with her competitor.
Café Paradise is about Suzy's fight to save her
business in spite of the odds. Sometimes, she
realizes, dreams have an expiration date and it
takes just as much courage to let them go.
Along the way, she must re-define the meaning of
work, family and romance so she can find her
own formula for happiness.

Book 5: **The Longest Nine Months**

In Getting to Mr. Right, Campbell debunked
the Prince Charming myth, only to meet a special
man who turned all her assumptions upside

down. Now she's married to Chand. But Happily-Ever-After turns out to be another illusion. Campbell deals with job burnout and struggles to find her place in the world. An unexpected pregnancy and its complications undermine her relationship with Chand and take her to a difficult crossroad. No matter which way she decides to go, nothing will ever be the same!

OTHER BOOKS:

Mourning Has Broken – A Memoir on Grief

Mourning Has Broken offers a moving and poignant look at grief and loss. In this collection of narrative non-fiction essays, the author speaks from the heart not only about the death of a dear sister but also about the mourning of a mother, a father, a dear friend, a career and a religion.

Readers who have known loss will find much to relate to in this book, and will particularly appreciate the author's ability to be frank and open and at times humorous about feelings that might be difficult to acknowledge.

Warning Signs

A psychological crime novel about obsession. Eugene's research into his criminal mind is not about the why, but how to prevent his horrific crimes. Angie, a young woman starving for passion sees Eugene as her savior from a lonely life of caring for her heroin addicted mother. How far is she willing to go in order to save her relationship with Eugene and his promise for a future together?

Detective Van Ray is on a vindictive mission as he attempts to solve the murders of young girls in Youth Protection.

Their lives collide in a mixture of mistrust, obsession and ignoring the warning signs. A psychological crime novel about human frailty and loneliness.

Just Before Sunrise

Homeless Maya is drifting on the streets, grieving the recent loss of her mother.

When she is offered the opportunity to prepare a lake-side house to be used as a half-way home for delinquent girls, she doesn't think twice.

She soon falls for Charlie, the attractive boy next door, who has a seriously dark side. She is drawn into his murderous schemes, doing anything he asks her to, risking her own safety for the promise of a future with him. When she finds herself party to murder, and she realizes he is more concerned with his older female accomplice than with her, she must learn to trust her instincts and use all of her courage to get out of their trap alive. Just Before Sunrise is a story about loss, survival. About loneliness, betrayals and desires. It is also about the relationship between an older woman and a younger man.

The Lilac Notebook

At age 40 Holly Baranov is in the beginning stages of fast advancing Alzheimer's. Unwilling to care for her, Holly's husband leaves her.

She moves out of her large middle-class home and into a small apartment near McGill University where she enrolls in a poetry course in the hopes of stimulating her brain.

There she meets Kim Harris, a thirty something beautiful but damaged law student and Amelia Rose, a twenty-year -old pole dancer in a seedy nightclub who wants nothing more than to graduate, teach high school, marry and raise a family.

When Amelia is found strangled in her apartment, Holly becomes involved in the investigation both as prime suspect and as victim.

ACKNOWLEDMENTS

I'd like to offer my deepest gratitude to the people who have helped with the various aspects of this book.

For her enthusiasm, support, helpful suggestions and careful edits I'd like to thank my editor, Thelma Mariano (http://www.u-unlimited.ca) for elevating this story to its flowing end product.

I also want to thank from the bottom of my heart all those who were here from the very beginning when Getting to Mr. Right was first titled Brenda's Disastrous Dates, then The Dating Club and was just a series of posts on a blog. Thank you Joanne, Sylvie, Louise, David, Geraline, Ursula, Jocelyne, JY.

Sincere thanks to my current blogging community for your support. You are too many to mention but you know who you are.

Many thanks to my writing groups who might not have seen the manuscript but whose exchanges on writing were motivating and encouraging.

Namaste to Suneeti Phadke for her extremely helpful input on Rishikesh and the Ganges.

Sincere appreciation to Claudia Rock who did part of the editing and to Jennie Nash, who partially worked on an early draft.

I am always grateful to Yang Ding's tech support and availability in helping me keep my website up-to-date.

Thanks also to Miruna Radulescu for the cover

Please visit me at:

Amazon - http://www.amazon.com/Carol-Balawyder/e/B00HVETKWM

Goodreads - http://www.goodreads.com/author/show/7704883.Carol_Balawyder

Smashwords - https://www.smashwords.com/profile/view/cbala

Website - http://carolbalawyder.com/

Blog- http://carolbalawyder.com/blog/